A Cry From the Dark

A Cry From the Dark

ROBERT BARNARD

This edition published in Great Britain in 2003 by
Allison & Busby Limited
Bon Marche Centre
241-251 Ferndale Road
Brixton, London SW9 8BJ
http://www.allisonandbusby.com

A catalogue record for this book is available from the British Library

ISBN 0 7490 0617 X

Printed and bound by
Creative Print + Design, Ebbw Vale

ROBERT BARNARD was born in Essex. He was educated at Balliol College, Oxford and after completing his degree taught English at universities in Australia and Norway, where he completed his doctorate on Dickens. He returned to England to become a full-time writer and lives with his wife in Leeds, Yorkshire. The couple are currently collaborating on a Brontë Encyclopaedia. In his spare time he enjoys opera, crosswords and walking the dog. In 2003 Robert Barnard was the recipient of the prestigious CWA Cartier Diamond Dagger, an award in recognition of a lifetime's achievement in crime writing.

To the two Alisons, Rick and Libby and Helen –
Helpers and Stimulators

Novels by Robert Barnard

Bones in the Attic
The Mistress of Alderley

Short Story collections

Death of a Salesperson
The Habit of Widowhood

Writing as Bernard Bastable

To Die Like a Gentleman
Dead, Mr Mozart
Too Many Notes, Mr Mozart
A Mansion and Its Murder (US only)

1
Crabbed Youth and Age

Eighteen and eighty sat regarding each other across the Holland Park flat, calculation and world-weariness instinct in the eyes of the younger woman.

"I've been so looking forward to meeting you," said Kerry Probyn.

That Bettina did not doubt. Never had she seen a young eye more fixed on the main chance. She could be useful to the young Miss Probyn's burgeoning film career, and therefore she was valued. And as soon as the film was made, marketed and shown she, Bettina, would prove to be one of the "base degrees" of the ladder by which she had ascended, and would accordingly be scorned.

"Let's begin," she began briskly. "I have a friend coming for tea at four. I hope the photographer will be prompt."

"Oh, he will," said Kerry, with a look that said they were both professional women. "You made it clear that he had to be."

Bettina smiled, knowingly, without replying.

"Well?" she said, when the silence had not been filled.

She looked at the girl across the table that was between them. She had distrusted Miss Probyn from the moment she had opened the door to her, perhaps from even before that. Miss Probyn had been brought to Britain by her parents when she was two. Her father was something high-up in the Legal Department of the Australian High Commission. She had been back to Australia for one year in her early 'teens – probably, Bettina suspected, to equip herself with an accent should any Australian parts come up. She had, Bettina had read, decided on a career in acting when she was eleven. She would have preferred a young actress with much better Australian credentials for the part of Liz in *The Heart of the Land*. She had sat her down on the other side of the occasional table, and would resist the photographer's inevitable attempts to photograph them together in an intimate closeness. Enough was enough.

"I'm awfully interested in your growing up," said the young woman. "In an outback town in Australia, with farming parents, going to a small state school. Just like Liz in the book."

"Liz in the book lives in Armidale, which is not an outback town but a prosperous rural town on the Northern Tablelands." Since Kerry Probyn showed no signs of being abashed, Bettina asked nastily: "Haven't you spent some time in Australia?"

"Yes, I was born there. And I spent nearly a year in Sydney."

"Sydney is a wonderful town, but it's not Australia," said Bettina, who had not seen Sydney or even Australia for the last forty years. "There is all the difference in the world between a New England town like Armidale and a little, parched, remote town like Bundaroo, fifty miles from Walgett – which back then meant fifty miles from nowhere. That's where I grew up. That's real outback."

Kerry pouted.

"I didn't get out of Sydney all that much. There was so much to do there ... But even if there are lots of differences, it's a book about a young girl, isn't it? There must be a lot of you in it, your reactions to things."

Bettina repressed a grimace at that last, slack phrase.

"I have been a young girl, and the book is about a young girl. That much is undeniable, but not very illuminating."

"The names Liz and Bettina are related, aren't they? They both come from Elizabeth."

Someone had been filling her silly head with the sort of nonsense academics used to spout. Bettina sighed audibly.

"Very sharp. Still, the fact that the two names have only one letter in common meant that I was entirely unaware of the relationship."

"And you got away from Australia, like Liz," said Kerry, her tone getting rather bellicose.

"I *left* Australia."

"And you never went back. I mean, that's got to be significant, hasn't it?"

Bettina's gaze was thundery.

"No. It might have been if what you say was true, but it's not. I have been back."

It seemed at last to get through to Kerry Probyn that the interview was not going well.

"Sorry. What I meant to say was that you never went back there to live."

"Oh no. I never went back there to live."

"Why was that?"

"I never intended to."

"You left, meaning to stay away for the rest of your life?"

"Yes."

Bettina intended that to be a full-stop, the subject laid to rest. Kerry Probyn, characteristically, failed to see it.

"I'm just wondering why," she said. "I can see that writers in South Africa during that Apart-thing had to leave the country to write the truth about it. But no one was forced to leave Australia to write the truth."

"Oh *weren't* they?" said Bettina. It was another full-stop, and again it was ignored.

"Perhaps finally, now that you're writing your memoirs, you will be able to tell the truth," she said, with an attempt at brightness.

"I have always told the truth. And I am *not* writing my memoirs."

Bettina registered happily that the "little chat" proposed by Corydon Films was going from bad to worse.

"Let me tell you a few things about Armidale, and the countryside around it, so you don't make the mistake, should you go there, of calling it an outback town," she said, with a brightness that was intentionally false-sounding.

The first paragraph of the memoirs that Bettina was not writing almost wrote itself. It had in fact been written almost word for word sixty-five years before.

By nine the sun begins its daily blaze over Bundaroo. If there has been a sharp breeze overnight, the dust from the tracks and homesteads on its borders is collected around the nest of buildings which is at its heart. The schoolchildren walk from the weatherboard homes in little knots of friends and allies on to the short bitumen strip, past the meagre wrought-iron pillars and balconies of Grafton's Hotel, past the vegetable and grocery shop run by Won Chi, past the wooden verandah of Bob's Café, then into the dusty playground of the brick-and-board school building. Behind them is flat, brown landscape, eucalyptus trees, and the blue shapes of mountains in the distance. Ahead of them lies the same, on either side the same too. The children have entered the world of boundless hopes and limited prospects that their parents have inhabited for years, and that they will inhabit for the rest of their lives.

Whenever she read over this paragraph she remembered that in the last sentence she had originally written "open landscapes and closed minds". She had substituted "boundless hopes and limited prospects" because the words she had first written seemed too cruel. Perhaps she would use them later in the memoirs. Now the substitution seemed to symbolise why she had left Australia. Not because of any system of state censorship. But because one censored oneself.

Particularly if one was sixteen, and doing one's first piece of real writing.

The photographer, who had come promptly with a PR woman and looked, like her, rather nervous, did all the things that photographers do on what is basically a publicity job. He took a series of shots of Kerry Probyn gazing from the windows of the first floor flat, over the beauties of Holland Park (in very soft focus), then a series of her gazing at Bettina's small Russell Drysdale, having first asked her which was the most valuable picture in the room. Then, more from tact than from any practical purpose, he took solo pictures of Bettina sitting in an armchair, hands in her lap, expression magisterial, looking every inch a great writer in the autumn of her days. Duty done, the photographer got down to the nitty-gritty.

"Now, if we could have some shots of you two together on the sofa," he said.

Bettina silently pointed Kerry Probyn to the sofa, she herself remaining aloof in her chair.

The photographer had failed to catch the clear messages of their body language.

"No, I meant both of you on the sofa, very much together, going over the book maybe. The book the film is being made from – I'm sure you'll have a copy here."

"We only met an hour ago," said Bettina. "I have been talking to Miss Probyn about what it was like to live in Australia in the nineteen-thirties – about weatherboard houses, dunnies in the back yard, and red-back spiders. She thinks anything about the Australia outside Sydney will be useful for her performance in *The Heart of the Land*. I hope it will. That is all. Photography, like any other art, should aim at the truth. To set up some kind of love-in would be dishonest because it would have no basis in truth. Now, can we please go ahead with this business as we are now?"

The photographer was abashed, but nevertheless opened his mouth to continue his attempts at persuasion. An almost imperceptible nod from the PR woman – but one perceived by Bettina – persuaded him that this would be unwise. He photographed them talking across the table – at first frostily, but as Bettina decided to make a concession, having got her way, with an attempt at warmth and friendliness. Well before four the session was over, and Bettina felt very glad that it was. She was also pleased that little Miss Probyn seemed to have had her dreadful teenage confidence dented by the encounter.

"Well, it's been wonderful meeting you," the fledgling actress said, as the photographer packed his heavier gear away. "Like a dream come true."

But a quaver in her voice belied her words, and when she made as if to embrace Bettina she changed her mind and actually shook her hand. As she turned to follow the other two her body spoke of gratitude that the ordeal was over.

"Oh look! Aboriginal art!" she cried, as she caught sight of a bark painting by John Mawurndjurl by the door. Her gesture brought a quick flash from the cameraman. Then she shot a glance at Bettina's face, saw that it was grim, and scuttled out.

"Oh look! Aboriginal art!" Bettina said disgustedly to the friend she called Hughie as they sat half an hour later over tea, sandwiches, fruit cake and gingerbread. "Such a false little thing! Still, I suppose it's a sort of advance that she didn't say 'Abo art'. We would have done back then."

"You wouldn't have called it art," Hughie pointed out. "The most you would have done was call them pictures."

"True," said Bettina, who often had to be reminded of attitudes all those years ago. "I wonder why I disliked her so instantly. Was it because she was convinced she'd be playing *me*? And though it's not true, there's a little bit of truth in it, and I don't want to be played by a forward little minx who's grown up in the Home Counties, who's spent a year in Sydney and thinks she knows all there is to know about Australia."

"Why was *The Heart of the Land* set in Armidale anyway?" asked Hughie. "It's not a town you knew well, is it?"

"Well enough. I had a holiday there with my Auntie Shirley when I was ten – when Oliver was born. And then another when I was sixteen – the one you know about. At the time it seemed the grandest place on earth. The shops! If you wanted anything you could choose which one to go to. I'd never realized there were places like that apart from Sydney or Melbourne. Of course I

19

had no money to speak of, so it was more to look than to buy."

"When I first met you I wasn't much more sophisticated," said Hughie smiling reminiscently. "I had been to Newcastle once or twice, but mostly it was tiny little villages near the farm, places with one shop apiece, and never more than a penny to spend."

Hughie did not need to tell Bettina that he was talking about the Newcastle in Britain, not the one in New South Wales. They had known each other so long, since Bundaroo in fact, that Bettina often felt they didn't need to talk – they could just sit and think together.

"The film will bring in a lot of money," Hughie said, biting into a slice of shiny gingerbread. Bettina had known he was going to say that. She shrugged.

"If it's a success. Clare's got a wonderful contract, so the money isn't coming in one big bung. She's an agent in a thousand. Still, I don't think it will be a success."

"How on earth can you say that?" Hughie seemed genuinely concerned. "Oh, I know: it was the girl."

"Not at all. The girl will do well enough. She'll have a Sydney accent which will be all wrong, and she won't look *drab* enough – but who cares about the accent, and who wants young girls to look drab? No, what I'm afraid of is that the whole *thing* will be wrong. That they'll be thinking of the international market and dress it and set it accordingly. If that's the case there'll be no chance of its being authentic. I'd be willing to bet that Corydon films it in the wrong area, gets the wrong sort of town, in the wrong sort of landscape, with all the people looking wrong."

"But that's the story of every film of a good book that Hollywood has ever made," said Hughie. "The Australian film industry is a mini-Hollywood these days. And only you will know."

"Well yes," admitted Bettina. "I suppose what I'm thinking is that it won't be an *artistic* success. But why should I care about that? The film will have a premiere, get some kind of distribution, probably come out on video, and that will be the end of it. The book will always be around."

"True. And you've done very nicely by the books ... very nicely in*deed*. But films are another thing – speaking financially. And one success could spark other successes. Merchant Ivory could take your books up ..." Bettina knew what was coming. "You have so many grasping people around you, my dear."

"They seem to grasp only in your imagination, Hughie."

"Clare, for example. She is obsessed with money."

"That's her business as my agent. She does quite nicely out of me as it is."

"Mark – even his father, your brother Oliver. I remember him as a delightful, solemn little boy, but who knows what he is like now? They all want their cut, you mark my words. Then there's Peter Seddon – you never really finished with him as you should have done. Not to mention – "

"Then *don't* mention them! I know perfectly well who my friends and associates are. I am not about to discuss my will with anyone. I have now more, much more money for myself than I need. I can leave something to everyone or nothing to anyone. You really mustn't *bore* me by going on about this every time you come round, Hughie."

Hughie looked abashed. She made him sound such a drag.

"I realize I go on, Betty, but you know I have your interests at heart. You ought to get yourself a literary executor, a sort of custodian of your writings – "

"And biographer?"

"Well – "

"You for example."

"I would be – "

"Hughie, I am not so pessimistic about my chances of living a few more years that I would appoint as my biographer and executor someone who is exactly the same age as myself."

"But – "

"Especially in view of the superior life-expectancy of women compared to men. Let's say no more about this. How is Marie?"

"Well, quite well ... Bettina, you know there's no personal motive in what I've said, no designs on you."

"Of course there's not, Hughie. You're perfectly well provided for, you and Marie. I do hope you're right about other films. I'd like some of the later books to be done, the ones set here. It would be so much easier for all concerned than traipsing off to the outback. And they're just as good, and often very funny."

Hughie had no doubt noticed the swerve to another subject, but decided to go along with it.

"I don't think you'll find London in the 'fifties and 'sixties can compete with Australia in the 'thirties for audience appeal."

"I don't see why not," said Bettina, who held her opinions obstinately. "They're very entertaining, and there are lots of sketches in them of real people – actors, writers and suchlike – and they are people readers always recognise."

"And most of them are dead, which is an advantage," agreed Hughie.

"Exactly."

"Still, Australia is remote. It isn't just the popularity of the early-evening soaps – interest in it goes a lot further back than that. And the outback is remote and strange even for a Sydney or a Melbourne audience."

"True. No one in Sydney thought to take little Miss Probyn inland to show her what it's like."

"I suppose," said Hughie, after a moment for thought and remembrance, "that a lot of its appeal lies in the fact that on the one hand it's strange, like nothing that people in cities know, and on the other it's manageable and graspable."

Bettina thought about that.

"I don't quite see what you mean," she said.

"An outback town – what is it? One short street, a few shops, a café maybe, and a hotel which is mainly a watering hole. A few small properties immediately around it, and larger ones further away. Two hundred, three hundred people in all – people with their noses to the daily grindstone, people with incredibly limited horizons and no idea what is happening in the wider world of Australia, let alone the wider world of everything outside it. It's easily knowable, like an English village a hundred years ago."

Oh no it's not, thought Bettina. You were an outsider, and you were treated as an outsider. You were there for six months at most, then you left. You thought you knew Bundaroo, but you hardly even scratched the surface.

Bundaroo made damned sure it kept its secrets from the likes of you.

2
Alien Body

Next day, in mid-morning, when Bettina was about to get to work on her memoirs – which she called in her mind her Memories – she was rung by her agent Clare Tuckett.

"Hello darling. Did it go well yesterday?"

Bettina raised her eyebrows at the handset.

"I'm sure you know *exactly* how it went yesterday, Clare."

"Only because I can guess, and because I know you."

"I don't see how knowing me could help," said Bettina, bridling. "I don't always hate eighteen-year-old girls. I just happened to hate this one."

"Yes, and I'd met her too, briefly, and I knew you'd hate her. But far be it from me to interfere with Corydon Films' plans. In any case a raging feud between the author and the star of the film based on her novel is just as good PR as a love-fest and a meeting of minds would be. Better. You know that by now."

"Oh yes, I know that," said Bettina, sighing at Clare's mastery of the black arts. "But it certainly wasn't in my mind ... Clare, have you heard anything about Hughie's financial situation?"

"Hughie's? I thought he was comfortably off ... Hughie is not really in my line of interest, you know. Only incidentally an author, but really a newspaperman, albeit of a rather grand kind."

"It's Hughie who makes it grand – it's one of his roles. Art critics aren't by profession grand."

"They seem so to me. How do they *see* what they claim to see in dirty beds and piles of bricks? But let's not get on

25

to that. I can find out about Hughie's finances. I wouldn't be doing my job if I didn't have plenty of contacts in the newspaper world. Why, in God's name? Are you worried he's on the rocks?"

"It's just the fact that he keeps going on about people battening on me, or being after my money when I die. It's been coming on over the last six months or so. It's made me wonder if he's banking on something substantial for himself, though of course he says not. I've always thought he had piles stashed away after that television series, but there's the new young wife, and – "

"Darling, she's nearly fifty, and they've been married nearly a decade. That's swapsie's time in Hughie's circle. Well, I'll make enquiries. If he's made you think about money that's probably useful. It's time you faced up to the fact that you're a rich woman."

"Oh nonsense, Clare," said Bettina in her brisk-common-sense voice. "'Rich' doesn't cover people like me these days."

"Not your book earnings maybe, though they come to a very nice sum as I should know. But the flat is worth a fortune, and some of the pictures would bring you a tidy sum."

'Those are Hughie's doing ... Perhaps it's them he's got his eye on. As for the flat: when I bought it Holland Park was the sort of area you wouldn't walk through at night."

"Don't I know it! I'm a Londoner, remember. Now nobody walks there because people might wonder why you weren't taking a taxi ... I'll make enquiries, darling. Meanwhile enjoy your newfound wealth."

"I will. But I enjoyed my flat and pictures when they weren't worth half as much. I don't see how their present value could make me love them any more."

"Work at it, darling. You'll find it can. I'll let you know as soon as I find out anything. Now get down to your memoirs."

"I am not writing my memoirs," said Bettina automatically.

"I'll believe you, thousands wouldn't. No. Amend that. Even if thousands believed you, I wouldn't."

As she put the phone down Bettina smiled, but the smile had a tinge of anxiety in it. She put her hand across the desk and painfully pressed the PLAY button on her new recorder. It began playing the last part of the first chapter, which she had dictated two days earlier. The tape recorder was not quite a necessity yet, though the rheumatism in her hands would soon have made it one. She had bought it to justify her assertion that she was not *writing* her memoirs. If she had not had this get-out she would have justified her assertion by the fact that she was writing her own story in the form of a novel, the only form she really knew. Both were pretty threadbare pretences. Novel or not, she was aiming to tell the truth – though perhaps not the whole truth, and perhaps sometimes the truth with an element of deception built in. *The Heart of the Land*, published in 1953, was a vaguely autobiographical novel, like most of her early fiction set in Australia. From a teenage boy-girl interest that was never more than tepid and was never going to go anywhere she had made a bittersweet romantic novel. The new book, the Memories, would be much closer to the truth, though she was acutely aware that the whole truth was not in one person. Others would have different perspectives on the events she was narrating.

Still, judging by the autobiographies she had read by politicians and actors for example, she was aiming at a level of truthfulness that was quite beyond them – dominated as they were by egos and concern for their posthumous reputation. Those would not be her reasons if she was ever economical with the truth.

The walk to school that day was a sad one. It wasn't often that her parents rowed, but when they did it was fierce. The atmosphere in the house was electric, somehow weighted down with their bitterness. These rows always left Betty with a conflicting mass of emotions: she blamed herself, blamed Bundaroo, and for some reason got all emotional about her little brother. "Man is born unto trouble," she said to herself, applying it to serious little Oliver, not remembering that if he was born unto trouble so was she herself. Self-pity was never one of her vices.

The cause of the row was Bundaroo itself. Her mother had realized years ago that the soldier-settler land they had been allotted was never going to give them more than a precarious existence, and now that employment in the cities was becoming easier to find she was in favour of cutting their losses. Her father was very conscious that they were far from building up the reserves of money that would be necessary to tide them over against falling world prices, crop diseases, climatological disasters and all the other perils of outback agriculture, particularly for a cow-cockie. But he believed that in the small world of outback New South Wales they were building up a network of mateships and mutual trust, whereas if they moved back into the city they would be friendless and anonymous if luck turned against them.

Betty's mother fought against this argument.

"You forget that if you're in strife out here all your mates will be in strife too," Betty heard her hiss as she left the house.

Though she was upset, she was also excited. When she

grew up and went out into a wider world – and any world had to be wider than Bundaroo's – Betty realized that the unexpected always attracted her, even if there was fear as she confronted it. Probably both emotions had their origins in the fact that anything out of the routine hardly ever happened in her tiny home town. Her world was Fort George, Bundaroo, and the more distant world of Wilgandra, the biggest property locally, which she had only occasionally visited. She saw the school bus rattle along the track from Wilgandra, dump the children of the station workers on the road nearly a mile outside Bundaroo, then take the equally rutted track to the township of Corunna, to fetch the schoolchildren from there. All as usual. Things that happened in Bundaroo happened every day. Today, though, an unusual thing occurred. Ahead of her on the road to town she saw a figure she did not recognise. It was a boy – she knew that by his walk, as well as by his short trousers – but not one of the boys from school. The trousers, the cut of them, struck her as out of the ordinary. She speeded up her steps so she caught him up with only a half mile still to go.

"Hello," she said. "Are you new?"

The boy looked round. He was about her age or perhaps a bit younger, with fair-to-brown hair and a worried, uncertain expression which he tried to hide by a strutting style of walking.

"Yes." From the one word she knew he was English. "We've just moved here from Victoria. My dad's the new manager of Wilgandra."

Betty had heard Wilgandra was about to get a new manager. Wilgandra's owner Bill Cheveley loomed large on the horizons of Bundaroo people, and Bill was a friend of Bettina's father – friend and patron, in fact, and one of those on whom he might have to rely if times of trouble were ahead.

"My dad's a friend of Bill Cheveley," said Bettina, eager to form links. "Bill was one of his commanding officers during the war. They're mates."

"Is your dad Jack Whitelaw?" the boy asked. Bettina nodded. "My dad says he's fed up with hearing what a good bloke Jack Whitelaw is."

"That's not a very nice thing to say."

"Well, he's new, and he thinks people are comparing him ... Sorry. I didn't mean to be rude."

"I suppose it is annoying, if he's new. But my dad *is* a good bloke. I'm Bettina Whitelaw, by the way. Betty."

"And I'm Eugene Naismyth."

"I suppose you're called Gene are you?"

"Not really. My mother thinks Eugene is a nice name and says I ought to be called by it."

"I don't suppose what your mother thinks is likely to impress anyone at Bundaroo High, do you?"

The boy looked shocked at her tartness, and then giggled.

"I don't suppose so."

"Still, on second thoughts I don't think Gene is a good idea. It's the same as Jean – and the boys might start singing 'I dream of Jeannie with the light brown hair.' That would really be a bad start. We can't call you Eu-ie though ... But we could call you Hughie. That sounds perfectly all right."

"Except that it's not my name. Surely the teachers will know that I'm Naismyth, E.?"

"We'll manage that. You've got to try and fit in. You've got that Pommie accent to live down."

Hughie looked crestfallen.

"I thought I'd lost it."

"It's sort of half and half," said Bettina kindly. "I expect they took the mickey at your old school, didn't they?"

"A bit. But I had a lot of good mates there." A conviction gripped Bettina that he had had no mates there at all.

"And of course you'd still speak English English at home, wouldn't you?"

"Yes, I do. My mother thinks – "

"Forget your mother. She's a bad influence. Parents usually are."

"It doesn't sound as if yours are."

"Things are crook at home at the moment."

"They're always crook at my home."

"Don't change the subject. I'm not the problem. We'll have you speaking properly in no time."

She sounded more confident than she was. There was something through-and-through non-Australian about Hughie. But she did her best, and introduced him to everybody as Hughie, including Miss Dampier and Mr Copley as they walked through the playground.

"This is Hughie Naismyth, Miss Dampier," she said. "His real name is Eugene but everyone calls him Hughie."

"Hello Hughie. Welcome to Bundaroo. I'm sure you'll soon settle in here. I'll see you for English at eleven o'clock."

Hughie expressed his gratitude to Betty.

"Don't mention it. New schools are always difficult."

"I know. You can imagine what it was like at Benalla."

That at any rate was fair-dinkum, more truthful than the claim to have had 'good mates' there. She must tell him that he shouldn't use the word 'mate' until he could say it like an Australian.

Friday night for Bettina, as often as not, was the Duke of Sussex pub in Holland Park Avenue. She walked to it as a rule, to prove that rheumatism hadn't gained supremacy over the whole of her body. Anyway, to take the bus for just a couple of stops and then have a walk at the end of it was more trouble than it was worth. In spite of what

Hughie had said, she had never been a taxi person by habit, only by occasional necessity. Anyway, she was one of those who had floated up with the property values of the area, not bought in at the current breath-taking prices. The newcomers' habits were no doubt inbred, but she wasn't going to change her own.

"Evening, Rod," she said to the young Australian behind the bar. "Nice evening for a change. Peter been in?"

"Been in half an hour, Mrs Whitelaw," said Rod. She didn't correct his version of her name. She had been a Mrs in her time, though so long ago it was something she often forgot. "He's in the Public having a game of darts. Want me to give him a shout?"

"No, he'll finish his game anyway. When he does, tell him I'm over there with Katie in her corner, will you?"

Katie Jackson had been Bettina's cleaning woman for twenty years before she retired and was replaced by a firm of contract cleaners who were not nearly as satisfactory, and not entertaining at all. Katie knew all Bettina's business, and provided running commentaries and leading articles on events of thirty years ago as if they were yesterday.

"Hello Katie," said Bettina, settling opposite her. "Got your corner tonight then."

"There was an American family come up wanting the other seats, but I give them the evil eye. Thought you'd be in, it being Friday. Is Peter here?"

"Having a game of darts. He'll be along soon, I expect."

"Good." Katie always made it clear she liked Peter much better than she liked Bettina, and her former employer accepted this with equanimity. "Worst thing you ever did was when you showed 'im the door."

Bettina, for the umpteenth time, cleared up the matter of events of twenty years before.

"I didn't show him the door. He went off with a bit of skirt."

"He'd 'a' come back when 'e was tired of 'er."

"I'm not a rest-home for tired fornicators."

"Hmmm. Peter was never more than instant sex to you, ready for it whenever you shapped your fingers."

"He was always a great deal more. I was very fond of Peter, and very upset when he walked out on me."

"You threw 'is clothes out into the street."

"That's what I mean about being upset. Ah – here he is." She lowered her voice. "Thank God you're here, Pete. We'd have been going through all that old news from the day you moved in to the day you moved out. Want a refill, you two?"

"If you're buying in," said Pete, bending to kiss her. "Are you well? The rheumatics keeping at bay?"

"They're no worse anyway. But I'm having to use a tape-recorder for the new book. I don't know if I'll ever get used to it. It's not the same as writing." She got herself up and to the bar with the three glasses held rather feebly in her hand. When she got back she said: "Katie's been regaling me with her opinions on the rights and wrongs of my chucking you out."

Peter nodded.

"Worst thing I ever did, walking out on you. She didn't chuck me, love, I walked. And when all was said and done, she was a tart. I could have had her and stayed with you – no problem."

"That's exackly what I bin saying," said Katie. "You should 'a' stayed together, or got together again."

Peter scratched his head. Bettina thought: he's trying to

imagine being with me for so long, and doesn't altogether like it.

"I dunno," he said. "Can't go back, can we? And if we'd come back together, who's to say I wouldn't have done it all over again? I'm daft enough."

"You are," said Bettina. "And I certainly wouldn't have had you back a second time. Hughie was saying only the other day that I should have finished with you entirely."

"Oh, Hughie," said Peter with contempt.

Peter Seddon was, or had been, a bus driver. He had been on Bettina's route for six months before, one night, she was the last on the bus on his last run of the day, and he had driven off-route to her flat and stayed the night there. The double-decker parked outside had ruined Bettina's local reputation. The next morning one of the residents had complained to London Transport, so Holland Park must have been on an upward curve even then. Peter had moved in, and had been loved – in Bettina's way – because he was funny, unbookish, loving and uncomplicated, with a life centred on his own preferences and pleasures. That he was not entirely faithful didn't worry Bettina at all, and she would have winked at his final bit of skirt on the side if he hadn't insisted on walking out on her. That had hurt. It had made her decide that her time for live-in relationships was over.

"Hughie is convinced that everyone except him is after my money," said Bettina.

"Probably are," said Katie. "You've got more o' that than sense, like most of you intellect-u-orls."

"I would be after your fabulous wealth if there was any chance of getting it," said Peter. "Correction: I would be if I was twenty years younger. At my time of life money's just a bind. A burden, like."

34

"Come off it, Pete," said Bettina. "You wouldn't say no to a whacking increase in your pension."

"'Course not. But *lots* would be a bore. Is Hughie hoping for the lot? That wife of his must be expensive."

"So far as I know Hughie has plenty and to spare. And in the past at least he's always looked after it. People who grow up with not much of it usually do."

"If you come from the moneyed classes," amended Pete. "If you come from the unmoneyed classes like I do you blue it as soon as you get it. Spend, spend, spend. Lovely!"

"Well, that's never been Hughie's way."

"You bet it hasn't. Too bloody arty-farty and airy-fairy for vulgar display. I often wondered whether he ever looked at anything except books and paintings, but going by the bits of fluff he somehow or other attracts he must do."

"Hughie's never wanted for female companionship," said Bettina primly. "But the turnover rate is high. I should think they quite quickly get bored."

"That's a fair bet. When you introduced us I was nodding off within the first sixty seconds."

"You're an extreme case. You've never read a book in your life, Pete."

"True. Not what you'd call a book, anyway. You should have told Hughie I don't go much on talk about Olivia Manning's spat with the literary editor of the *Sunday Yawn*."

"I've spent my life trying to get Hughie to fit in with other people, instead of expecting them to fit in with him. It's never had more than a momentary effect. So you think there might be something in his idea that people are after my money?"

Peter shrugged.

"Where there's money there's people after it. Who does he suspect? That nephew of yours?"

"Mark, you, Clare – everyone I know, I think. It's a bit of an obsession with him."

"The remedy's in your own hands. Tell everyone you know that you're giving it to charity."

Bettina screwed up her face.

"Oh, that *sounds* a good idea, but I can't think of anything I feel that strongly about. I'm not the Lady Bountiful type. And I like to think of people having a bit of a blue-out after I'm gone."

"Well, tell them you're leaving everyone a nice little token to remember you by and that's that."

"That still leaves all the rest of the money. What am I to leave that to? The British Museum? The Society of Authors? The bloody government?"

"Well, what about the Australian government?"

"What has the Australian government ever done for me?"

"You could do it just as a way of gaining time. When you find out who covets your dosh and is thinking of murdering you for it you could think again."

"Oh I don't think even Hughie's feverish brain is entertaining the idea of murder."

But when she got back to the flat that night it wasn't that part of the conversation she remembered – because, after all, if you didn't care much about money while you were alive you couldn't get hot under the collar about what happened to it after you were dead. It was the conversation about Hughie that stayed in her mind, and how she felt she had acted as his interpreter to the world, or had somehow stood guard between him and it, that she remembered. She stood at the window thinking about this, looking over the darkened expanse of Holland Park. Then, when she had sentences firmly in her mind, she went into her study and switched on the tape recorder.

Betty walked home that afternoon with Hughie and her best friend Alice, and when Alice went into her slightly run-down home on the outskirts of Bundaroo she walked on with Hughie alone. They talked about the day, the English class, the teachers, the other kids at the school. Somehow or other they got on to music, and Hughie told her that they had records of Beethoven's Seventh at home, conducted by Toscanini. Betty very much wanted to hear them, wanted to play them over and over so that the music was imprinted on her soul (she thought like that in those days). Hughie said he'd ask her over when the family was properly settled in. But when his way parted from hers and he waited for the bus beside the dry, rutted track that led to Wilgandra she shouted after him:

"I shouldn't mention the Beethoven records at school."

The burden of her morning walk weighed down on her again as she walked the last half mile to home, and she decided to slip quietly to her tiny bedroom (though in that house all noises could be heard everywhere, even silences). However as she went through the front door she heard the familiar voices, talking normally.

"We've been married a while now, Dot. We've seen a lot of dry gullies. And we've always come through."

"I've always supported you, Jack. You've got to admit that."

"You have, Dot. I'd be the first to say it."

"And I've done it because I trust you."

"I just feel that if hard times come – "

"*Harder* times."

"OK. Things haven't been easy – too right they haven't! But

if things get tougher, you need mates about you. In the city no one has mates. They have acquaintances, neighbours, even family, but they don't have mates. We'd be alone. We could become dolers, sundowners. It doesn't bear thinking about."

"I suppose you're right, but – "

The reluctance in her mother's tone was palpable. Betty thought it was time to burst in on them all sunny and smiling, to show her gratitude for the end of the row.

"Hello Mum, hello Dad!"

"Well, look at the time!" said her mother. "I haven't even thought of tea. Have a good day at school dear?"

"Not bad ... There was a new boy there."

"Who was that?" It was her father who spoke. He was always half-jealous when she spoke of boys.

"His name is Naismyth. His father's the new manager at Wilgandra."

"Oh yes?"

Her father's tone spoke volumes. Betty knew as well as if he had spelt it out in flowing sentences that Hughie's father had not made a good start as Bill Cheveley's manager, and probably that the family as a whole was not liked out at Wilgandra. His sense of fairness would not allow him to say any more, but he couldn't keep the truth out of his tone.

Soon all of Bundaroo would know it. And Hughie would have one more black mark against him, to add to his accent, his Englishness, his devotion to "culture", and his total foreignness to outback customs and ways of looking at the world.

3
Ghosts

"Hello, Auntie Bet? You OK?"

The voice was male, young, and broad Australian.

"Hello, Mark."

She tried to inject some enthusiasm into her voice, though he probably wouldn't notice one way or the other. Mark didn't. If anyone was making a film on the Narcissus myth, Mark would be a natural for the part.

"I've been meaning to pop by and make sure you're still in the land of the living, and I will do, this week or early next. I just haven't had a minute recently."

"Oh, that's good," said Bettina, adding maliciously: "Are the parts beginning to come in?"

"No, it's more this personal trainer lark. It's a soft cop – all perks and no work. Charging around from posh hotels to posh flats and houses, then on to posh gyms. Sounds a drag, doesn't it? But I suppose that sort of thing's not your scene, is it, Auntie Betty?"

"It certainly doesn't sound like it."

"You mentioned parts. I thought you might be able to help there, Auntie B." Bettina left a silence. This was what she had been expecting since she heard his voice. He was forced to come out with it explicitly, since she refused to ease the transition. "I hear they're going to make a film of *The Heat of the Land*."

"*The Heart of the Land*. Since it's set in Armidale the heat is fairly moderate. There is a part for a young man, but he's quite a lot younger than you."

The heroine of her book had a brief and bittersweet romance with the school's cricket captain. Bettina had portrayed him as a willowy young man perpetually in white flannels. She certainly hadn't imagined him as a lumbering mass of muscle and self-love, which pretty well summed up her nephew Mark.

"I can look anything from seventeen to forty, Auntie Bet."

"Maybe. I can mention you to the film company, but that's *all* I can do. They'll make their own decisions. And all the filming is going to take place in Australia."

"Oo-o-oh – really? I thought the interiors would be filmed here."

"Definitely not."

"Of course I want to go back to Australia – naturally I do. But all the action is here at the moment – "

Being personal *something-or-other* to people with more money than sense, thought Bettina. She interrupted him.

"Well, you have to make some sacrifices for your Art," she said. "Or alternatively you could sacrifice your Art for the good life. The loss would be great to Art, but – "

"Don't be sarky, Auntie B," said Mark, and she was surprised that he was actually listening. "And another thing. There's Dad."

"Your father?"

"He's coming over. Should be here in a couple of weeks' time. That's if the bargain tickets work out."

"Oh, that *will* be nice," said Bettina, genuinely pleased at the prospect of seeing her baby brother again.

"That was what I was really ringing about," said Mark, who clearly had had no interest in her well-being and little hope of a part in the film. "I was going to ask a favour of you, Auntie Betty."

"Ye-e-es?"

"I know you don't like people to stay for too long, and

40

that's fine – he'll stay here with me. But I wondered if you could take him around the plays and operas and that sort of cra– thing, just now and again, could you? Save me. I mean, I would do it, but I'm busy most of the time, and I couldn't afford to lose customers by standing them up. And you know it's not my thing."

"Yes, I know it's not your thing, Mark."

"That's beaut, then. What with Dad being a bit of a cul-ture-vulture and you being the same, that suits everyone, doesn't it?"

Bettina wondered what sort and degree of a culture-vulture Oliver could have turned out to be, and how he could have produced or nurtured a brainless lump like Mark. Perhaps she had better ring him up and sound him out on what he might like to see.

"I'd be delighted to show him around and take him to things," she announced gladly.

"Gee thanks, Auntie Betty. You're a sport."

I hope *not*, she thought.

As she pottered around the flat for the rest of the after-noon it occurred to her to wonder from time to time why she reacted so badly to her nephew. Things had got off on to the wrong foot when he had arrived in London eighteen months before. He had been warned that she was a working writer and never had guests for longer than a week, but he had made himself and his copious luggage at home in the flat and displayed a clear inten-tion of staying there as long as he could string it out. In those first days in Britain he had made determined attempts to break into the acting business there. He was not without credentials, though nearly so. He had had three months ten years earlier in *Neighbours,* as the resi-dent hunk. His contract had not been renewed. The experience had not cut much ice in Britain. Since then he had made a living as barman and bouncer, swimming instructor and rugby player with a minor side, PE teacher and "personal trainer" – with no doubt some extra income from selling his body to whomsoever was attracted by it.

Bettina pulled herself up. She had no evidence whatever that Mark sold himself on the side. The only experience of him that had given her the idea that he might was his habit, in that one week in her flat, of going around the place in his briefs or – on one occasion only, when he had been the object of her wrath – in only a jock-strap. She had felt uneasy with him. It was as if he was offering himself to her – at her age! – in lieu of rent. That sort of aggressive male sexuality made her uneasy.

Still made her uneasy. It made her realize that she had never got over that terrible night in Bundaroo. It wasn't enough, never to have gone back. To put it for ever behind her she would have had to have had no people like Mark who could remind her of it. In this day and age, she said to herself, that was unlikely.

It was two weeks after Hughie began at Bundaroo High that Betty walked to school with him and Steve Drayton. Steve was from Wilgandra, where his father was a stockman, and he only walked with them because he had designs on Betty's friend Alice Carey, and thought that through Betty he might attain what he coveted: Alice's partnership at the leavers' dance in December, her brilliant revision notes for the end-of-the-year examinations, slices of her mother's well-thought-of passionfruit sponge, and beyond that her heart – and beyond that still her bed, or at least access to her knickers. Betty rather liked Steve. He was down-to-earth in a way she approved of.

"Alice Carey's brilliant at geography," Steve was saying. "I can never make head nor tail of it. I wish it was just maps, and 'What's the capital of Austria?'"

They were approaching the bitumen strip of Bundaroo's main street, and Betty saw the brawny form of Sam Battersby outside the Grafton Hotel, rolling empty barrels round to the strip of waste land at the back. Sam was the landlord, and thus had a pivotal position in Bundaroo life. She changed her position so that the boys were between her and the Hotel.

"Whatcher doin' *that* for?" demanded Steve. "I was talkin' to you."

"I don't like the way Sam Battersby looks at me," said Betty, keeping her voice low.

"Looks at you? Listen to ya!" said Steve, taking no such precautions. "He's just lookin' at the kids goin' to school. Not much happens in Bundaroo."

"This happens every day," said Betty.

"Betty's right," said Hughie. "He does look at her."

Steve seemed about to make some jeer at the newcomer, but he bit it back. Sam Battersby had upended a barrel on a low dray outside the front entrance to his hotel, and had planted his big fleshy arms on it, and his beer belly against it, and was gazing at them as they walked past.

"See?" said Betty.

"Come off it! It's just ordin'ry," said Steve, but not with great conviction.

"It's not ordinary. It's horrible. Watch the side window of Bob's Café. It reflects the Grafton."

As they walked they gazed surreptitiously at the little café's window. Sam Battersby had not changed his position, but his head was turned in their direction, and his protruding eyes were watching, fixed on Betty's retreating back.

"Well," said Steve. "I suppose you're right. But I've never noticed it before."

"He doesn't watch you," said Betty.

The next weekend it was Masonic Night in Walgett. Betty's father had been sponsored as a Mason by Bill Cheveley, so that he could drive him there and – more to the point – back. Bill had never much liked driving, since four long years as an ambulance man during the war. He had once driven into a tree on the way back from Walgett when he'd drunk too much. Bill paid for Jack's services as a chauffeur by making his car available to him whenever he had need of it. Jack only had to go into Bundaroo and phone Wilgandra from the Grafton Hotel and it was brought over by one of the stockmen. Whether he would have joined the Masons if left to himself was doubtful. Betty had heard him ridiculing the ritual one night when he'd thought she was asleep. "Grown men dressing up like high-class waitresses," he'd said. "Makes me split a gut laughing." But Bill Cheveley was more than a mate. The two men admired each other, and they had between them something that was almost as intimate as a marriage.

That evening Bill Cheveley brought along a guest. Hughie's dad Paul Naismyth was a Mason, initiated back home in the North of England, and Bill, who was a man who took obligations seriously, had felt obliged to ask him as his special guest. To him the Masons were about fellowship.

"Good to meet you at last," said Naismyth, shaking Jack Whitelaw's hand. "Heard a lot about you from Bill – all good, of course."

"Is tea all right for you?" said Dot, not expecting to be introduced, and not being. "It's what Jack and Bill usually have before the drive."

"Whatever comes out of the pot," said Paul Naismyth. "And this will be the young lady my son Eugene's been talking about, is it?"

44

Betty just smiled, and Naismyth stretched his arms above his head, then took up his cup and drank.

"I needed this," he said. "I've been all day trying to get a hand's turn of work out of that lazy hound Kevin Drayton."

Betty felt immediately an access of tension in the room. Paul Naismyth had transgressed, had passed over one of those unmarked boundaries. He was too new, and too English, to criticise one of the established members of their little community. And since Kevin Drayton did not have the reputation of being idle, everyone in the room could have guessed that he was probably engaged in some kind of passive resistance to the new manager.

"Now we're just waiting for the Rev," said Bill Cheveley, stepping into the silence, "and then we'll get going."

"Oh, is the vicar a Mason?" asked Paul Naismyth. "We have a vicar in the Hexham lodge, but mostly the C. of E. people steer clear of us."

"Michael does too," said Cheveley. "He thinks people would be confused by the double allegiance as he calls it. No, he has a sister in Walgett, and he sometimes comes along so he can drop in for an evening."

"I see."

"Sam Battersby asked if we had room, but I had to say no."

"Good," said Betty, under her breath.

"I thought we couldn't squeeze a third rear, and that a big one, on to the back seat … Ah, that looks like Michael now."

The Reverend Michael Potter-Clowes was riding his bicycle through the gathering dusk down the rough dirt track. He was shaken about so much that Betty thought he'd have done better to walk. He was a long, thin, birdlike man, unmarried, who was looked after by a widow who came in to cook and clean for him. He was generally liked or tolerated in Bundaroo, and thought of as a bit of an eccentric, or a throwback. He was a hoarder, and he had a great collection of back numbers of the *Bulletin*, which Betty sometimes went along to the shabby wooden house that served as a vicarage to read – loving, especially, the cartoons and jokes, but seriously reading her way through the political stuff as well. She liked the Reverend Potter-Clowes well enough, but they were never entirely easy with each other. Betty knew he thought her very bright and didn't know how to live up to his assessment.

"Ah Betty!" he now said, when he had been introduced to the newcomer and had made enquiries about his wife and son, "I have some news for you. The *Bulletin* this week says that in a fortnight's time they will be launching a special competition for young people."

"Oh," said Betty flatly. "It will probably be some awfully difficult quiz that you need encyclopædias and things to find the answers to."

"No, it's not. It's apparently a competition to find budding young journalists. It'll be just like writing an essay, I should think – a bright, entertaining one. That's very much up your alley, isn't it?"

"Well, it could be. Yes – that might be interesting."

"Betty would make a very good journalist," said her father loyally. "She notices things."

"So what do you think about the Czech situation?" the vicar asked, turning to Bill Cheveley.

"Oh, don't you worry about Czechoslovakia," put in Paul Naismyth. "Country like that – only existed for twenty years. Nobody's going to rush in and fight for a country that's just a name. It's so remote nobody gives a damn about it."

"So was Sarajevo," said Betty's father. Now Betty knew for certain she thought Hughie's father a blatherskite. There was another awkward silence. Then the ill-assorted little group of men began to make their way to the Holden waiting outside.

Later that evening Betty's mother said to her, when she came in from putting little Oliver to bed:

"When they said Sam Battersby wasn't coming tonight, you said 'Good'."

"Yes."

"Why?"

Betty waited for a while before replying.

"I don't like the way he looks at me."

Betty's mother seemed about to say something, then thought better of it. The Grafton Hotel and what went on there was men's business. This was something that seemed to straddle her world and her husband's.

Thinking back on things later Betty decided that that week was the one when matters began to crystallise. When what was to come was started on its accelerating course.

The phone call from her brother Oliver came two nights later. Bettina had been intending to ring him, and wished she had: she wanted to ask him if he'd like to stay for a few days, and it would have looked better if she had called especially to invite him. She realized she was appearing grudging, and blamed Mark for it. He was not the reason for her preferring not to have visitors who stayed in the flat, but he had certainly strengthened her dislike of it. And she had loved her baby brother, been so protective of him, in those long-ago days in Bundaroo.

"Ollie! I was just about to ring you. I get so confused about the time differences and was afraid I'd ring you when you were asleep."

"It's early morning here, and I know you're something of a night owl, Betty. And it's Thursday – your tomorrow."

"Oh, it *is* so confusing. I should know, and I'll try to remember."

Bettina was very conscious that what she was saying revealed how occasional the contacts had been between them – between her and anyone from her Australian past. With Oliver the contacts had been, quite often, just once a year, and never more than twice. She launched herself into a spiel she had been preparing in advance, and, realizing that in her effort to appear welcoming, she was gabbling, tried to rein herself back.

"Ollie, I wanted to say that I'd love to have you to stay here for the first days of your holiday. You know how itchy I get if I can't get down to the writing in peace, but it's been so long, and it would be so nice if we could actually be together, really get to know each other. *Again* – because we really did know each other once." Conscious that Oliver might point out that this was until he was about five, and that he'd developed a great deal since then, she began gabbling again. "And then we could plan what you'd like to see while you're over here. The London theatre is not what it was, but it's still pretty good, and I'd need to know the sort of thing you like – and then of course other sorts of things: concerts I'm not too good on, but I can find out, and then there's art exhibitions, places of course – "

"Hold your horses, Betty! One thing at a time. Now as to plays, I'm old-fashioned, and I like good strong plays with meaty situations."

"Ah ... Maybe one of the Priestley revivals. Or Tennessee Williams? Strong plays don't get written much these days."

"Either would be fine. And then I've *never* – I'm ashamed to say this – seen Shakespeare on stage. I suppose I've been saving it till I could see something really good."

"Right. That should be possible – depending on what plays are being done."

"I'm not fussy about the play."

"Well, you should be, Ollie. If you've only one chance to see really well-done Shakespeare it shouldn't be, say, *Timon of Athens* or *Two Gentlemen of Verona*. Luckily they're not often done."

"Then a concert at the Albert Hall, and an opera at Covent Garden. It's a question of experiencing the places as much as anything, but it would be nice if the opera is something mainsteam."

"That might be a problem with opera. Mainstream operas at Covent Garden tend to get booked up by Corporate Sponsors, I don't know why. The people who come find anything more complicated than 'O Sole Mio' heavy, so you might just as well sit them down in front of a Stravinsky or a Berg as a Puccini. Still, I'll do my best."

"And ..." Here the hesitations became long enough to be awkward. "Going back to the staying with you in the flat ..."

"You'd prefer to spend your time with Mark," said Bettina, breaking in on him. "I really should have thought of that. You haven't seen him for yonks, and – "

"No, it's not that ... Not entirely ... It's just that ... well, here goes: I've been hoping to have someone to travel with me. Judy couldn't face the long air trip, and Cathy couldn't get the time off work ..." Those were Ollie's wife and daughter, women Bettina hardly knew. She waited, her stomach feeling oddly churned up. "Well, I've never told you this, but we've been seeing quite a lot of Sylvia these last few years. We've ... come together, and get on very well."

Bettina tried without success to put her voice into neutral.

"I take it this Sylvia is – "

"Sylvia Easton. Yes. And – well – the long and the short of it is, she's always wanted to make the England trip, but never felt like doing it on her own. And the upshot is, she's coming with me. Mark hasn't known about this. I've only just told him."

"I see. This does rather change things, Ollie."

"Yes. I can see that it does."

Her voice took on a protesting tone.

"It's not that I don't want to meet her, have her with us when we do the theatres – " (though, I *don't*, she thought), "but staying here in the flat, that's a bit different."

"Yes, I thought it mightn't be a good idea," said Oliver. "After everything."

After *nothing* would describe it better, Bettina thought.

"But perhaps I'd better have time to think about it," she said.

"No – look, I feel I've rather landed you in it. Last thing we would be happy with is a fraught situation. We'll be perfectly all right at Mark's. He's got a mate on the floor above with a spare bedroom. I can sleep there."

"And Sylvia will sleep in Mark's spare room?"

"You should hear your voice, Betty! Sylvia's not a young woman, you know. And Mark's perfectly safe with women. Doesn't have a lot of luck with them, if the truth be known."

Not entirely sure what he meant, Bettina put the matter of Mark and Sylvia out of her mind. What she felt in the hour between the call and her bedtime was a sinking sensation of chickens coming home to roost.

50

4
New Horizons

The approaching arrival in London of her brother Oliver and the unknown woman to whom she had given birth long ago gave Bettina several disturbed nights. It also had the odd effect of seeming to spur Bettina on to greater, more concentrated work on the book of memoirs that was not her autobiography. She could not pinpoint exactly where this stimulus came from, since it would surely have been more logical to suspend work and see what the new Australian impulses likely to result – congenial impulses, at least as far as her brother was concerned – would do for the book. Then one day, over the large breakfast mugs of tea with which she invariably started her day, she realized why it was: she wanted to get *her* memories of Bundaroo, *her* notion of what it was like, down on paper before her life was invaded by the Australia of today. She had no reason to think that Oliver was haunted by memories of the town in which he had spent his earliest years. The other visitor had never been there so far as she knew, nor lived in any comparable outback small-town. She was aware that the changes to Australia since her youth had been enormous. What she had to capture was the outback of 1938 – the heat, the smells, the poverty, above all the attitudes of mind. She had to get down the tiny details of what she could remember. Later on she could dust them off, like an archaeologist with his fragments of pottery, winkle out the dirt from the patterned surfaces, and display their purpose and significance.

* * *

The day Betty went out to visit Hughie at Wilgandra was a red-letter day for her. Any visit to Wilgandra would have been something to remember, for she had been taken there perhaps three or four times in her life, or since she had begun having memories. She had not been for three years, not since Mrs Cheveley became something of an invalid. The day had been arranged by Hughie on their walks to school: Mr Naismyth would borrow the Holden and come and get her on the next Saturday. She would spend the afternoon at the manager's house, have her tea there, and then he'd drive her home.

Betty had not relished the thought of two twenty-mile drives with Mr Naismyth, whom she had not taken to, and she had exacted a promise from Hughie that he would come too.

"You needn't worry about my dad," said Hughie. "He's harmless."

"I'm not worried," she said, not entirely truthfully. "I'd just rather talk to you."

It was a fine day, the September sun glowing rather than beating on the dusty landscape.

When the Holden arrived soon after one, Mr Naismyth raised his hand to Bettina's father on the other side of one of the near paddocks as if he was an old friend, and nodded to her mother when she opened the door to them. It was Hughie's first time in Bettina's home, but he couldn't find much to say about it. On the drive to Wilgandra they chatted about their English homework (a short appreciation of "Oh to be in England", for which Hughie had a definite advantage, Bettina felt), and about the forthcoming *Bulletin* competition for budding journalists.

"They wouldn't pick someone who's only been in the country for under a year," said Hughie. "What could I write about?

Though I would quite like to write about Australian art, if we can choose our own topic."

"What do you know about Australian art?" asked Betty.

"I saw a bit in Melbourne, after we landed. Most of it was on a level with Mr Blackfeller's pictures – the ones he paints for the city shops – but there was some interesting stuff too."

"We should do more Australian stuff at school," said Bettina, who decades later was to greet the news that her novels were now set for the Leaving Certificate with a distinctly mixed reaction. "Just do the English stuff for a sort of background study."

"Yes, we should," said Hughie, as if he belonged there.

"Well, you have been setting the world to rights," said Mr Naismyth when they arrived at the manager's house, half a mile from Wilgandra itself. "I haven't heard Eugene talk so much since we left the Old Country."

Clearly he hadn't been listening to them, only registering that they were talking.

In the kitchen Mrs Naismyth welcomed them, but said she couldn't shake hands because hers were all eggy.

"I'm making some custard tarts for poor Mrs Cheveley – doing them in the English way. She said she'd have loved to see you, dear, but she doesn't feel up to talking at the moment."

That was all to the good. Mrs Naismyth was friendly enough, but a bit too ladylike for Bettina. She and Hughie retreated to the main room of the house, where Hughie had already wound up the gramophone, and had the records of Beethoven's Seventh piled up beside it.

"It's rather dark and mysterious at first," he said, with a touch of condescension, "then it becomes a sort of whirling dance."

His words had the ring of something he'd read. The Naismyths must own books on music, Betty thought. She

53

could hardly get her brain around the idea of *books* on *music*. They certainly didn't have any such thing in the Bundaroo library. In fact, that tiny collection had so few books on anything that it only opened for two hours on Saturdays.

Hughie put the first of the records on the turntable and lifted the arm. When the music started Betty found it not really mysterious at all (she later found he'd confused it with something he'd read in the same book about Beethoven's Fourth). It was more sort of mathematical, she thought, as if getting ready for something. Only when that something started did she become gripped, and standing there in the middle of the floor she had the first of several visions of a dance, sparked off by Hughie's words, with powerful bodies first in joyful motion which gradually took on a feeling of controlled frenzy. She hardly noticed when Hughie changed the record or announced a new movement. The dance became full of slow-paced menace in the second movement, then gradually increased in Bacchic fire for the last two. The bodies in her vision, now all but unclothed, were leaping and writhing and expressing a terrible, unnerving sort of rapture. When the music ended Betty took a minute or two to recover her sense of who and where she was. Looking at her hands she found they were shaking, and she tried to hide them.

"Play it again," she said. "Please Hughie, play it again."

Hughie sorted through the records, then put the first one on again.

This time the dancers appeared only intermittently in her brain, and she became more conscious of the shape of the music, the way the themes presented themselves, then changed and developed, and intermingled. She was more conscious, too, of Hughie – of experiencing this wonderful music *with* someone. Of course he knew the music and she didn't, but she had a sense of it beginning to etch itself on her brain, the tunes and the shapes of it becoming part of her as it must be part of him.

"That was even more wonderful," she said when it finished. And she was about to beg him to play it again when Mrs Naismyth's head appeared round the door.

"Can't you play something *nice* for your guest, Eugene? Beethoven isn't the thing for hot summer afternoons, surely? What about John McCormack or Richard Tauber? Or *Eine Kleine Nachtmusik*?"

"*Eine Kleine Nachtmusik* isn't the thing for hot summer afternoons," said Hughie. But he said it when his mother had shut the door again.

He put on *Fingal's Caves* and some Chopin. When they saw his mother disappearing in the direction of Wilgandra, carrying a wicker basket with something wrapped in dazzling white cloth inside, he lifted the arm of the gramophone and they played the Seventh again. Betty couldn't remember when she had had a more thrilling day.

During the Mendelssohn and the Chopin, which she might have liked if they had been played after something other than the Beethoven, Betty looked at the pictures around the room. Most of them were watercolours of English landscapes, alternately lush and wild ("Lake District and Northumberland" said Hughie). Betty thought the little pictures nice but rather ordinary. The only large picture in the room was an oil, depicting a jagged, prickly, unsettled landscape.

"It's mine," said Hughie. "My granddad bought it for me. He said he wanted to give me something that would be valuable when I was thirty and had a family, but that my dad wouldn't be tempted to sell before then."

That statement bowled Betty over. She didn't know what to say, so she said nothing, but she looked Hughie in the eye to show that she had registered.

Betty was an honourable girl, and she paid for her exciting afternoon by being especially nice and charming for the Naismyths over tea, which Mrs Naismyth called High Tea ("You can't call it dinner because it's just cold, but with some quite nice things"). She offered Betty the bathroom to wash her hands, and she was glad she did, because she could use the wonderful toilet soap called Parma Violet, wrapped in a pretty little paper package, which had the most beautiful smell Betty had ever known. She knew that Phil Pollard at the shop stocked it only for Mrs Cheveley, and had been quite disconcerted when Mrs Naismyth bought the last bar for herself. He had had to apologise to the greater lady for having to send her a bar of Colgate instead. It had become a matter of comment in Bundaroo, as almost everything that happened there did.

Over cold ham and cold meat pies and custard tarts (which didn't taste any different from custard tarts made the Australian way, but Betty said it was very nice of Mrs Naismyth to go to so much trouble for the invalid), Betty thanked the Naismyths for inviting her out and letting her listen to their wonderful gramophone records.

"I'm passionate about music," said Hughie's mother. "With Eugene it's more art, but I'm passionate about *music*."

"I did like the pictures on the wall," said Betty.

"They're by my Auntie Frances," said Mrs Naismyth. "She had a wonderful eye for a good watercolour subject. About Mr Sutherland's ugly landscape the less said the better. But Eugene says it's good, and Paul's father who bought it for him says it's good, so who am *I* to have an opinion? They're the experts."

"He bought it for me because he knew I'd appreciate it," said Hughie, and they looked at each other again. The censored version for family consumption, Betty thought. She found it difficult to come to terms with the fact that Hughie's father was distrusted by his own father, who in his turn had made this clear to Hughie himself. Betty herself was not over-burdened with relatives and had always rather idealised the large family unit. She was invariably loyal to her own father and mother when speaking of them to the outside world. But then, she had never had any grounds for being anything else.

On the way home Betty and Hughie talked non-stop, except when Betty begged Hughie to sing her the tunes from Beethoven's Seventh so they stayed in her mind. Sometimes Mr Naismyth joined in these, but mostly he kept quiet. Betty's father was outside the house when they pulled up, but Mr Naismyth just raised his hand and said:

"You've got a really bright kid there."

"I know." Betty's father tried to keep his voice neutral, but Betty knew that there was an unspoken "without being told it by a condescending Pommie bastard."

"Got to get the car back to Bill," said Mr Naismyth, and drove off.

Sunday should have been an anti-climax – and was, but not so much as Betty expected. They all went to church, and Betty as always met up with lots of schoolfriends there. The Naismyths were there as well, and Mr Naismyth, whose first time at the church this was, made no attempt to hide his bore-dom. Not many of his schoolmates spoke to Hughie. He had had a brief period of acceptance when he had taught a group of boys the rules of what they called soccer. By now they had reverted to their own game, which Hughie called Rugby and they called football. Hughie was neither popular nor unpopu-lar in the school, merely disregarded. He gave every appear-ance of not minding, but Betty thought it was probably an appearance. Hughie, she divined, was an actor. Actors needed audiences.

After the service, the Reverend Potter-Clowes singled out Betty in his greetings and farewells to his congregation at the door.

"Betty! I wondered if you'd like to come round when you've finished your Sunday dinner. I shall be off to Corunna to take a service about three, so you can have the place to yourself. I thought you ought to do a bit more prospecting into my old *Bulletins* – see the sort of thing they like."

"May I, Mum?"

"Of course, Betty."

"Then I'd like to, please. But you wouldn't disturb me if you were there."

"Oh, I do bumble in and out if I need things, as you know. And Corunna only gets a service once a month. I can't let them down, can I?"

Betty thought he probably could, but she just thanked him and said she'd be there by three.

When she got to the little weatherboard vicarage, Mr Potter-Clowes bumbled – as he called it – through to the study with her – a room, Betty always noticed, where the works of theology and spiritual speculation were outnumbered by volumes of the *Bulletin* and *Punch* (both, Betty suspected, sources for the jokes the vicar regularly injected into his sermons). He brought her tea, with a plate of biscuits and a slab of gingerbread, and pointed out, as he always did, the volumes of *Bulletin* for the past fifteen years, and the pile of more recent editions loose in the corner.

"You really should dip into some of the old and some of the recent ones. Research your market. I once met a real writer – in the trenches – and he said that was what would-be writers always needed to do, but very seldom did."

"Did you fight in the trenches?" asked Betty. This was new to her.

"Eventually. I tried to be an objector, but as time went on I couldn't believe any more that keeping out of the war was any sort of answer ... We shall be celebrating Armistice Day soon. 'Greater love hath no man than this, that he lay down his life for a friend.' So true."

"But wouldn't it be even greater if he laid down his life for an enemy? Or for someone or something he didn't really care about one way or another?"

The Reverend Potter-Clowes seemed perplexed.

"What have you in mind, Betty?"

"Well, Czechoslovakia, for instance. Or England. No one really seems to like England or the English very much, but the men go off to fight for her."

"Ah, our conversation the other night. I don't think you'll find your father's friend is right about Czechoslovakia. In the end and even if you don't know much about a country, you find you can't just shut your eyes to what is being done to its people ... Ah, there's my lift to Corunna. Do put on the light if you need it, but I don't suppose you will."

Betty smiled as he left the house. Electricity was Michael's little meanness. He used it as little as possible. She called him Michael to herself, getting it from her father, but she had to be careful not to use the name aloud. She settled down with a ten-year-old volume of the *Bulletin*, then changed to more recent issues when she got bored, enjoying the controversies about living issues which she had heard about on the wireless. She was digesting the information about the competition for young journalists when Potter-Clowes returned.

"I'm just finishing," she said, getting up. "There's a limit to what I can take in in one go."

"Of course there is – but don't go on my account. Did you find it interesting reading?"

"Oh yes – I always do. But some of the people who write in say some very strange things."

"I expect that's true of people who write to all newspapers and magazines."

"One man wrote in saying the dole was utterly wrong because birds don't have any such thing. It's a bit hard if we're never to have anything the kookaburras don't have, isn't it."

The vicar laughed.

"The *Bulletin*'s got itself a very sharp reader in you ... You know, it's wonderful to think that Bundaroo has thrown up such a keen brain and a creative intelligence such as yours is."

"Oh ... I don't know – " Betty squirmed a little.

"Dear girl, don't be embarrassed. It's very clear to me that you have it in you to be something exceptional. Whether you *do* become that special being is in the Lord's hands – and your own, of course. But I feel very blessed that in my little parish there is someone who can think – think *through* matters that other people just accept. It's a great joy for me."

As she started on her way Betty felt burdened by the vicar's high expectations for her. She felt they were something she could never live up to. By the time she reached home, however, she had squared her shoulders and lifted her head. Oh yes, she could!

Turning the Off button on her tape recorder three days before her two visitors were due to arrive, Bettina fell into a reverie. She knew what had happened to Michael Potter-Clowes. He had got another parish at the beginning of the war, but one hardly more impressive than Bundaroo and the surrounding townships. His time as a conscientious objector probably didn't help. But what about the others from her childhood in Bundaroo? Her friend Alice Carey, for example? Or Steve Drayton? Or

Mr. Copley and Miss Dampier? Had the latter got married and concentrated on home and children, or had she stayed with a job she had a real talent for? Bettina had an idea that at that date you were forced to give up your job as a teacher if you had children.

Another age! But she wished she knew something about those people. She was cut off by what happened at the Leavers' Ball of 1938. That was when her life changed entirely.

5
The Here and Now

The next day, with only forty-eight hours to go before
Oliver arrived, Bettina received a letter with Australian
stamps on it, and in an unknown handwriting. Tearing it
open and going straight to the signature she confirmed
what she had already suspected. It was from Sylvia
Easton. She put down the pages, conscious that her heart
was beating faster, and took two swigs from her breakfast
mug of tea. This was a situation that seemed more fiction-
al than real: she had last seen Sylvia when she was two
months old. Now she must be in her late fifties. This was
the first time she had seen her handwriting. She had
never received, and never wanted to receive, a photograph or any other memento of her. She chewed slowly
through a piece of toast and apricot jam. Then she felt
strong enough to read the letter.

Dear Mrs Cockburn,
    Oliver tells me that he's discussed with you our plans to
visit London. I am glad these are not upsetting for you, and
that you agree it would be best if we stay at Mark's flat,
though we both look forward to your company at plays
and concerts and whenever else you can spare the time.
    May I suggest that we meet as strangers, since that is
what we in fact are? I am a friend of Oliver and Judy, and
I'm coming because Judy felt she couldn't face the long
flights again at her age. All this is true, and reason enough
for you to receive me politely but with no special warmth.
I genuinely feel excited at meeting one of Australia's fore-
most novelists, but nothing more than that.

I think it is for the best if it is on those terms that we meet – as well-disposed strangers.

With best wishes,

Sylvia Easton.

Over the rest of the morning, which was mainly spent making notes for her next chapter, Bettina thought about the letter. She decided she approved of it. This was probably because the proposal suited her down to the ground. Emotionally and practically it had every advantage. One thing there had been no question of was showing emotion at her reunion with Sylvia. If she had felt no love for her at her birth, had felt no impulse to get in touch with her during her now-quite-long life, it would have been rampant hypocrisy to pretend any pleasure at the prospect of meeting now.

The tone of the letter, too, suited her. Matching the proposal itself, it was distant. No, that wasn't quite the word – matter-of-fact was more like it. Or business-like. They would meet, they would talk about plays and operas, about present-day Australia. The tone of the letter was exactly right for such a prospect.

She wondered why her daughter had addressed her by her married name. Hardly anyone used it these days – hardly anyone knew of her marriage, for a start. She had used the name Cockburn during the year or so of her marriage to the inadequate Cecil. In those days every married woman used her married name. But she had not published anything at that point, so she had not been burdened, as Agatha Christie in her heyday had been, with the name of a man from whom she had long been parted.

Perhaps that is how they refer to me in Ollie's household, she thought. She could imagine that Judy, whom she had met only once, was quite hot on respectability. A married name was a badge of respectability, particularly for a woman who had a child. Or was Sylvia Easton trying to register some kind of claim? She dismissed the thought. Hughie's notion that she was surrounded by leeches and potential leeches should not be allowed to gain a foothold in her brain. That would poison whatever relationship they might manage to achieve.

Nevertheless the notion came up again the next day, when her agent Clare Tuckett paid her one of her occasional breezy visits. She steamed in, waving little envelopes.

"Tickets, darling. And in particular tickets for Covent Garden – and for the Golden Pair singing in *Tosca*. I can tell you I had to use every *ounce* of nous, influence, skullduggery – you name it, I've had to use it. Officially you'll – or rather *we*'ll – be part of a corporate booking from British Gas, so we'll be surrounded by people who are either asleep or talking. I felt I had to go along, after all the strings I'd pulled."

"I'll pay of – "

"Of course. *Have* you got a cigarette, darling? Thanks. Light? Oh yes, now I got tickets for Colin Davis and the LSO, for the Royal Shakespeare in *Julius Caesar*, *South Pacific* at the National (can't think what's national about *South Pacific*, can you?), and a big, vulgar concert of lollipops at the Albert Hall. So that takes care of five evenings. Anything else is up to you."

Bettina was as usual flabbergasted but grateful at having her responsibilities and choices pre-empted for her by her agent.

"Clare, I didn't expect you to do anything other than the Covent Garden – "

"All part of the service, darling. These cigarettes are

vile – why do you smoke them?" She stubbed hers out and absent-mindedly took another from the packet. "Apart from Covent Garden I got three tickets for everything. I didn't think your nephew Mark would be trailing along, from your account of him."

"Oh no, Mark won't be with us. Quite apart from anything else, he's a would-be actor, and taking him to the National or the Royal Shakespeare might suggest reasons why he's not getting any work."

"Bitch," said Clare approvingly. "He sounds wonderfully stupid. If he's in some general plan to murder you I can't see him staying out of police hands for long."

"That *is* a comfort. Anyway it's not a plan to murder me, just to get my money."

"Since you're much too sharp to be swindled out of it, the one thing suggests the other. Have you got your will all in order and as you'd like it to be?"

"Well, not really. It's years old, and some have died – "

Clare cast her a piercing glance tinged with contempt, then marched over to the phone, dialled, and arranged a meeting with her solicitor for that afternoon.

"We'll want it finalised, and signed and witnessed on the spot. It probably won't be a final one, but it's urgent that it's done, and is valid."

She banged down the phone.

"Clare, it really isn't that urgent."

"Of *course* it's urgent. Leaving aside Hughie's scaremongering, you're over eighty." A thought struck her. "Oh, by the way, I can't get any rumours that Hughie is in financial low waters. It's probably just senile suspiciousness. Now Bettina, you've got till three o'clock to decide what you're going to do with what you have. Write it down if you can, so we can just *tear* through it.

Oh – that reminds me: you're dictating things these days, aren't you?"

"Yes. I bought myself a tape recorder."

"Hmmm. Not the safest of records."

"Why not? You hear of people who've lost thousands of words from their computers."

"That was long ago, darling. Everyone has back-up disks nowadays. Have you had what you've done already transcribed?"

"Oh I don't know that it's really ready for that yet, but I have got the name of a very good person who – "

"So the answer is no. Give me all the tapes so far, and I'll have them duplicated."

"Clare, I'm sure there's a studio nearby who – "

"Darling, it's all part of the service. We have a lot of old crocks like you who dictate their books. We know what needs to be done – we have a standard drill. Anyway, we'll charge you the earth. Now, when we've done that, your very good little woman – *bound* to be a woman, I presume? And cheap as dirt – can collect them and begin the work of transcribing. And when you have a new tape ready – no, a new *chapter* ready – she can bring it in, then collect it when it's been duplicated."

"You're going to an awful lot of trouble, Clare."

"Darling, you haven't written a book in seven years, and you've only been with Tuckett and Mancini for ten. We can't live off little pieces you write about your first book for *The Author* or celebrity paragraphs on your favourite city for the *New York Times*. You've got to throw us a bit of meat now and then."

"Don't pull the line that you only keep me on out of charity, Clare. You'll do very nicely out of reprints and film rights."

"After a *great deal* of spadework and a lot of hard bargaining. Anyway, all I'm saying is a real book to sell and promote will be a nice change. I have no intention of letting you be murdered."

"That's comforting to hear. Though I've no intention of letting myself be murdered either. You don't just give up because your eighty-second year is just around the corner. I'm not going to lie down and die."

"I'm sure you're not, darling. Knowing you you've got a Kalashnikov stored behind your front door. Now, get me those tapes and I'll be on my way."

When Clare was on her way, with the tapes stuffed into her handbag, Bettina luxuriated in the pleasant feeling of being looked after. Of course Clare was protecting her investment, but she felt sure that real liking was involved too. If the memoirs she was not writing proved to be a good commercial proposition then Clare would be well rewarded for years of support, tender loving care, and sheer cheering up. It was nonsense to see Clare as a person who was battening on her except in the obvious and accepted professional way. Meanwhile there was the wearisome and worrisome matter of the will. Bettina made some coffee and prepared to come to some decisions.

Clare turned out to have some unexpected business that afternoon, so she sent a secretary from the agency whom she knew Bettina was fond of to take her to the solicitors'. She arrived at a quarter to three, and by then Bettina had made up her mind. Twenty minutes later she was spelling out the terms of her very simple new will to the agency's lawyer: equal legacies of £5,000 to her brother Oliver, to Sylvia Easton, Hughie Naismyth, Peter Seddon and Katie Jackson. The rest, and all future royalties from her books, she left to the National Portrait Gallery. It was the place in London where she felt happiest.

That settled (for the moment, and until she got a better idea), she got herself prepared, materially and mentally, for the arrival of her brother and her daughter. The last time Ollie had come to Britain he and Judy had done the flight in one. That was in 1977, and though they had left Mark and their daughter with Judy's parents, they had been exhausted for days after their arrival. After a week in London they had flown on to their real destination, Los Angeles, to visit Judy's brother. By Ollie's account at the time they had arrived there all but dead, and the foul air had made sure that they hardly made any recovery during their two weeks there. This time Oliver had scheduled a stopover in Singapore. Bettina was informed of their intentions by a very casual Mark.

"They get to Heathrow at seven in the morning, Auntie Betty. Dad reckons they'll both need eight or ten hours' shuteye, which at their age is probably spot-on, wouldn't you say? I've got something on most of that day, so I wondered if you could lay on the tucker that first night."

Lay on the tucker, thought Bettina disgustedly. Mark's Australian accent and vocabulary had got broader since he arrived in London. Probably he was hoping this would get him any Australian parts going. He was certainly not likely to get any English ones. Quite apart from anything else he looked Australian, with his enormous body, his jutting-chinned face, cleft chin, and his daunting air of healthiness.

"I'll be delighted to see them and give them dinner," she said. "Will they come by taxi, or will you bring them round?"

"Oh, whatever. I'll see what I've got on," said Mark, obviously determined to have *something*.

Bettina had a day to prepare a meal, since she had no intention of meeting the visitors after a day spent toiling over her stove. She had never made a great thing of entertaining, though she was a competent enough cook. Feeling she would have enough emotionally on her plate that evening to need help with the mechanics of it, she rang Katie and arranged for her to do the serving out and the washing up afterwards. She prepared a casseroled carbonade, all but the bread topping, then went down to Kensington High Street and bought gravlaks and some ripe nectarines to make a sorbet with. She also bought in some good wine – she usually bought Australian or New Zealand, but thought that would be silly in the circumstances. She surveyed her purchases with satisfaction when she got back to the flat: they would fit the bill nicely – something mid-way between the fatted calf and a Barmecide feast.

Not, thinking of the former, that Sylvia was in any way a prodigal daughter. If anyone had been prodigal in their relationship it had been the mother.

They arrived around seven, watched for from Bettina's first floor window. Mark drove them to Holland Walk and then pointed them to the door. He had a genius for doing things in ways that got Bettina's hackles up. But since he was not there to freeze she put him out of her mind and gave the visitors a proper welcome.

That was very easy with Oliver. He had certainly gained a lot of weight since she saw him last: though by no means short, he was by now distinctly roly-poly, and with his good-humoured, tolerant expression he looked almost Pickwickian. She hugged him with real warmth, and then shook hands with his companion.

"It's so good of you to come," she said.

"Not good at all," said her daughter. "It's wonderful to be able to visit Europe with a companion to take some of the strain. Luckily that suits both of us."

She was spectacled, greying, but with a trim figure she had not let go to seed. Her stance was not exactly prim, but there was something of the schoolteacher in it – something that spoke of simple codes, firmly adhered to. Bettina felt she could probably respect what she saw, but reserved her judgment on whether she would like it. She was just sitting them down and preparing to get them drinks when Katie let herself in with her old key and bustled through. She was dressed in a dreadful old black dress, too short and tight, that she had used when, long ago, she had used to "help out" in grander houses than this one.

"I'll do the drinks," she announced to Bettina. "This'll be your brother, will it? What will it be?"

"A beer will be fine."

"And you're – ?"

"Just a family friend," said Sylvia firmly. "I think I'll have a medium sherry."

"Can see you're not family," said Katie, whose eyesight had always been poor. "And you'll have a g. and t. will you, Bettina?"

"Thank you, Katie," said Bettina, smiling with her eyebrows slightly raised in her guests' direction. When Katie had gone through to the kitchen she said: "Katie is an old friend."

She had thought it was the right tone to adopt, but she sensed uneasily that it had not gone down well with her guests. "Not really a servant, but a friend who helps out now and then" should, surely, have been acceptable to democratic Australians, and it was nothing but the truth. She had the idea, however, that her daughter had diagnosed hypocrisy – thought that it was better if you paid anybody to do things for you that you spoke of them, thought of them, and treated them, as servants.

Talk about theatre and concerts lasted them until dinner. Bettina told them what she'd got tickets for, and got them the theatre pages of *The Times* to show them what else was on. As they went to table Bettina realized she hadn't asked them about their flight over.

"Well, I'm real glad we decided to stop over a night," said Ollie. "If we'd just had the normal half hour or so in Singapore airport I think they'd've had to drag me back on to the plane."

Bettina sympathised.

"Yes, people tell me it *sounds* like a good idea to do it all in one go, but that really it *isn't*. I always went back to Australia by sea, but I do remember one long-distance flight long ago – I think it must have been to California, or maybe Rio – and on that you had bunk beds for sleeping."

"Things have got worse rather than better, then?" asked Sylvia.

"Oh much. Take food. Now you get tiny little pieces of this and that on a plastic tray. Then you had proper meals served from salvers. The only thing that I can think of that's got better is the air hostesses. You do get real women now, often older ones, not over-painted dummies."

"Going by sea must have been wonderfully different," said Sylvia.

"It was. Three weeks was fine, but if it took five that was too much of a good thing. I wished I'd got off at Perth and taken the train – dry, very dry, land instead of water would have been a nice change."

"Did you go back to Australia often?"

"Deaths," said Bettina briefly. "Mum had cancer, but I had plenty of warning and got there in time. Dad had a minor heart attack, then another three days after I arrived. That hurt. I would have so liked to have had plenty of time with him before ... before it happened. I loved them both, but Dad believed in me so much."

"He was always talking about you," said Oliver.

"Yes – I'm sorry about that."

"No, not at all. It was always interesting, learning what you were like. In fact, I knew you from what Dad told me, rather than from my memories. Those ended when war came ... or at least when you came to Europe."

"That's right. I did that at nineteen. We'd been talking about war so long I'd already made up my mind: I knew that being part of it was the right thing. Then quite soon it was war correspondent in Europe, then the army and that was my fate sealed."

Or not quite, she thought, as perhaps Sylvia thought too. That summary missed out one or two important developments.

"Here's the stew," said Katie, coming in and plonking it down on the table. "Smells horrible rich."

"That's the brown ale it's cooked in," said Bettina.

"Hmmm. Personally I think alcohol is for drinking," said Katie, "or using for a rub."

"Well, I'll drink to drinking alcohol," said Bettina, raising her glass. Her thoughts were on the track of old times, as they were every day as she wrote, and she said:

"Perhaps it was best that I didn't see too much of Dad before he died. I have the feeling that he was putting on a last show for me, that he must have been broken, defeated."

Oliver shook his head vigorously.

"No – not Dad. Why did you think that? Because of the drought, and having to sell the property?"

"Yes, I suppose so. And Mum dying. I knew that hit him hard because I was there, and I thought maybe he wouldn't ever really recover. Because though he pretended to be happy, working out at Wilgandra – "

"He was happy," insisted Ollie. "I never saw him so contented as when he was managing for Bill Cheveley. And you know what? I don't think he'd ever really believed in running his own property. I think he saw through those soldier-settler schemes early on. They were too timid, too penny-pinching. None of the properties was really viable, not when the crunch came. And that drought was the crunch for a lot of them." There was the sound of the phone ringing, but Bettina was fascinated and let Katie answer it. "He was happy with Bill because they worshipped each other, and because it was a weight off his own shoulders. Dad had faith in himself, but he couldn't carry through a project he never really believed in."

Katie's head appeared around the door, and she looked at Oliver.

"It's for you," she said. Oliver appeared mystified and hurried out to the hall. Bettina looked at Sylvia.

"Who on earth knows he's here, apart from Mark?" she asked.

"I can't think," Sylvia replied, wrinkling her forehead. "We've both been fast asleep all day. Though I suppose

Judy could have guessed, particularly if she tried Mark's number first."

"Oh, that'll be it," said Bettina. But as she spoke Oliver came back into the room, still looking bewildered.

"It was the police," he said.

"The police!" both women said.

"I don't understand. They say they've got Mark in custody ... Can you be arrested for driving too slowly in this country?"

"Well, not as a rule," said Bettina. "What exactly did they say?"

"It was a phrase I didn't really understand. They said he'd been arrested on suspicion of kerb-crawling."

6
Concerted Action

The next half hour was quite hectic. Bettina rang Peter Seddon, made sure he hadn't been drinking, then asked him if he would drive her brother to the West Kensington Police Station, where Mark was being detained, and offer support and know-how while Oliver went through the necessary formalities to get his son released on bail. While they waited for him she explained to Ollie what kerb-crawling consisted of: pestering women to have sex in the car. He was quiet for a time, trying to take it in.

"I expect he was just trying to be friendly," he said at last. "Chatting them up and that."

"Yes, that's what kerb-crawlers do for starters," said Bettina. Then, not wanting her brother's first evening to be more spoilt than it already was, she added: "But you could save Mark's face by saying you're sure that that's all it was, and that he doesn't understand the British laws."

"Yes ... Yes, that might help ... I'm sure he didn't mean any harm. Mark's always been a bit of a problem – the comedian of the family – but there's no harm in him."

"No, no, I'm sure there isn't," said Bettina, speaking against her better judgment. "Ah, that'll be Peter."

When they had got Ollie off Bettina came back into the flat and raised her eyebrows at Sylvia.

"Well, I don't know what you'd feel about a sorbet. Maybe we do need cooling down a bit."

"No, that's Mark," said Sylvia, and they both laughed. When Katie brought it in it was clear she had been listening.

"Well, I won't say a word about what's going on," she began.

"Good," said Bettina.

" – but Mr Mark is the last person I'd've thought would need to go kerb-crawling for a woman."

"Then obviously you're wrong, aren't you?"

"I'm not wrong so often as others that think themselves a lot cleverer than I am," said Katie complacently.

When they were alone again, Sylvia said: "You don't like Mark, do you?"

"Not much. Well, not at all, frankly. I can't think of many women who would, in spite of Katie, even ones who go for brawn. He's so obviously in love with himself, completely taken up with it. There's no room in Mark for any other passion."

Sylvia didn't entirely go along with that.

"As Oliver said, he's regarded as a bit of a comedian at home."

"I can't remember him ever having the company in stitches at his droll witticisms."

"I meant unconsciously. You weren't supposed to laugh, but you did."

"Well yes, I can imagine that. But I didn't laugh."

"You found him – what – threatening?"

Bettina answered without hesitation.

"Yes, that was pretty much it. Any young man who walks around an old lady's flat in a jock-strap has either no sense of what nudity implies or he assumes he's God's gift to any and every woman."

"He's certainly got no idea of the fitness of things," said Sylvia. She opened her mouth to say something else, then thought better of it.

"What were you going to say?" Bettina asked.

"Oh, nothing ... It would have sounded as if I thought you over-reacted to Mark's blokeishness, which wasn't at all what I meant ... To tell you the truth, I was going to ask if you thought you were still scarred by ... that early experience."

"Yes," said Bettina at once. She let Katie bring in the coffee, then go out to resume noisily the washing up. "Not in the obvious way, maybe. Horrible experiences like that affect different people in different ways. I took a while to recover, but recover I did. But, like any other experience, it leaves a sort of residue. You *are* changed, you are not what you would have been if you had never gone through it ... I'm talking awful clichés, aren't I? All the men in my life – and that's another cliché, isn't it, but what I meant was all the men I've loved or just gone to bed with – have either been gentle types, real *lovers* in the best sense, or men who just took sex as a matter of course, something to be enjoyed in a non-guilty way. Peter Seddon whom you just met was like that, the latter type. But what I've always shrunk from has been the aggressive type or the – I don't quite know how to put it best – the self-advertising type. Swaggerers."

"Don't you think Mark may be just that? He swaggers. Having to go kerb-crawling shows how empty the swagger is. I've never thought of him as posing a threat."

Bettina shook herself.

"I expect you're right. But I do think that the one thing is very close to the other. For example, if Mark's vanity was under attack – and he's one mass of vanity – I believe he could well turn aggressive. He couldn't bear not to preen himself at the very thought of how wonderful he was."

"You're the novelist, the people person. Look, I think

I'd better be going. I still need to catch up on sleep. Such a pity your lovely dinner-party has been disturbed – I was really enjoying myself."

"There'll be others. Will you be all right in Mark's flat? You'll probably be disturbed when he and Ollie come home. There'll be all sorts of ructions and recriminations."

"Do you think so? For all we know, being arrested for kerb-crawling may be all in a day's work for Mark." The two of them giggled.

"Well, it may be for Mark, but it won't be for Ollie. He'll surely want to chew it over, give fatherly advice or whatever."

Sylvia looked at her.

"You don't really know Ollie, do you?"

"No, hardly at all. Ollie was an afterthought, or rather a mistake I suspect. When I left home to go to Armidale he was only four."

"Right. Well, nothing fazes Oliver. He accepts whatever fate throws at him. If Mark has been pestering women Ollie will say he's just been silly and he'll learn from his mistakes. There certainly won't be any rows and ructions."

Bettina thought as she rang for a taxi that this was carrying nonchalance too far. Still, Mark was well out of swaddling clothes, and as unlikely to take good advice from his father as from anyone else. He was his own man, in the worst possible sense. And she herself, having never had a child that she would take responsibility for, was the last person to pass judgment.

When Peter rang her on his mobile after dropping Ollie and Mark he said, with a complacency that annoyed Bettina:

"You wouldn't think a bloke like that would have to pay for his pleasure, would you?"

"No, you believe in getting paid, don't you, Peter?"

"Come off it, Bettina," he protested. "I've always stood my round."

"That was the fig-leaf. I always paid for the food and booze while you were living here."

She regretted saying it as she went to bed. She didn't want to become one of those women who were congenitally sour about men.

When she came to sit down at her tape recorder next day, Bettina remembered the conversation with Sylvia about aggressive male sexuality, and she began her reminiscences with a tiny incident that she had had no intention of including in those gleanings of her past, something so minor that it had no significance beyond the fact of the man that it dealt with. And that was very significant indeed.

The message was given them on Saturday morning in the General Store run by Phil Pollard, a shop generally referred to as Phil's. Everyone went into Phil's on a Saturday morning, so he was often the bearer of messages. When he told Betty's mother that he had one for her she knew at once – and Betty did too – that it must be from Wilgandra. And that it was for Jack, rather than for either of them. The doctor who served Bundaroo, Corunna and two other small townships had advised Bill Cheveley to get hold of a new tablet that he thought would be beneficial in Mrs Cheveley's illness. When she heard this Betty vaguely wondered what Mrs Cheveley's illness *was*, and if anybody really knew. Bill had phoned the chemist in Walgett and they had the tablet in stock, so he wondered if Jack Whitelaw would drive him there. Both women knew Jack would do anything for Bill.

"You go to Grafton's and get your father," said Betty's mother. "I've got to go and have a word with the vicar about the Christmas party in the church hall."

"Oh Mum! Do I have to?"

"Now don't whinge Betty. No harm can come to you. I've got Oliver, and all you've got to do is ask someone to bring him out to talk to you."

That was precisely what Betty hated doing.

To make matters worse, when she approached the main door of Grafton's Hotel, Sam Battersby emerged from it to take a breather in the sun during a lull in customers' orders. There he stood, fat and leering, and Betty had come so close to the entrance that she couldn't change course and go round to the back.

"Well, well, young lady. This is an unexpected pleasure."

"I've got to speak to my Dad." The request came out, as intended, more rude than merely business-like.

Sam Battersby's leer broadened.

"No problem about that. When I've just finished my smoke I'll go in and get him for you."

"Please, it's urgent."

"Now what could be urgent on a lovely Saturday morning when everyone's enjoying the sunshine buying little things for Christmas? Let's you and me just have a little chat and – "

"It's a message from Wilgandra. Dad's got to drive Bill to Walgett to get some medicine urgently for Mrs Cheveley."

He scanned her face, to see whether she was lying.

"Oh well ... Bill's a good mate ... We'll just have to postpone our little chat, young lady." And he lumbered off into the smoky, dark, male-filled Saloon Bar behind him.

"Anything wrong?" asked Jack Whitelaw when he came out.

"Bill Cheveley wants you to drive into Walgett to get some new medicine for Mrs Cheveley," said Betty, this time not having to stretch the truth.

"Oh, right ... What I meant was, anything wrong with you? You looked sort of ... upset, like."

"I don't like the way he calls me 'young lady', or the way he thinks he and I should have a 'little chat'."

He walked on for a bit.

"It's not much, is it, Betty?"

"No, not when I say it out ... But it's not just what he says, it's how he looks at me."

"Yes, I can see that. Well, I'll wait here for Bill and the car. That could be them in the distance. Look after your mother. We should be back by sundown."

But Betty did not go at once to join up with her mother and Oliver at the vicarage. From the edge of the little township where she had left her father she walked back along the strip of bitumen greeting schoolfriends, some with parents, usually mothers – the fathers were in Grafton's, asserting their superiority to such concerns as shopping – some in little knots by Phil's or Bob's Café, or even by the little shack at the far end where Mr Blackfeller swapped stories with anyone who passed. Betty walked quickly past the hotel, then went up to a group of about her own age outside Bob's.

"I haven't seen Hughie, have you?" she asked. One or two boys gave exaggerated shrugs.

"His mother was in Bundaroo yesterday, I think," contributed one of the girls. "Her Ladyship probably did the family shopping then."

"What do you want with a mardarse like Hughie Naismyth?" asked Herbie Cox. Herbie was born in Nottingham, and his father had never lost his native dialect in the twelve years the family had been in Australia. Herbie picked up the words from back home, and liked spreading the words of contempt as an alternative to the Australian ones.

"Hughie's not a mardarse," said Betty. "He taught you lot soccer."

The shrugs came again, still more exaggerated.

"Soccer's a game for cissy boys anyway," said one of the others. "You don't want to go with that Hughie. He's useless."

"He's a sight more use than thickies like you," said Betty, and she walked away quickly.

Immediately she kicked herself. She was not going to help Hughie by abusing his classmates. She had been thrown by what she had just heard, which was what she had been dreading. The suspicion of Hughie, momentarily lightened by the boys' interest in the new game, had softened first to indifference, but was now hardening again into disdain and dislike. Soon there could be one of those minor school vendettas – not frequent things, but always a danger where incomers were concerned. Bundaroo was a small town with a very small-town dislike of anything unfamiliar, unknown.

As she made her way down the street there was a shout from the little knot of teenagers she had left.

"Only thing that nancy could play would be bloody *Beet*hoven!"

"*Bate*hoven," Betty turned and shouted, and again realized she'd done a foolish thing. If there was going to be a vendetta she knew she had to be on Hughie's side. But it would be so much better if there was no vendetta, and all she had done in the last two minutes was to harden antipathies.

She wondered how they had found out about the Beethoven afternoon, but it turned out to be quite simple. When Mrs Naismyth had gone over with the English-style egg-custard to

84

the Cheveleys house at Wilgandra she had not seen the invalid but had given it to the full-time cook and housemaid who had been so necessary since Mrs Cheveley's health had failed. This was the mother of Steve Drayton, wife of Kevin the stockman whom the new manager had taken against, so conversation was inevitably short and stilted. In the course of it Mrs Naismyth had said that her son and Betty Whitelaw had got together "and were playing Beethoven, would you believe it?" It was a remark somewhere between a boast and an apology. Mrs Naismyth was a woman who was never sure of herself, her values, or her place in the scheme of things. The remark was reported later to the Draytons, father and son, and thence circulated around Wilgandra, and was carried into Bundaroo.

When she saw her mother leaving the weatherboard vicarage Betty went over and took charge of Oliver.

"Dad's on the way to Walgett," she said, and her mother nodded.

"The poor lady needs anything that could bring her relief, so I'm told," said her mother.

"Oh Betty, I've got something for you," said the Reverend Potter-Clowes, taking a sheet of exercise book from his pocket. "The competition was in this week's *Bulletin*. I'm an awfully slow reader, because I sometimes get ideas for sermons from it – "

"I know," said Betty.

"I'm sure you do! I couldn't keep anything like that from a sharp girl like you. Anyway, I've copied it all out, and you can really get thinking."

As they walked back through Bundaroo and out towards home, Betty noted that the Naismyths had arrived, probably driven by one of the stockmen in his old jalopy (Paul Naismyth had talked about getting his own car since he arrived, but had not yet done so). Paul was shopping with his wife, perhaps because he realized he wouldn't be made welcome at Grafton's, or possibly from a sense that officers didn't mix socially with the other ranks. He had a lot to learn about Australian democracy, which in the outback was real, and more than skin-deep. Paul Naismyth, however, did not talk or act like a learner.

As they walked past Bob's Café Betty saw that the little knot of her schoolmates had been joined by Hughie. They weren't ignoring him, but whenever he spoke they looked him in the eye and didn't respond. It was a technique she knew very well. She sometimes thought she knew everything there was to know about Bundaroo. Quite soon she was to realize that her knowledge was as skin-deep as Paul Naismyth's understanding of Australian democracy.

The topic of Bundaroo and the *Bulletin* competition came up the next night, when she, Oliver and Sylvia went to the concert of classical pops at the Royal Albert Hall. She knew the Hall was the attraction, so she suggested that they meet in the bar half an hour before the concert was due to begin, so that if they felt like it they could do a bit of walking around before the music started.

"Beethoven's *Leonore* number three," said Sylvia, looking at the programme. "At least I know that. And then there's the *Elvira Madigan* concerto."

"Betty was famous in Bundaroo for playing Beethoven – on the gramophone, that is – with her friend Hughie," said Oliver. "It was part of the local folklore after she was gone."

"I don't see anything outrageous or contradictory in that," said Bettina. "I see Bundaroo, or at least the country around it, as spare – rather grand and terrible. Not unlike."

"That wasn't quite how you saw it in the *Bulletin* piece," said Sylvia. Bettina shot her a glance.

"Good heavens! You haven't gone rummaging around in libraries to find that, have you?"

Sylvia smiled, and nodded her head in Ollie's direction.

"A family heirloom," he said. "We got it when Dad died. It was much-thumbed even then. He showed it around a lot."

"Of course, Dad would. We were given five copies, along with the prize – the little silver cup, I mean. The *real* prize was a hundred pounds and the trip to Sydney. I've still got one of the copies. Mum and Dad had one, and so did the Cheveleys and the vicar. That just left one, and I gave it to Auntie Shirley in Armidale. I was living with her by then, and she made sure I was practically a local celebrity."

"But in the piece you concentrated on the narrowness – how limiting the place was," insisted Sylvia.

"I dealt with it, but I covered it up pretty well. You're sharp to see how important it was. If I'd plugged it too hard I would never have won first prize. I had to balance it with a lot of stuff about the closeness of the people, the sense of community, the church and school pulling the place together, the monotonous grandeur of the landscape. The narrowness of people's horizons was a very minor part of the piece as far as space went. I was going all out for that prize."

"You knew even then you were that good?" asked Ollie.

"I knew I had to get away," said Bettina. She might have elaborated on that, but suddenly she said "Good Lord! Speaking of my Bundaroo past!"

Her companions looked towards the other end of the bar, where Hughie, his wife by his side, was coping with two grey-haired ladies. Bettina knew fans when she saw them, and these had obviously bearded Hughie, determined to tell him how much they'd enjoyed his television series *The Rise of the Modern*, now all of twelve years old, and dating back to the time when television took its educational role seriously. Hughie's wife Marie, immaculate in her blonde perfection like a Hitchcock heroine targeted by birds, stood resolutely beside him, her smile fixed in place as implacably as each strand of hair. After a minute or two the fans backed apologetically away, and Hughie turned in their direction, raised his hand to them, then, seeing in Bettina's face permission, edged his way over, followed by the determined Marie.

"Hello, Bettina. This must be Oliver. I remember you when you were just a dirty face and sticky fingers. I'm Eugene Naismyth – Hughie – this is my wife, Marie. And you must be Sylvia Easton. We haven't met, but it's good to see you over here. Did you have a good flight? *Is* there such a thing as a good flight from Australia to Britain, I wonder?"

"I've only known two," said Oliver. "All I know is, I prefer it with a stopover."

"True. But how ghastly you feel when you have to get on the plane again *after* the stopover. Marie knows. We go to Australia regularly, and it gets worse and worse each time – one other symptom of aging."

"Do you have relatives there?" asked Ollie.

"No, no. I'm a sort of ambassador in this country for Australian art – an expert, if the truth be known, who knows *rather* more than some of the specialists back there. I go back regularly to make sure I keep up with the art scene."

"I don't suppose there was much of an art scene when you and Bettina were going to school in Bundaroo, was there?" asked Sylvia.

"Oh, definitely a burgeoning one," said Hughie. "I'd been in Melbourne, and noticed it. I thought I was the expert because I knew more about it than anyone in Bundaroo, which was a very *small* degree of self-praise. Anyway, I nurtured Bettina's taste."

"Oh dear, don't let's go back into pre-history," sighed Marie Naismyth. Her speciality was calculated rudeness. "You know, all Hughie's wives have had to live with Bettina as a third in the bed."

"Metaphorically speaking," said Hughie, covering up for her rudeness. "Our friendship has always been exclusively aesthetic."

"Too right," said Bettina.

She had been aware over the past two days that her accent was regaining some of its old Australian overtones, and now she exaggerated them deliberately. Hughie, on the other hand, who owed some of his television popularity to the cut-glass enunciation of old-fashioned upper-class usages, had put on his most dated and precious tones to welcome the newcomers. Bettina wondered how far both developments were deliberate, how far unconscious. They were interrupted by the sound of the bell.

"Here we go for popular culture," said Hughie.

"Oh dear," said Bettina, "I was intending to take them around the building before the concert, and now there won't be time."

"If you would like a tour of this great monument to Victorian uxoriousness," said Hughie, "you can have one in the interval with a moderately well-qualified guide."

"Oh yes – yes please," said Ollie and Sylvia, as they moved towards the auditorium. Bettina was pleased to get out of that chore, because really she knew very little about Victorian architecture, and she had other things on her mind. She pulled Sylvia back.

"How is Mark facing his disgrace?" she asked ironically.

"Disgrace? He seems quite unaware of any. He just says 'All in a day's work' and grins. I'm still trying to work out what that's supposed to mean."

The concert proved more to Bettina's taste than she expected, with a performance of the Mozart by a young Norwegian pianist that was a revelation. But in the second half, full of familiar and bouncy short pieces, she wondered about Hughie's unexpected appearance. She had told him on the phone all the things that they were booked for. Most of them were for long-running shows, or, as at Covent Garden, part of a series of performances. The concert was the only ticket they had that was a one-off, the one thing where Hughie could be sure of meeting Oliver and Sylvia.

One thing Bettina was sure of: the last sort of cultural event that Hughie would normally wish to be seen at was an Albert Hall concert of classical lollipops.

7
Painted into a Corner

The audience at *Tosca* was predictably "brilliant", which meant in Bettina's view well-heeled, either by inheritance, the sweat of their brows, or via some infernal financial nous that she could not begin to understand. There were faces that she knew in the foyer and crush bar, people she could flap a brief greeting to, but she thought Oliver and Sylvia would be happiest just looking rather than being introduced, so they found themselves a space and contentedly sipped their drinks. Sylvia certainly observed the dresses with a clinical, appraising eye, suggesting not that she would ever dress like that herself, but that she was glad to know that this was what people did wear these days to smart events in London.

"It's good to have seen an audience like this," she murmured.

"Once," said Bettina.

Their seats were not of the grandest, being in the Amphitheatre Stalls, but four of them had set Bettina back more than she cared to think about. She wasn't mean, but she did like to feel she had got value for her money. What was the point of subsidising a theatre for the superbly-well-heeled, she wondered, conscious that she would be accounted by many as one of that company herself. Clare slipped into her seat beside them only as the lights were going down, so there was no chance of doing more than make muttered introductions.

The first act got into its stride quickly, and Bettina was glad it was an old, traditional production, with monumental sets and a tenor of the stand-and-deliver persuasion – delivering, indeed, rather more, in the form of long high notes, than Puccini had stipulated. Then Tosca arrived, jealous and demanding, and the temperature rose. Ollie sat forward in his seat, and Sylvia stiffened into renewed attention. By the time the act ended they were so involved that Bettina wondered they could forebear from booing Scarpia.

They collected the drinks they had ordered and found a corner of the crush bar where they could watch and listen as well as talk.

"Are you enjoying your stay?" Clare asked Sylvia. Bettina was interested that she couldn't quite keep the note of metropolitan condescension out of her voice.

"So far very much. Everything so new and unusual."

"We're enjoying this tremendously," said Oliver. "I gather that we've got you to thank for getting the tickets." Clare gave a wave of dismissal.

"All part of the service."

"I'm sure it's *not*."

"For some authors," amended Clare.

"I know one can't expect it to be in English, with international stars," said Sylvia, "but I wish I knew *exactly* what was being said at each point."

"The theory is that you study the libretto in advance," said Clare.

"But if I did it thoroughly I'd have to do it listening to discs of the music, and by the time I was *really* well-prepared I'd know the opera so well that it would have lost some of its impact," said Sylvia.

"You're quite right," said Bettina. "Audiences these days don't want to *follow* the action, they just want to *wallow* in the music, with a vague idea of what's going on. And that suits the singers, who don't have to bother about getting the words across. They should be having that audience agog with the 'what happens next?' excitement. They've got it wrong, you've got it right."

It was the first time she had expressed even implied praise or fellow-feeling for her daughter. Sylvia flushed with surprise, and to cover the embarrassment of the moment Clare said:

"And where else are you going while you're over here?"

"We hadn't thought of anywhere else but London when we were planning the trip," said Ollie. "But now we've been wondering whether we couldn't slip in a few days in Edinburgh."

This was news, and rather enticing news, to Bettina.

"Edinburgh in April!" she said. "It could be lovely, depending on the weather. Much nicer anyway than Edinburgh in Festival time, though of course there won't be as much to do."

"Do you know Edinburgh well?" asked Sylvia.

"Once upon a time I went there fairly often. Now, I'm afraid, it's many years since I was there. The usual thing: old age."

"Why don't you come with us – if we can fit in the trip with all the theatre and concert tickets."

"The tickets can be changed, or ignored," said Bettina firmly.

"Then you'll come?"

"I'm very tempted ... But would you two want an old person with you? One who keeps having to cry off things and go back to her hotel to rest?"

"Why should we mind?" said Ollie. "We're old people ourselves. And if we do stand the pace, you can cry off: you get your rest and we plough on doing the sights."

When the bell went and they all began to troop back downstairs, Sylvia and Oliver in front, Clare whispered to Bettina:

"If you are going to traipse off to Edinburgh, make sure I have all you've dictated of the book before you go."

Bettina looked at her, bewildered, then laughed.

"I'm afraid I've passed on some of Hughie's paranoia to you, Clare. Why on earth should I be under any sort of threat?"

Clare didn't answer, but gestured towards Ollie and Sylvia. Bettina felt something like anger rise in her, in spite of her long friendship with Clare.

As they were sitting down, Bettina bent across over Ollie and said to Sylvia:

"You're quite right about translation. It's the only way to really get the impact of an opera. Verdi refused to let the Paris Opera give the premiere of *Otello* in Italian. He knew it had to be in French to make its proper effect."

She was not making a contribution to the age-old debate about the proper language for opera performances. She was making, for Clare's benefit, a gesture of solidarity with her daughter.

She had a long history of making gestures of solidarity.

As November advanced, the heat in Bundaroo began to assume its fierce summer glare. For some it was welcome. For others it was feared – Betty and Hughie among them. From early in the day armpits and the small of the back became itchy in the dry heat. All visible skin began to re-assume the tan or the raw red of the previous summer. Tempers were frayed. Little things began to assume ridiculous importance, irritations festered and became grudges. It was summer again – the summer when Betty would leave school.

As Bundaroo High moved towards Christmas and the end-of-year leaving exams, feeling against Hughie crystallised. It wasn't so much what was said – in fact an absolute minimum was said *to* him, and he wasn't much discussed when he wasn't there. The youngsters didn't need to discuss him, because they knew what they thought about him. Their collective judgment was formed from a variety of impulses and time-honoured reactions, but the main ones were the feeling that he was *different*, and was not making an effort to prove otherwise. Hughie was also affected by the wider feeling in the community that Paul Naismyth was a no-hoper posing as an efficient leader and manager, a man whose engagement had been one of Bill Cheveley's few mistakes, one who would be taking the road to Sydney or Melbourne and the boat back to England before many months were over. That second judgment, at its most extreme, shaded off into the view that Naismyth was a smooth-talking crook. As often happens in schools, Hughie suffered for the reputation of his parents.

Nobody, not even Betty, was quite sure how he was affected by the general hostility and contempt. Hughie walked nonchalantly to and from school, apparently quite unconcerned if he had no one of his own age to talk to. He made friends with the vicar, who was always happy to have some intelligent conversation, and he discussed art with Miss Dampier. The latter's essay topic on "Oh to be in England" had resulted in especial praise for Hughie's effort, which in its turn led to muttering about his unfair advantage. Miss Dampier had tried to neutralise this by a follow-up topic on what pupils would choose to regret if they were away from Australia, what they would remember and long to experience again. Miss Dampier had long been frustrated by the fact that syllabuses for New South Wales schools dealt entirely with English history and English literature, with barely a nod to the nationality of most of the pupils. Hughie didn't help matters, though, by muttering "endless mutton and the dunny man calling" as she was elaborating her theme. Miss Dampier diagnosed a boy who was terribly unsure of himself, and who felt the need to make periodic aggressive gestures.

Hughie's best friend, however, was at this point Mr Blackfeller, also known as Alfred, and by an aboriginal name no one could attempt to pronounce. He was generally genial, though a man of few words, and when Hughie went to talk to him after school and look at his pictures, the visits mostly consisted of them both sitting contentedly together in the little patch of garden in front of his shack while Mr Blackfeller smoked his pipe and uttered the occasional monosyllable.

The gift of Mr Blackfeller which brought him most local recognition was not his painting but his prophecies. These prophecies (which, perhaps fortunately, were never about people, always about greater events) were passed around in Bundaroo and the nearby townships, generally scoffed at, but – if not believed – widely *registered*, referred to, kept in the back of people's minds.

"Mr Blackfeller says we've got a big drought coming," said Betty's mother one day over breakfast. Jack Whitelaw's cup went down with a crash on his saucer.

"Bloody hell, Dot, you don't believe that flaming con-man, do you?" Jack Whitelaw's language always became stronger when a nerve had been touched.

"Oh, I don't know – "

"He'll say anything for sixpence. It's just made up, like those trashy romantic books you read."

"Well, if he's saying there's going to be a drought he's not telling people what they want to hear, that's for sure."

The justice of that had to be admitted.

"Too right. He'll not get many sixpences in his palm for forecasting a drought in this neck of the woods."

"Anyway, everyone says he foretold the Great War."

Jack slapped his knife across his plate. He never liked people talking about the Great War.

"Oh yes? And what's he supposed to have said? 'Great storm cover whole world.'"

"Well, it did, didn't it?"

"He could have been talking about another Great Flood. If people had believed him they'd have gone away and started building themselves flaming arks! Bloody hell, Dot, I'd've expected a bit more sense from you ... What's he said?"

"Something about a great thirst on the way."

"There's one of those every Saturday in Grafton's."

"He's a clever fellow," protested Dot.

"Oh, he's that all right."

Mr Blackfeller presumably did not fill Hughie's head with his Cassandra-like prophecies. Hughie had read a book on Nostradamus. He said the prophecies of that sage were so vague you had to be downright cracked to believe them. Hughie just sat there with him, telling him things now and then (Mr Blackfeller liked information), and sometimes being invited into his shack to see his latest paintings aimed at the Sydney market, and other more private ones that Hughie found much more interesting.

"He's got those ones that he does and sends to Sydney and Melbourne. Dealers of some kind there give him a few quid for them – it's a market, and he knows what they want," Hughie explained to Betty. "But he's got these others, ones he keeps in an old cardboard box, and those are the real thing – strange, abstract-like pictures: not much colour, and they seem at first to be just patterns, and then he points out things – the moon, trees, stones, a snake. The ones he sells are quite good in their way, but the ones for himself are wonderful."

"Would he show them to me?" asked Betty.

"I don't know. This is for your article, I suppose?" Hughie sometimes spoke of her article as if he was jealous of it. "He might show them to you if you came to see him with me. The sad thing is, though, that the ones he values himself are the ones he can sell to Sydney and Melbourne. He doesn't think anything of the real stuff. My dad gave me five pounds for my birthday and I bought three of them for that – he wanted to give them to me and not take any money, but I insisted he take it. The other ones may gain in value – no one's giving their money away if they buy them. But it's the strange ones that will be really valuable in fifty years' time."

Betty couldn't think in terms of fifty years, though if anyone had told her that in fifty years' time she would be an esteemed novelist living in London she would probably have thought that life was going to give her everything she had ever dreamed of. She said:

"How can you know what they'll be worth in fifty years' time?"

Hughie shrugged.

"Twenty, maybe thirty. It all depends on when Australians wake up to what Australia really is."

Betty had this in common with her schoolmates: she didn't like Hughie assuming, with Pommie over-confidence, that he knew what Australia really was. She certainly didn't feel Hughie was one she needed to talk to as she meditated her article for the *Bulletin* competition, which could account for the tone of voice he assumed when speaking about it. He was still one of her best friends, and she was still his only one, but as she got possessed by her subject he got sidelined in her life, and she hoped (without worrying too much about it) that he could get all the companionship he needed from his adult friends, more suitable matches for his sophistication. Betty wildly exaggerated in her mind the sophistication of a Northumberland farming community, and had no idea how Hughie's apparent cultivation and worldly wisdom had been patiently gleaned and put together from the wireless, from such newspapers as he could pick up, and from any relations, neighbours and friends of his parents who might drop a relevant crumb in his path.

So it was with schoolfriends other than Hughie that Betty sat down and communed when she was collecting and sifting material for her article. One day after school Betty sat in the playground with some of her best friends in the school and read them the draft of her first paragraph.

"By nine the sun begins its daily blaze over Bundaroo ..."

When she came to the bit about "open landscapes and closed minds" she substituted on the spur of the moment the words "boundless hopes and limited prospects." When the little group began discussing what the rest of the article should contain, one of her friends – Alice Carey, her best friend – suggested that she go and talk to Won Chi at the vegetable shop, and another that she should talk to Mr Blackfeller about his prophecies, and describe the little aboriginal reserve two miles out of town. These suggestions seemed to justify the change she had made in the wording, but one voice demurred: "Surely you should be concentrating on the Australianness of the place, not on the outsiders." The remark seemed to justify her original comment.

"It's a bit funny if aboriginals aren't considered Australian enough to get in," she said in a deceptively mild tone of voice.

"Well, Australia like it is now," said the boy, who was Steve Drayton.

The subject of the aborigines in the area came up again, from an anecdote told her by Hughie one day on their walk to school. He had been buying a slab of fruit cake in Bob's café the day before when Bob had opened up on the subject.

"You the boy I see talking to Mr Blackfeller all the time?"

"That's right."

"Can't see what you two have to talk about."

"Oh, we talk about his pictures, mostly."

Bob spat decorously behind the counter.

"Them daubs. I don't call them pictures ... Still, I suppose he gets himself a living by them, unlike most of his bunch."

"He doesn't charge enough for them," said Hughie.

"Is that right? You'd know, would you? ... See here, young man, you want to be a bit more careful who you mix with. Mr Blackfeller's all very well in his own world and with his own people, but he wouldn't be allowed in my café, and he wouldn't be allowed in Grafton's, and that tells you something, doesn't it?"

"Oh, yes, it tells me something," said Hughie.

Betty relished the anecdote, but some part – some small part, she insisted to herself – wished it had not been Hughie that it had happened to, that he had not been the one to make that last, barbed remark. That part of her understood – even shared – the resentment of her schoolmates of the outsider, particularly the outsider who would say what he thought even if it meant assuming a superiority to the people of his host country. But Betty had glimmers of understanding of the personal uncertainties, the divided nature and loyalties, of the boy who said it. The exchange did not find its way into her article.

It was a few days after this that Betty, at the end of the school day, was following some yards behind Hughie through the playground when she heard a little chorus from the younger children from the primary section, a glorified hut at the far end of the playground near to the river bank.

"Here comes the nancy boy, here comes the homo!" the angelic voices sang out in unison. It was the development that Betty had most feared, but one she had known in her heart was bound to come. Hughie gave no sign of reacting to the children, beyond a stiffening of the shoulders. Betty considered whether to stop and say something to the children, but then wondered what on earth she could say. They didn't even understand what the words meant that they were using.

She speeded up her walking, and linked arms with Hughie just outside the gate.

The performance of *Tosca* stayed with Bettina when her arthritis kept her awake that night, and over her breakfast of scrambled eggs. She dwelt particularly on the second act, with Scarpia's study so conveniently situated next to the torture chamber. How Puccini, for all his horrible hang-ups, did sometimes ring the bell: the apparently innocuous setting, concealing something monstrous. The unspeakable being done while around it normal civilised life seemed to flow on as usual.

There had been no Scarpia in Bundaroo. Though what Sam Battersby had been after was not so different.

She walked slowly through to her study and sat down at her desk. The events she was chronicling, the small-town feeling against Hughie, against all the Naismyths, was so apparently petty, so insignificant set against the Grand Guignol of torture and summary executions that had lodged in her mind since last night. But it was the same feeling that in the Southern states of the USA had led to lynchings, and in Nazi Germany and the East European countries had led to consequences which her mind, most minds, could not yet grasp the full horror of.

She leant forward to turn on her tape recorder. Then she stopped and sat back in her seat. The machine was not where it should be. It had been moved. Not by much, by maybe two or three inches, but moved it had been. It was no longer in exactly the best position for her old arthritic hands. The cleaning firm had not been in since the previous morning, and in any case were sternly forbidden to do anything about her desk. She remembered coming out in the night to go to the lavatory. The light had been on in the study, and thinking she was becoming forgetful in old age she had come over and switched it off. She shivered at the memory.

The machine had not moved itself. Someone had been in.

8
At Sundown

"I'm taking Dad to a club tomorrow night," said Mark to Bettina when she called in at his flat in Earl's Court to collect Oliver and Sylvia to take them to the Barbican.

"To a *club*?" said Bettina, her mind toying with all sorts of possibilities about the sort of club concerned.

"Yeah – show him a bit of the London scene. Sylvia thought she'd give it a miss."

"I'm not surprised. I'd give it a big miss myself. Do you think your father can cope with more than ten minutes of the sort of club I think you mean?"

"'Course he can, Auntie Bet. He's a tough old bird, and he's very young at heart."

"But is he young at ear?"

Mark looked at her, his thought processes almost audible, then decided it was a joke and laughed.

"Dad'll cope, you'll see. And if he doesn't like it he can slip out as soon as he wants. There's plenty of pubs in the vicinity, not to mention other amenities."

In the interval of *Julius Caesar*, when Ollie had slipped off to the Gents, Bettina said to Sylvia:

"I can't think why Mark would want to take his father clubbing."

Sylvia shrugged.

"Oh, I'm sure he'll take it in his stride. The pill-popping and drug-taking won't faze him – if he notices it."

"I wouldn't be able to stand the music. Mark says there are plenty of pubs around. I don't think drinking alone in a London pub while your son tries to chat up the birds in a nearby club is much of a night out."

"I think Oliver just likes knowing what sorts of things are going on. Like a novelist, maybe."

Bettina laughed.

"At my age I've become very choosy about the sort of experience I can be bothered to cultivate ... Mark seems to be quite unfazed by the kerb-crawling charge."

"He is. He just says it's a good way to pull in the chicks. The fact that it's illegal he says is 'just silly'. Mark is very unfazable on the surface."

"I'd like him more if I was sure it was only on the surface. What goes on under the surface? Does anything? I wondered when he told me he was taking Ollie to a club what sort of club he was talking about. I discarded the Garrick or the Athenæum, but I did wonder if he meant a gay club."

Sylvia shook her head confidently.

"I've told you, Mark is mildly heterosexual. So far as I can see he is interested in conquests to boost his own opinion of himself and his desirability. The conquests are always female. Whether he'd say no to an approach from a man I don't know, but that's different."

"True ... You'll be on your own tomorrow evening. Would you care to come out for a meal?"

There was only a tiny pause before Sylvia answered.

"You don't have to, Bettina."

"I know I don't have to. I'd like to."

They looked each other straight in the eye, something they did not do very often.

"In that case I'd like it very much," said Sylvia.

Then Ollie came back, and by common and unspoken consent they kept their dinner date to themselves.

Bettina chose for their first meeting on their own a new restaurant off Kensington High Street. It had not yet received extravagant plaudits or brickbats from the burgeoning tribe of restaurant critics, so it did not attract the crowds of punters that both kinds of notice bring with them. There were two or three empty tables between them and the next diners, so they could talk without that buttoning-up effect that closeness to strangers brings with it. They walked there, and Bettina, like many older people, welcomed the presence of someone to guide her, restrain her at crossings, and cope with the manifold hazards of the London streets.

"Well, I *hope* Ollie is enjoying himself," she said as they settled over their menus, "but I certainly wouldn't bank on it. I'm sure Mark is going on his merry way without a thought for his father. He's that sort."

"Probably," agreed Sylvia. "But that may be what Ollie would prefer."

It occurred to Bettina that parents and children, in particular neglect of customary duties between them, was not the happiest choice of subject. They talked over the menu, which was fashionably eclectic, and Bettina ordered for both of them, with an Alsace wine to follow their gin and tonics.

"Verdict so far on your trip?" Bettina asked, sipping her gin.

"Fabulous. Enchanting. Exciting. All the words the advertisers and travel writers use. It's been what I always had in mind, the thing I had to do eventually. A lot of younger Australians think in terms of visiting Asia these days – "

"I suppose it's cheaper," said Bettina dryly.

"Well, it is that, but I think they genuinely feel that that's where Australia's future is. I sympathise, but I can't follow suit. I suppose I'm more interested in the past. Our past is here. It must be a generational thing."

"Both my parents talked of Britain as 'home'," said Bettina. "In my father's case those feelings had been reinforced by the war – the First World War of course. That had an effect on me. When I felt the need to get out of Australia it was inevitably England I came to. It had to be an English-speaking country, and one I could relate to quite easily. Quite soon I felt confident enough to start writing about it. And don't say I never returned to Australia, as a silly young actress said to me the other day. I have been back."

Sylvia left a second's silence.

"I know you've been back," she said. "But they've always been duty visits, haven't they? Deaths?"

"Yes," said Bettina bleakly, feeling cornered.

"You've never been back to travel round, see what it's like *today*, go to see areas you've never seen before."

"There are plenty of *those*. Dad and Mum never travelled. No, I haven't been back for that sort of visit."

Sylvia left a silence again, obviously asking: why not?

"A writer of my kind," said Bettina, slowly and carefully, "stores up experiences. You conserve the old ones, and you go into new ones only if you think they might be useful. That's why I'd never go with Mark to clubs, to listen to vile music and watch young people taking drugs. It would upset me, but more important: I would never use it. And you have to be careful not to complicate old experiences, so that you become unsure what is *then* and what is *now*. If I ever use Australia again it will be *my* Australia of the inter-war years. To experience the Australia of today would unsettle me, and unsettle my memories. I *know* Bundaroo as it was then. Bundaroo as it is now is of no interest to me whatsoever."

"I think I see," said Sylvia, equally carefully. "So it's not just a question of ... what happened then?"

"The rape. No, it's not just a question of the rape. Though I got out soon enough, and never regretted it. The thought that I might have lived on there, seeing him walk around the town as if nothing had happened makes me shiver. Though as it turned out he left the town soon after anyway, the man who is thought to have done it. No, my Bundaroo is the sum of all my days up till the day of the rape."

"Were there any results of ... of the rape?"

Bettina looked at her, then shook her head.

"Have you been listening to rumours? Ollie knows the truth."

"Ollie was so young at the time."

"There were no results, as you call it. I went to Armidale, to a sister of my father, because I couldn't bear to go on living at Bundaroo with people being nice to me on the surface, but looking at me out of the corners of their eyes and talking about me out of the corners of their mouths. It wasn't to have a baby or anything like that, though of course I was terrified at first ... If there were results they were less ... tangible. I certainly never went back to Bundaroo willingly."

Sylvia took a deep breath.

"One of the results was that you didn't want children, wasn't it?"

This was it. Truth-telling time.

"Yes ... All the first weeks I was in Armidale were a sort of preparation for if I was expecting. I tried on my Auntie Shirley's make-up to see if I could look older – for a possible visit to an abortionist. Then I realized that if I did go to some back-street fixer in Sydney or Newcastle I would need money. I broached the subject to my Aunt, and she was shocked at first, but gradually she came round to my way of thinking. But by then it was becoming clear that I wasn't pregnant."

"But the experience got you used to the idea that you didn't want children?"

Bettina thought, wondering whether to protest that this was too bald a statement, then decided against it.

"Yes, it did. I knew precisely by then what I wanted to do in life, wanted to be. Though I went to Europe, later joined up, went through as much of the war as my age allowed, it was all a question of getting experience, and going through or getting to know about things I could *use*. I was going to be a writer, and that was that. When I got pregnant with you it coincided with a telegram to say that my mother had cancer. Cecil, my husband – your father – didn't have many uses, but he had some influence in military transport. He got me on a flight to India via Egypt. There was a wait for the first plane, then one for the second. Another wait in Bombay for a boat to Perth – that took a fortnight – then the train across the Nullabor Plains. By the time I'd seen my mother, talked, tried to bring my Dad out of his misery, the pregnancy was ... well-established."

"Too late to have an abortion, you mean?"

"I suppose so. But anyway I was so used to it that I was reconciled to having it ... *you*. Not to bringing you up or anything but to having a baby. In any case, getting an abortion then, in Australia or England, wasn't easy. To be honest, I don't think I thought about it much that time around."

"I'm glad you didn't. I've had a good life, on the whole."

Her gratitude seemed misplaced. Bettina hurried on.

"But as I say I knew I didn't want a child for life, with all that that entails. You probably know what happened. Bill Cheveley had friends – your parents, people who couldn't have children of their own. I trusted Bill absolutely on people he knew. He went wrong with the Naismyths senior, but that was because he took someone else's recommendation. My dad arranged it, and came to Europe with his sister to fetch you – still a small baby. I'm afraid I didn't feel much. Not the sort of emotions a mother is meant to feel."

"Too late for you to agonise about that now," said Sylvia.

"Much too late. Funnily enough the thing I remember most from that time has nothing to do with being pregnant. It was something my mother told me, in bed, in the hospital at Walgett. She was in great pain from the cancer, but all the time I had had the idea of something on her mind, something she wanted to tell me. Then one day, when the pain was a little easier, she did."

"What was it?"

"She told me that she and Dad had met through a lonely hearts column in the local newspaper. She was working as a waitress in a café in Lismore. He was just back from the war, and living in Casino. They met up, liked each other, and went on from there. She was afraid I would find it ridiculous, but I didn't. It seemed rather touching. 'I couldn't have got a better man,' she said, 'not anyone straighter or more faithful. I've been a lucky woman.' It taught me – if I needed teaching – that there were other kinds of marriage than the kinds you read of in romantic novels. After the funeral I went straight back to Europe and sued for a divorce. As I said, Dad and Auntie Shirley came over and got you in 1947, when you were still a baby ... I'm glad, so very glad, that you've had a good life. But please remember you've nothing to thank me for. Quite the reverse. Thank your real parents – that's what they were – thank Bill Cheveley, thank my Dad who took it up with him when he knew I was pregnant. But don't, ever, shame me by thanking me."

By the middle of November the heat in Bundaroo was dominating everyone's daytime and night-time existence. Temperatures reached the hundreds, and the sun blazed down with a ferocious intensity. The inhabitants of Bundaroo who were not born there wished they could wear more clothes, not fewer, to protect their skins from the scorching and incessant attentions of that tormenting orb, burning and dessicating all the exposed skin. Like a dictator arrogant from years of power it ruled their lives – this in the run-up to examinations and the end of the school year. And with the sun came the flies – always around, always an irritant. And the flies were just the most all-pervasive of an upsurge in insect and animal life that was seldom joyous, seldom cause for celebration, but more often an intrusion that most people wanted to be free of. Everyone at Bundaroo High was on edge – Hughie and Betty not the least, though they both made endeavours to hide it.

"There must be something you could do to help Hughie," said Betty.

She had gone to see Miss Dampier about a knotty grammatical problem in her article: "each of the shopkeepers has their own speciality" she wanted to say, to avoid the awkwardness of "his or her" (though, truth to tell, there were no female shopkeepers in Bundaroo apart from Mrs Won, when her husband was away, setting up a Chinese restaurant in Lismore), but she had an awkward sense that this was not allowable, and might be the sort of thing that someone at the *Bulletin* head office might seize on. There was a lot about the *Bulletin* that she did not understand, such as its determination to refer to New Zealand as Maoriland, and even to abbreviate it to ML rather than NZ.

"Don't you think that might do more harm than good?" asked Miss Dampier. "It might work in junior school, but Hughie is a bit old to have a teacher fighting his battles for him."

"I don't want there to be any fighting," said Betty.

"I was speaking metaphorically," said Miss Dampier. "I think you could help Hughie more than I could. Try to persuade him to fit in better."

"Why should he fit in?" asked Betty, uneasily conscious that this was precisely what she had tried to accomplish. "He's grown up in a different country, and been educated at a different sort of school. Of course he's different. We could learn from him."

"But he really doesn't make much *eff*ort – "

"What should he do? Play football – what he calls rugby – and get his teeth knocked out so as to be one of the boys? Or hit sixes to the boundary in white flannels?"

"You know Bundaroo doesn't run to white flannels," said Miss Dampier.

"It's not going to happen. Hughie's not against sport, but he just can't be bothered. He is interested in Australian art."

"*That* isn't likely to win him many friends apart from you," said Miss Dampier. "He doesn't *have* to be so *different*, you know. After all, Herbie Cox was born in England – "

"And he was *four* when he came out here," said Betty, scornfully.

Miss Dampier was later to prove a tower of strength at the time of the rape, but on this occasion Betty thought she failed her. Her admirable attempts to infiltrate an Australian element into the English-dominated literature syllabuses of the New South Wales education authorities was welcome and exciting to Betty, but she felt her attitudes had spilled over into the larger areas of life, making her instinctively unsympathetic to Hughie's predicament. Betty hadn't meant her to do anything obvious, such as call people together and try to broker peace. That would inevitably be doomed to failure. But she had thought she might do something more subtle, to emphasize that Britain and Bundaroo could benefit and learn from each other. She wasn't sure what this subtle gesture might be, but she thought a teacher ought to be able to devise something.

Hughie's isolation from the rest of the school was now (Betty apart) complete. The juniors shouted mockingly at him as he walked alone, and sometimes even plucked up courage to do it when Betty was with him, shouting "homo" and "mummy's boy" and "mardarse" at the backs of both of them. In class if he said anything, there was always a suppressed snigger, and his comments were never taken up. In the playground, on the school bus, on the walk to Bundaroo, he was totally shunned.

"It's like the Jews in Germany," said Betty to Mr Copley, who taught her maths and science.

"You're exaggerating a little, Betty," said that mild man, devoted to fact and exactness.

"They all lose so much, not talking to him and listening to him."

That Mr Copley had to agree with.

"That's very true. All education is a matter of talking and listening and profiting by it." He added, in a rare indiscretion, "I blame his father."

For in truth Paul Naismyth was not helping his son, his wife, or anyone else, especially himself. He was not so foolish as to believe that an Australian sheep and cattle property could be run exactly as if it was a Northumbrian farm. But he was stupid enough to believe that Australian rural workers could be handled in the same way, with the same methods, as he had used with English farmworkers. And he would not be told – not by Bill Cheveley, Kevin Drayton or anyone else at Wilgandra. "I've run a property back home," he would say. "Trust me – I know what I'm doing." At first no one asked the obvious question why, if he'd done it successfully, he was now in Australia. Quite soon politeness wore thin, deference still thinner, and the question was thrown at him by stockmen and shearers alike. His matinée idol good looks soon modulated into petulance and impotent rage. His only response was to glower and turn on his heels.

The story went around town that he was about to be sacked. The story was self-generating, mere wishful thinking, and it spread the more readily for being what everyone wanted. Bill Cheveley knew that he had to be loyal to his appointee, and he always said that the murmurs were nonsense, that Paul was doing a fine job and was a dinkum bloke. But his loyalty was – had to be – finite. He was watching events, cataloguing the relationships that broke down, even noting the social gaffes of Naismyth's uppity wife. He knew that the likelihood was that Paul couldn't change his ways. Then the end would have to come, and he wouldn't be able to recommend the man for any other job in Australia. That would be to do the dirt on his own people, the property owners. It would, in any case, be to the benefit of all if the Naismyths took the journey home again. And the ones who would benefit most would be themselves, or so Bill thought.

It was on the night that Betty put the final, finishing touches of polish to her article for the *Bulletin* competition that the Whitelaws at Fort George received a visitor. As the recession had slowly, painfully, begun to give way to slightly better times, the number of men and women roaming the outback in search of work, dole, or just a meal and a rough bed for the night had grown fewer. It was a while since Fort George had seen a sundowner, but it saw one that evening. The sun, in fact, had an hour or two of fierce assertion left in it and the temperature was in the high nineties when the man appeared. Jack Whitelaw had gone in Bill's car to Walgett, for important negotiations with his bank manager (another Mason). He was not yet back when a man sauntered down the road from Bundaroo and banged with his fist on the door – not threateningly, but just enough to make his presence known.

"Sure I was wonderin' whether you had a job of work for me, and a bite to eat in exchange," he said when Dot Whitelaw opened the door. She frowned at the sight of him, but not discouragingly.

"Haven't you been here before, a year or two back?" she asked. "My husband had you mending some fences, let you sleep in the barn?"

"There now, he must have kept you away from me, for I never met you that time. I was wonderin' why I seemed to remember the property, but couldn't call to mind the charmin' lady of the place."

Dot paused for a moment, then giggled.

"There's no charming ladies in this part of the globe! But come on in. I think my husband must have eaten in Walgett, so there's a bit of Irish stew going begging. I wouldn't know about work. That's for Jack to say." She ushered him through. "But I can see you don't go hungry, work or no work."

Poor as they were, her instinct was to share at least some small portion with those less fortunate. And she was always grateful for company, whatever shape it took. They were in the kitchen now, where they ate most of their meals, and she sat him down at the table.

"Well now, isn't this cosy – and tasteful at the same time," said the sundowner, looking around him. He was a man of medium height and sandy hair, with a good-humoured face, bearded, and with a sparkle in his eye. But for his clothes and ragged pack one might assume he was a person living the best possible kind of life. Betty had come out of her bedroom carrying Ollie, and stood in the doorway watching the newcomer as if she were a bemused five-year-old.

Dot had been ladling food from three large saucepans on the range. She put the plate down in front of him and sat at the other end of the table. It seemed an age since she had had a conversation with someone she didn't know.

"Now isn't that the best Irish stew I've had since I left me native shores."

"I think Jack took a plate of stew to you in the barn when you were here before," said Dorothy.

"Did he now? Then your cookin' just gets better and better!"

Dot giggled again.

"I think you remember perfectly well coming here before," she said. "We do try to be hospitable to ... people like you."

"Sure an' I know you do. We men of the road, we do remember folks who are good to us, but we don't bring it up, in case they think we're going to make a habit of callin'. For myself, I just put on a friendly face, because that's what folk like to see, and where's the harm in that?"

"Is that why you put on an Irish accent too?" asked Betty. The man stopped in his tracks.

"Sure that's a razor-sharp mind the young one there has."

"Not much gets past our Betty."

"Joey O'Hara at school has an Irish father, and your accent doesn't sound right," explained Betty. "I didn't hear you talk when you were here before, because me and Mum just watched you and Dad from the window."

"Then like I said it's a clever soul your dad is, if he keeps you both locked away, because it's a gracious lady you have for a mother, and you'll be a bobby-dazzler breakin' men's hearts in a few years' time, that you will." He paused again in his eating, which was as enthusiastic as good table-manners would allow. Then he went on in an ordinary voice. "I'm sorry for the accent. I do it all the time when I'm with strangers, and it becomes second nature. People do like it. Most Australians have a relative who's Irish, and as often as not they're favourites – an uncle who's a bit of a card, or a gentle sort of fellow who's in the Church. So it ... works."

"How did you come to ... do what you do? Did you lose your job?"

"Not as such, no. The fact is, I went to war."

"Jack went to war too," put in Dot. "My husband."

"I know. I remember him telling me. He was under Monash, but he didn't get there till 'sixteen. I – mad bastard that I was – worked my passage to England as soon as the war broke out, and I was in France by late November. I dunno what made me do it. I had a brute of a father, but I really went from the frying pan to the fire ... You'll know from your man that it's not a thing to be talked about ... Like a hellish dream ... It took all of us different. When your man came back he obviously wanted to settle down, put it behind him, get back to normal. That meant having a family, being his own boss. I tried normal, but it didn't work for me: job, promotion, house, children – I couldn't face getting into that kind of rut. It was all a cheat, a con, from my point of view. And that's why I'm a sundowner, young lady. The only thing that's real for me is where my next

116

meal is coming from, and where I lay my bed. That's all my poor brain can cope with."

Betty nodded. The man shook off his mood in a moment.

"And you meet some types on the road, I can tell you. Last week in Moree I was talking to some children in a little park near the church there, telling them stories of the road, of some of the dogs travellers have, some of the wild animals that make friends with us (I made a lot of that up, but the littlies loved it), and we were having a famous time, and the kiddies were laughing and gurgling, when up comes this police constable – seventeen stones if he's an ounce, all beer belly and blubber, and he says: 'Here, you can't entertain in a public place without a licence!'"

"Entertain," said Betty, outraged. "Just telling stories to children?"

"You hit the nail on the head, young lady. He has his brains in his boots, that one. So I said to him: 'I might need a licence if I were collecting money, but how much do you think I could get from this lot? A couple of farthings at the most, and then I'd give it back to them because I don't rob wee things like they are.' Anyway, he wouldn't see reason, and he tried to break up the meeting or move us on, and the children got so angry, because I'd never finished a story I was telling them about being woken up by a goanna and a funnelweb spider having an argument about which was the uglier, so things started to get nasty – not *really* nasty, you know, but funny nasty, because they were angry kids, even though the eldest was no more than seven, and there was this great fat representative of law and order – "

The sundowner was interrupted by the sound of the door opening, and Betty's father coming home. One look at his face told the women that the talk with the bank manager had gone well.

"Well, if it isn't Al Cousens!" said Jack Whitelaw, coming into the kitchen. "Have your travels brought you here again?"

It was typical of Betty's father that he'd found out the sundowner's name on his last visit, and remembered it until this one. He sat down and they began talking about the year that had just passed. Betty, a child again, was bursting with a natural storyteller's curiosity.

"But who was the uglier, the goanna or the funnelweb?"

Al Cousens screwed up his face in thought.

"Well now, young lady, I'm not sure I'd made up my mind about that. I think it was a case of 'How happy could I be with either, were the other ugly-looking b – brute away.'"

They all laughed, and Dot put on the kettle to make another pot of tea.

Going to bed that night Betty's head was filled with thoughts of a sundowner who said "uglier" rather than "ugliest" for a comparison between two, and could quote from – well, she wasn't quite sure *what* from, but she knew that "How happy could I be" came from literature of some kind. She thought Al Cousens was a lovely man, and she knew her mother thought so too.

And, quite suddenly, there came into her mind the thought that her mother would have liked to go to bed with the sundowner. And also the complementary thought that, even if a safe opportunity presented itself, nothing in the world would have persuaded her to do it.

9
Heatwave

Now we're getting there, thought Bettina, as she settled down at her desk. She had thought of little else all night but the approach of the day that cut her off for ever from Bundaroo, and the world it represented. There were so many other things, better things to think about: her pleasure in Ollie's company, yes and Sylvia's too, and anticipation of the approaching trip to Edinburgh. But no: she was back in that sweltering summer of 1938, as November melted into December, Leaving Certificate was sat in the enervating heat, and the night approached of the Leaving Dance.

In the morning Betty heard her mother singing from the kitchen.

"I wouldn't leave my little wooden hut

For you-oo! For you-oo!"

She wondered as she dressed as to whether the words had any significance, then decided that this was one of only three or four songs that her mother launched into when she was in singing mood, so they couldn't have.

Before setting off for school, Betty put her competition entry into a large brown envelope she had begged from Miss Dampier (the Department of Education was very protective of its stationery, but Miss Dampier was rather excited about the competition, thought it could redound to the school's credit, and made an exception "just this once.")

It was the day for the dunnyman to collect the cans from the little hut at the back of the house ("Dig 'em deep and dig 'em wide" her father always said, but on his deathbed, in Ollie's house in Melbourne, he said that being shot of dunnies was the best thing that had happened to him in his last years). Normally Dot welcomed the dunnyman as another face to have a chat with. Today he made the mistake of pushing his face against the wire grill on the kitchen window.

"See you've got one of those no-hoper travellers to fix yer fences."

Dot fired up at once.

"He's not a no-hoper. He's one of the nicest, gentlest people."

"Have it yer own way, lady. But don't say I didn't warn you if yer rams get out and eat all yer pretty flowers."

"Jack'll make sure his work is up to scratch. I expect he's done fences scores of times. He doesn't want something for nothing. He's fought for his country."

"There's plenty has done that," said the dunny-man. And he turned back to his odiferous cart and began the three mile journey to Bundaroo.

When Jack came in for a bit of early breakfast, Dot recounted the conversation to him.

"You shouldn't have said that about fighting for your country," her husband said, slicing into his sausage. "Syd Southern was at Gallipoli."

"Yes ... Well, I'm sorry. But *he* shouldn't have said what *he* said. A lot of the sundowners are old soldiers."

"Too right," agreed Jack. "It takes you like that sometimes. And you're right about Al being a good worker. I know that from last time he was here, or I wouldn't have given him work now. He'll be here for a couple more days."

"You're a good man, Jack Whitelaw. Better than that Syd Southern – I can't do with him."

"You can't do without him," Jack pointed out.

"No, well ... You should have asked Al in for breakfast."

"I did. He said he didn't want to bludge."

"There you are then. That's the sort he is. I'll put a sausage and some bacon in a bag for him, and a few slices of bread."

Walking to school Betty decided that her parents were kindly people – like Bill Cheveley, or the vicar, or Mr Blackfeller, who had a word for everyone and never took offence. She contrasted them in her mind with Mr and Mrs Naismyth, or Bob at the café, or the horrible Sam Battersby. They were always needing someone to look down on, sneer at, or pick a quarrel with. She thought too about Al Cousen, who was a sundowner, yet one of the most charming people she had ever met. And he spoke – when he was not putting on an Irish brogue – the most beautiful English. He'd said his father was a brute, but perhaps he was one of those civilised brutes, or one of those who used their religion to justify their cruelties. She shivered. Like Mr Murdstone, she thought. But mostly on that walk she thought of her competition entry, going over many of its phrases, wondering if they were the best she could have chosen, rather glad she had sealed the envelope so she could indulge in no further indecisions.

When the midday break came, Betty went and bought a stamp from Miss Dampier in the staff room.

"Would you like to put it in with the school mail?" she was asked.

"No, that's all right. I need a walk."

As she walked into the blazing noonday sun towards the post-box near Mr Won's fruit and vegetable shop she wondered why she had refused the offer, and decided it was because she didn't want her participation in the competition to become a school thing. It wasn't – it was *her* thing, done entirely *by* her, its opinions her own responsibility. Yes, her friends had made suggestions, but it was she who had decided which ideas to accept, which to forget about. The article had her stamp on it, and hers alone.

When she had let the big envelope fall with an exciting plop into the box she bought a quarter of cherries from Mr Won and began to walk back to school. Suddenly, all responsibility for the competition entry having passed on, a new realization struck her: the Leaving Certificate was in three weeks' time. She had told her parents and her teachers that she was still hard at work preparing for it, but in reality the competition had taken over most of her spare time. If she was going to do what was expected of her she needed to use all the hours left to her to revise, revise further, then re-revise. With a sudden swerve she changed course and headed for her friend Alice Carey's home.

Alice went home for her dinner at midday. She was one of the few High School pupils who were in a position to do that. She was eating, in fact, when she opened the door to Betty.

"Alice, I've just had an awful thought. It's Leaving Certificate in three weeks' time."

"Well, you must be the only person in the school who could forget that."

"Not for*get*, I mean ... well, just with the competition and that ... I just wondered if I could have a loan of your geography notes, just for the night."

"Oh those," said Alice, who knew they were perfect. "Steve Drayton's got those."

"Well, when he finishes with them? – "

"Oh, he'll be a long time. He's not as quick on the uptake as you are Betty. Must go."

And she shut the door. Other times Betty had called on her at lunchtime she had been invited in, just to talk with Alice and her mother while they were eating, perhaps to have an orange squash. No longer.

Alice, clearly, after three months of neglect, was no longer

122

Betty's best friend. She now had no best friend, unless it was Hughie – and best friends, almost by definition, were of the same sex.

Betty squared her shoulders. She could do without friends, and she could cope with the Leaving Certificate without help from anyone. Part of her said that how she did in the Leaving was no longer of any great importance.

That evening she said to her parents:

"I'm going to have to put my head down to work for the Leaving."

There were a couple of sharp glances at her.

"I thought you were keeping up with your school work," said her mother.

"Well, I was ... But there's revision, loads of revision. I'll just have to go into purdah, like a nun."

"I think that's a Sultan's missus does that," said her father. "Or missuses. We thought you were set to do really well in the Leaving, darl."

"I'm sure I'll do well enough to get into Teachers' College."

"That wasn't what we had hopes of," said Jack Whitelaw. "That's just high-grade drudgery, the sort of job you get from there. We believe in you, Betty. We believe you can be better than a small-town teacher. What about repeating final year? Maybe going to Armidale, where the schools are better. You could live with your Auntie Shirley. She'd be pleased to have you."

It was the first time Armidale had been mentioned. And the first time anyone had raised the possibility of her living with Auntie Shirley, of whom her recollections were very dim. Dear old Shirley, as she later proved in the crisis: a bit slow on the uptake, but sturdy and trustworthy in her support. Shirley, who had helped to relieve her of her baby, when eventually the time came.

"I don't know," said Betty. "Maybe it won't be necessary ... Maybe I'll do really well in the Leaving."

But doing well in the Leaving wasn't what she'd been thinking about, dreaming about, at all.

"I've heard rumours about your Hughie," said Clare, one day when she called round to discuss whispers of interest from BBC Television in one of her later, London-set novels.

"He's not my Hughie any more than I'm his Betty," said Bettina in a mock-tired voice. "What sort of rumours?"

"That he's got himself a new romantic interest."

Bettina considered this.

"I'm not altogether surprised. It's a while since the last one. It's something that Marie has had to put up with in the course of her marriage. And to be fair to her, she has put up with it. She knew about it before she married him. She'd been one of his dolly-birds. I think his affairs give her a handle, something to use to get the upper hand in all the things that really matter."

"And what are they? Money?"

"Of course. If you've seen Marie you'll know that money is something she sets great store by. She uses a lot of it. And who is the lucky girl?"

"I didn't say she was a girl, but I suppose you know your Hughie. She is. She's a librarian at the South Kensington Library. Distinctly glamorous with peach-painted lips and a South African accent. That's how she was described to me. She's working her stay here, after graduating from the University of Cape Town."

"I see. Well, lucky old Hughie."

"Of course she's in it for something or other."

"Of course. Maybe he's her entry-key to Fleet Street.

But all the same, lucky old Hughie. I might go and take a look at her when I get back from Edinburgh."

Clare sparked up at once.

"Edinburgh? Is that decided? When are you going there?"

"Next Monday, with Ollie and Sylvia. For five days."

"Will the flat be empty?"

"Of course it will."

"Couldn't you get someone to flat-sit for you?"

Bettina pondered.

"I suppose Peter would do it, if I slipped him a few twenties."

Clare paused for a few moments, in thought.

"I notice," she said, "that you don't pooh-pooh the idea and say I'm out of my mind. Why not, Bettina?"

"Well," said Bettina carefully, "it may be my imagination – " she pulled herself up. "No, it's not my imagination. I found that my desk had been – I don't know – searched, investigated, mucked about with. The tape recorder had changed position. And my cleaners hadn't been in, or anyone else that I know of, who would have been in the place legally ... If only I still had Mr Growser. He was worth a hundred pieces of modern electronic surveillance."

"Amen to that. A Jack Russell beats laser beams any day. But you could hardly have left Mr Growser in the flat while you were in Edinburgh. So get Peter."

"I'll see what he says. It was probably some burglar who didn't know what he was looking for."

"And didn't take anything? Or even disturb anything while he was searching?"

"He certainly didn't take anything – but then you can't expect a burglar to be up on Australian art. Why should he trash things and make his visit obvious if he'd no need to? He wouldn't want to leave more traces than he could help."

"He'd trash things because he'd be working fast, and any competent burglar knows how not to leave traces of himself behind."

"Well, all right. Perhaps not any ordinary burglar."

As it happened Bettina decided to go to the Duke of Sussex pub the next day at lunchtime – a Thursday, which was Peter's pension payment day. It was Katie's too, and the three sat around one of their favourite tables and wondered whether to have a pub lunch. When they had decided they would, Bettina told them she thought an intruder had been in her flat, and put the plan that he should act as a Jack Russell-substitute to Peter.

"I could do a Jack Russell bark," said Peter, and promptly did one, to the consternation of the other drinkers. "Nasty little brutes, your Mr Growser among them. I'd be happy to do it the week after next, if that would suit."

"It wouldn't. We're fitting in five days in Scotland between other things we've got booked in London. It's got to be Monday to Friday next week, because we've got the hotel booked as well. Couldn't you cancel whatever pressing engagements you have?"

"No, I couldn't, and don't be sarky, Bettina. It doesn't suit you, and it's not nice to assume I just exist to be at your convenience. I've had a week's holiday in Bournemouth booked for months. Special rock-bottom prices for pensioners. They only offer it because nobody but pensioners fancies the English seaside these days."

"Oh well, if Bournemouth is more important to you than me – "

"It is. Bournemouth *with* a friend." And he winked.

"I'll do it for you," said Katie. "I could fancy a bit of luxury: the run of the freezer, turn the central heating up if the nights get chilly. Can't do a Jack Russell, but anything else Peter can do, I can as well."

Bettina doubted that, but thought that the main objective in Clare's suggestion was to have someone in the flat – someone to turn a light on, maybe ring 999 if they heard a noise.

"You're on," she said.

On her way home, full of pub lunch and feeling adventurous, Bettina made a substantial detour and went to the South Kensington Library. She had been a borrower there for nearly fifty years, but she hadn't been inside for three or more. The older she got the more she enjoyed re-reading old favourites already on her shelves. When she entered the place she hardly recognised it: there seemed to be fewer books, more "areas" – places for people, mostly children, to do things in. Borrowing no longer seemed the first priority, and she wandered round, genuinely bemused, until she fixed on her prey, a healthy-looking young woman with peach-coloured, bow-shaped lips. She was replacing an armful of books on the crime shelves.

"I'm sorry to bother you," said Bettina, in that voice that had more touches of Kensington matriarch than it did Australian, "but it's many years since I was here … The art books are no longer where they were."

"The art books? They're on the wall, over there," and she pointed.

"Thank you. I see. It's a book on Australian art I wanted."

"Oh yes?" There seemed to be some constraint in the voice, though the young woman went on putting books back on the shelves.

"It's one by Eugene Naismyth. He had a series on television some time ago."

"That was years back."

"So you saw it?"

"No-o-o ... I'm too young. But I've heard of the series."

"I do hope the book's still available."

"If it's in stock it will probably be on the shelves. Television borrowing doesn't go on for more than about six months after the programme is shown."

There was a sort of reluctance in the pretty-mouthed woman's voice. Bettina smiled her thanks and pottered off. She found the unwanted volume – which she had a personally-inscribed copy of at home – and then went back towards the crime section, having noticed the peach-lipped one on the desk. A Reginald Hill, a Caroline Graham, a Michael Z. Lewin and a Peter Robinson had been shelved upside down on the various shelves where she had seen the librarian placing books.

The girl was in love, she thought. Or, more likely, in some other kind of relationship with the still-surprising Hughie.

The two weeks left before the Leaving began was indeed a period of almost monastic austerity for Betty. She drew up a plan of reading and revision, consigned one subject (Geography – she hoped Alice would feel guilty, but didn't bank on it) to the mental dustbin, knowing she could get only the barest of passes in it however hard she worked at it so late in the day. The rest of the subjects she read up methodically, pursued any interesting trails in the meagre school and town libraries, and read in her bedroom into the night. English she hardly touched. English she felt sublimely confident in.

Two days before the first exam she put away her books and

had two days walking around her father's farm, the animal paddocks close to the house, the grain fields stretching their not-quite-profitable-enough length until they met the fields of another soldier settler, a cockie her father was on terms of alternating hostilities and ceasefires with. As she was renewing acquaintanceship with the animals her brain was active with phrases she might use, strategies she might employ in essays, new approaches that might or might not be looked on with favour by the men with the marking pencils.

The weather continued baking hot – exhausting for a newcomer like Hughie, taken more in their stride by those like Betty who were used to it: the outback gods were not going to abate their usual ferocious attack merely for a few teenagers facing the most important examination of their lives. If, of course, it was that. Children from Bundaroo were not expected to do particularly well, and when their results were mediocre they quite soon got dead-end jobs and began their unspectacular way through life. The last student at the High School to get good Leaving results had been Sam Battersby's daughter, and she had taken off at once for Newcastle and had never been back.

Betty intended to take off, not for Newcastle but for Sydney. But she did intend to come back, often she told herself, to where her roots were. The limited horizons were sometimes comfortable, for a short time.

When the exams started she began to feel better than confident. Even in Geography she felt she performed creditably, in part due to all the reading she had done in the *Bulletin*. Her total lack of understanding of geometry was balanced by a splendid performance in algebra (she *knew*, and had her feeling confirmed by going through the paper with Mr Copley).

Occasionally, when the exam was in something that was not studied at Bundaroo High, they had time off. On one such afternoon Betty took one of her father's old nags and rode over to Wilgandra. Then she and Hughie played music again while Mrs Naismyth was at the Cheveleys' house taking tea with Bill's wife, who was feeling better, or thought she was, and was blessing the new tablets prescribed for her. They played Beethoven – the *Pastoral*, which Betty thought lovely, but a bit long in places – the *Egmont* Overture, and *Leonore* number 3. Hughie explained about the trumpet calls, and that moment went straight to Betty's young heart: liberation! The knocking-off of chains! She insisted that they play the Seventh again.

"All right," said Hughie, getting down the records from the wall cupboard. "I never get tired of it. Did you know it's been called 'The Apotheosis of the Dance'?"

"Oh," said Betty, who was not well up in apotheoses.

But his words had an effect, because when the orchestra began the urgent, frenzied motion of the first movement Allegro, Betty stood up, not quite knowing why, and suddenly the dancing visions she had had when she first heard the music seemed to take control of her limbs, and she began a weird but passionate sort of dance. Hughie, beside her but separate, in his own world, began his own dance, which was his own interpretation, and as the frenzy increased so did their own ecstasy, but it was a solitary, adolescent ecstasy, each of them wrapped up in themselves, trying to encompass what the music was saying *to them*. When the movement ended they sat down, embarrassed, knowing they could not wind themselves down to the spirit of the slow movement. Betty gave a little giggle, but Hughie seemed not to notice.

The music finished, and they sat in silence. When they saw Mrs Naismyth approaching at the end of the half-mile walk from Wilgandra itself, Hughie put on "Hark, hark, the lark", but when she came into the house she seemed too preoccupied to notice. That had been more than a tea-party, Betty thought. Hughie obviously thought so too, because he went out into the kitchen and started a low conversation with his mother.

"She really should have been talking to your father," Betty heard her say. "Or Bill should. He shouldn't work through us women. And how can she say your father shouldn't order the men around? He's the manager, isn't he? Who's going to give orders if he doesn't?"

Betty felt mean and dirty at overhearing the Naismyths' troubles, though she hadn't consciously listened. She shouted a farewell to Hughie and went out to her horse.

The day of the last Leaving exam was celebrated by a few of the pupils. One little group went and caused a rumpus in Mr Won's shop – some sending him hither and yon for little-called-for items, while others did some minor shoplifting. Mr Won knew perfectly well what was going on, because something of the kind happened every year, but the young people's custom during the rest of the year was worth too much to endanger it by making a fuss. The real celebration, more decorous and supervised, was the Leaving Dance the next evening. This was held every year, the last event of the High School year, and supervised by teachers. It had been called a Ball until two years before, when the students had protested that this was a ridiculous title when only about fifteen candidates took the Leaving in Bundaroo. And anyway a Dance sounded more fun, even if it wasn't.

Betty, along with most of the other girls, didn't have a great deal of preparation to do, no agonising about what to wear: she wore her Best, and that was that. In this the girls had the advantage of the boys, most of whom didn't have a Best, though they might acquire one when they got a job, or when they stopped growing. Betty experimented with her mother's make-up while Dot was at a meeting of the Church Ladies, but she decided she looked too much like a doll, and she settled for a dab of powder and a dash of scent. Saturday ought to have been a day of excitement with the Dance as its climax, and perhaps for some of the pupils it was, but for Betty the day was an anti-climax. She had done her best, done well she thought, but now there was nothing much in her life except waiting for the results. And waiting for the announcement of the winner of the *Bulletin* competition. This, doubtless due to what her mother called "a feeling in her bones", was the really important thing for Betty.

The Whitelaws went into Bundaroo that evening by foot. By six o'clock the heat of the day was lessening, and they knew they would meet up with other families doing the same. By the time they reached town two other little groups had joined them, so when they passed Alice Carey's house, and she emerged, there was enough of a group for her to join in without having to make it too clear that she and Betty were no longer close. As they gained the bitumened strip and walked towards Grafton's Hotel Betty whispered to her father:

"You're not going there, are you, Dad?"

It was not a pathetic plea of the child to its father in a melodrama to stay off the booze, and was not taken as such. On high days and holidays in Bundaroo there was a secret arrangement that everybody knew about that, after the regulation six o'clock closing, the back room at Grafton's would open, and drinks would be served and tallies would be kept on a slate, to be paid in the subsequent week. More people got stinking drunk after closing time than ever did in the steady-drinking daytime. Jack Whitelaw thought for a moment, then said:

"Maybe I'll go with your mum and have a bite to eat at Bob's."

When they got to the other end of the township Betty didn't feel she had to rush to the school hall. She knew what it would be like because she had seen it decorated for the Leaving Dance the previous year: tasteful streamers, the odd balloon, and a touch of Christmas since the littlies would be having their end-of-term party there in a week or two's time. She and her parents lingered with the other groups as the light faded, watched the little band arriving – in truth a trio, but much loved in Bundaroo, where they played at all such occasions and were prized as one of the best little groups in the North-West of the State. As the band, waving to old friends, entered the schoolyard the Naismyths arrived in the Cheveley's Ford. Betty had an odd sense of watching them as if they were strangers, almost characters in a book: she saw that Mrs Naismyth's manner was slightly wrong, as if it was the other parents who were outsiders, and she was welcoming them as hostess. She saw that Paul Naismyth's manner was becoming tinged with aggression, and she wondered (Hughie seldom talked of home) what sort of a father he was. She thought she had got a clue when she heard him say in a low voice to his son: "I'd've thought you'd've made some male friends by now." When she saw Hughie fix himself on to Steve Drayton, whom he hadn't talked to for weeks, she thought it was time to join them, though she recognised that she was less and less use to Hughie the more she became identified with him in their fellow-students' minds.

And so, together but unspeaking, the three of them went into the little school assembly hall, followed in a slow drift by the other Leaving candidates, by one or two of the last year's Leaving takers who had begged a ticket, and by one or two friends of the pupils from round about who tried to get into any occasion going. In the hall the tables were laid with jellies and cakes, sandwiches and biscuits, and a side-table held lemonade and orange squash. As they inspected it, Miss Dampier and the Headmaster arrived, he clutching a large case in which he had an accordion which he could all too easily be persuaded to play.

The band was now tuning up and playing snatches of dance tunes they were all familiar with, sending lively strains into the night down this end of Bundaroo, to balance the sounds of laughter and argument fuelled by beer that came from Grafton's at the other end. Most of the men were there, but Jack Whitelaw was with the other group, mostly mothers, tucking into pie and chips at Bob's café. The parents' role as chaperones ended when the dance started, because the headmaster, Miss Dampier and Mr Copley – not to mention some formidable refreshments ladies – would see that all was well and seemly in the school hall. Chaperoning would only begin again around half past ten, when the young people would start to straggle out into the street, ready to be escorted home.

Till then no harm could come to them, surely.

10
Thunderclap

The Corunna Trio finished their tuning and started the evening off with the *Merry Widow* Waltz. The Corunna trio knew what they were doing. A traditional waltz was the first thing learnt at Mrs MacKenzie's dancing classes in Corunna. These classes were eagerly attended by the girls of the area, less so by the boys –the ones that did attend were only there under the impression that dancing was the way to get girls. Many of the boys who did not attend (and family finances rarely stretched beyond the girls anyway, and dancing was really a girls' thing, wasn't it?) were taught by their classmates, and for many of the lads of Bundaroo their first real feel of a girl happened to the strains of the Merry Widow Waltz or the Blue Danube.

Betty took to the floor with Hughie. Both of them knew the steps, and after a single circuit of the little hall they were doing them with confidence and brio. Their showmanship, their consciousness that they made a good-looking couple, brought its inevitable reward: "Just look at those two – don't they just think they're the cat's whiskers!"; "Thinks her poopie doesn't smell that Betty Whitelaw – always has." Betty and Hughie danced on, smiling at each other if at no one else. "I don't care," said Betty to herself. "I'm enjoying it, I'm doing it well, I could be a wonderful dancer some day and so could Hughie, and why should we *hide* it just because some of the cow-cockies are *jealous*?"

When the *Merry Widow* had had a good outing, the trio changed tempo to a veleta, and Hughie and Betty made for the food table, chattering and laughing. Some of the others did the same.

"Are we allowed to eat with the star performers?" asked

Steve Drayton, addressing no one in particular, as if posing an abstract philosophical question.

"Suit yourself," said Betty. The moment she'd said it she wished she'd said "Oh, don't be silly, Steve," or something personal.

"They think they're Fred Astaire and Ginger Rogers," said Alice Carey.

"Got to do something like dancing if you're one of the queer brigade like him," said Steve.

They did not dance for the next half hour, but stood around eating sandwiches and cake, and drinking lemonade, behaving as if the world would end if they stopped talking. When their talk got down to the personal level Hughie said that Steve Drayton was uncertain about his own sexual tastes, which Betty thought unlikely, and that Alice had probably nourished gnawing feelings of jealousy for years as the less interesting partner in her friendship with Betty, who thought that made sense.

Needless to say no one asked Betty to dance, and Hughie knew that anyone he asked would refuse, or just turn away. You could tell that by the expressions on their faces. Even many of the faces on the dance floor turned in their direction in the middle of gracious, Mrs-MacKenzie-tutored motions with looks approaching hatred, or with theatrical grimaces of contempt. Betty felt her blood stirring. It was clearly time for them to take to the floor again – this they both realized without saying so: standing talking for too long only underlined their status as pariahs.

Suddenly the trio seemed to respond to their instinct. With a scrape and a twiddle they ended their current foxtrot, and the leader announced in a stentorian voice: "And now for our medley of songs from the shows!" The medleys were popular – the parents and other assorted adults who came and went at these evenings, forming a little knot at the door, loved them and hummed along with old favourites: the less enthusiastic dancers left the floor gratefully and pounced on the refreshments, and only the adept who could keep up with the ever-changing tunes were left in the centre of the hall floor. The tunes could range from old music-hall favourites to the Barcarole from the *Tales of Hoffmann*, and the trio prided themselves on keeping up with the latest hits on Broadway and Shaftesbury Avenue.

They began with "Bill", and they emphasized the yearning, painful qualities of the tune, and that clutching at the heart-strings got to Betty, made her feel she had to play it out somehow, give it some physical embodiment. She went towards the floor where only two or three couples were left, and her hands went above her head and her body began to gyrate in a routine that was expressive of longing, that was partly sexual, partly a lust for anything new, surprising, unknown – anything that was not Bundaroo. She had hardly begun when Hughie left his station by the wall and began his own dance – slow, unshowy, introspective, as before out at Wilgandra, near to Betty but not with her, exploring the unknowable, or maybe the inexplicable strangeness of love. Perhaps on a signal from their leader (Betty was conscious only of her own body) the trio kept with the yearning, frustration, unhappiness: they slipped into "Smoke Gets in Your Eyes", and Betty's own eyes glinted with recognition and Hughie gave her a brief grin of mutual understanding, and their bodies speeded up as they tried to give expression to a cynical resignation that they knew about, could identify with, but had never really felt themselves – and even as they danced they felt a performer's sort of elation.

Two of the couples on the floor walked off, and as they went by they said "Show offs" and "What do they think they look like?" Now there was only one other couple, Ed Malone and

Kitty Horne, unwilling to give up any opportunity of licensed bodily contact (in the succeeding twenty years they were to increase significantly Bundaroo's population, and Kitty continued the good work even when Ed was with the Australian army in New Guinea), but they preferred the darkness and anonymity of the edges of the dance floor, and left the centre to Betty and Hughie. As the trio edged their way into "Summertime" the languorous heat of the day entered Betty's limbs and the enervating nothingness of a place where the sun sucked out all desire for activity except the purely sensual, and Hughie made gestures towards his classmates that were slow and minimal (and kept from the eyes of the parents clustered around the door), but verged on the obscene.

Then the trio launched into "Anything Goes" and Betty and Hughie, as with the Beethoven Seventh but in reverse, could not cope with the effervescent after the steamy and languid, and, talking and laughing, they left the floor.

From the doorway there came a smattering of applause.

"*Didn't* they make an exhibition of themselves?" said Alice to Steve Drayton.

"If only they could see themselves," said Steve. "Flaming galahs!"

But Miss Dampier, sensing trouble like an educational weather-vane, came over from the door where she was swapping words with some of the parents, and said:

"That was really wonderful, both of you. So unusual!"

"Out of this bloody world!" came a mock-upper-class accent from somewhere around the food table. Miss Dampier seemed to feel she ought to say something, respond in some way to the obvious hostility from the rest of the Leavers, but, unable for once to think of anything to say, she wandered off, looking back nervously.

"There's your parents just come in," said Betty to Hughie.

"Thank God they weren't here ten minutes ago. These hicks have nothing on them when it comes to ignorance and nastiness if their beloved only son steps out of line."

"They'll probably hear about it from the other parents."

"Not them! We don't talk much with the natives ..." The thought seemed to make him nervous, though. "Still, maybe I'll pre-empt it."

They were now at the doorway, where the little knot of parents and others were talking freely among themselves. Hughie went over with a self-induced air of confidence.

"Hi, Mum. Hi, Dad. You should have been here ten minutes ago. Betty and I did a solo spot. It was a real laugh."

"Oh, it wasn't – it was lovely," said one of the mothers. "It was so artistic, and very tasteful."

"Excuse me," said Betty, smiling but determined, pushing her way through the little throng and out into the fresh air. Sometimes the attitudes of Bundaroo made her feel as if she was suffocating.

Outside was better. Outside had a tiny touch of cool in the air. Betty looked around her. She gazed over towards the lights of Bob's Café, where some parents were standing in the entrance, under the verandah, chatting and laughing. Probably coming over to take a look at the performing seals, she thought. She wanted to be on her own – not watched, not questioned, not jeered at by her one-time friends. If she was different from them – which was the substance of their jeers, at Hughie as well as herself – then she didn't want to be like them. She walked away from the school gate and the little main street beyond, round the back of the High School building with the assembly hall built on to it, then towards the primary section, which was a small wooden building little better than a shack.

One thing about inland Australia: land was cheap. The Bundaroo School did not have lavish facilities, but it had plenty of playground space. She stood between the school she was now leaving and the school she had started at when she was five. Back in the hall the music had started up again, and she could hear the thump of heavy shoes on wood. She felt, suddenly, very tired. Her solo dances with Hughie had not been physically exhausting, but they had been a gesture, a defiant slap in the face at attitudes and prejudices that she loathed, but which seemed endemic in her friends. The gesture had left her feeling alone and drained. She wondered if she had been right in thinking she would come back often to Bundaroo. It could only be to see her parents, whom she loved. If they moved, she now felt, she would never set foot in the little town again.

There was hardly a sound to be heard, beyond the beautiful ripple of water and the distant rhythm of dance music. There was a rustle in the long grass, as one of the creatures of the bush reacted to her presence. She began to feel cleansed of the spite and jealousy in the school hall. She turned towards the slow dribble of water that they called the river, which had only once in her lifetime swelled to the raging torrent that everyone said it was capable of. A little wattle fence separated the littlies' playing area from the rough-grassed bank leading down to the river. Here it was very dark, and well away from all the futile bustle of a tiny town on one of its gala nights. She ought to have felt frightened here, but she did not – only a sense that the best thing that Bundaroo offered was the space to be alone.

The attack came from behind – an arm around her neck, then tightened so savagely that she choked. For the rest of her life even a tap on the shoulder from behind would terrify her. She tried to scream, but the arm was still against her windpipe, holding her, rendering her helpless, her cry no more than a whimper.

140

"Stop it!" she whispered hoarsely. "It's not funny! Who is it? Steve?"

But now she was being turned around, and now the darkness was no longer a friend. Her dress was being torn, brutal fingers searching underneath it, ripping away her knickers. She heard gulped breathing, smelt a smell she recognised, smelt it with nausea and fear, then felt her legs being forced apart. She tried kicking, but her feet went wide of the mark and she felt something hard and terrifying entering her, and a hand across her mouth preventing her screaming. Some long-ago advice in a woman's magazine her mother took told her she should fight no more, should relax and hope to take the edge off "the vile beast's ferocity."

Minutes later she lay in the undergrowth at the foot of the fence, bleeding and sobbing, conscious of footsteps running away. Part of her wanted to lie there, hide, put a temporary stop to her life. But something else told her to get away. Who knew who else might be there in the darkness around the Primary School? Who knew whether some of the male members of her class might not be lurking in the darkness, just to watch, or to take their turn? She must run, or it could happen again.

She dragged herself to a sitting position. It felt as though her legs would refuse to support her, but she managed to kneel, then to push herself upright, then to take a step. Then she began to run, clutching her torn and bloody dress around her – first towards the High School, still alive with music and lights, then suddenly swerving away from it, nauseated by the thought of appearing before her fellow pupils as she now was, beaten, degraded, humiliated. She ran round the school, round the hall, then towards the school gates and out into the street. Down the far end of the main street she saw the lights of Grafton's, and shuddered. Nearer, marginally more of a refuge, was Bob's Café. Maybe her parents were still there. She ran, still sobbing with rage and shame, till she made the verandah and could throw open the door. She had no sooner entered than she heard a woman scream, heard footsteps coming towards her, felt protective hands even as she felt herself floating out of consciousness.

When, reluctance gripping her like a vice, she drifted back into awareness of what was going on around her, she heard her father's voice, but instinct with a blazing fury she had never heard before, say: "I'm taking her home. Where's that Naismyth? We can use Bill's car."

"What about Sergeant Malley?" came Bob's voice.

"Sergeant Malley can come out to our place. Where was he when he was needed? Grafton's I bet. And tell him to get hold of Dr Merton. Come on Dot. We're taking her home and putting her in her own bed."

Someone at the door said: "That's the Naismyths coming back now."

A way was made for her father, and she heard him from further off saying: "Paul. I need the car. We've got to take Betty home."

"The car? Well, I don't know. I suppose Bill – "

"*Look*, you fool!"

Betty, on the floor, turned away, almost wanting to hide her bloodstained dress from him, but she heard Naismyth say "Oh, my God" and run to the door. As they helped her up and then through the door and out to the street she heard the voice of Miss Dampier saying the same words, and was dimly conscious of her turning in the street and running back to the school to put an end to the Leaving Dance.

So they drove her home and put her to bed, and in the first part of a long, sleepless night, with the only noise the odd car, she heard the drone of her parents' voices, then her father talking to Sergeant Malley, then her parents again, and at last silence, intense silence, and only the sound of her own thoughts.

In the morning her mother brought her tea and toast in bed, and said that Sergeant Malley was going to get an inspector over from Walgett. The case was too important for him alone, he thought. Betty agreed. Sergeant Malley was a fine rugby player and that was about it. His brain was either in his shoulders or his boots. The thought of being questioned by him made Betty want to vomit.

On Monday morning Bettina met her brother and daughter on the forecourt of King's Cross, having said goodbye to a distinctly complacent Katie at the door of her flat and taken a taxi to the station. Her body was alive with pleasure anticipated. The ten past ten train to Edinburgh was not too crowded, and Bettina, Oliver and Sylvia were able to settle themselves round a table for four without much danger of their being joined by an intruder. Bettina had not booked them into First Class because she thought the others should be observing British people, and in First Class you never overheard anything of interest and could only look at a selection of the decaying and the dubious, mostly male. She had an old-fashioned view of pin-stripe-suited businessmen travelling on expense accounts: she thought they should get a real job, earn an honest living. On her trips to literary festivals and promotional events Bettina always travelled Standard Class, and she didn't see any reason to change her habits.

"What's this about a buffet?" asked Ollie as they sped through the desolation of Stevenage. "Or shall we wait for the trolley?"

"The water for the tea is nowhere near boiling on the trolley," said Bettina. "I thought we might go for a proper lunch later. It can be quite pleasant if they manage to get everything on the menu loaded on to the train. I'll settle for a proper cup of tea for now."

"I'll make for the buffet, then," said Ollie. "Coffee for me, tea for Betty – "

"And tea for me too," said Sylvia. "I've decided I don't like English coffee."

"Is Ollie horribly henpecked at home?" asked Bettina, as he scuttled off in the direction of the buffet. "He seems to think he should be at the beck and call of females."

"If you listened to family friends they'd probably say mildly so. But if you looked at the decisions made in the marriage I'd guess that rather more than fifty per cent would be Ollie's – engineered by him."

"Engineered – yes, I recognise that," said Bettina. "I think I do it myself. The trick is, you organise things around you so you get what you want."

"In your relationships with men?"

"Oh those! I'm not sure I got what I wanted in those. I was thinking more of the rape. After the rape." She could talk of that, the determining factor in her life, quite matter-of-factly with Sylvia now. She didn't even lower her voice. Other people had as much right to hear interesting things on a train as she herself did. "I think after it happened I *used* it. I don't feel terribly guilty about that. I'm sure any woman who had had that done to her in a little, inward-looking town would feel as I did: they would want to get away. So one of the things that influenced me over the days that followed – not the only thing by a long chalk, but one important one – was the desire to leave Bundaroo."

"And you succeeded in that."

"Yes. I can't feel altogether good about it, because it

meant a degree of cutting myself off from my family. We loved each other, but we could never be *close* again, because we couldn't be together. And that hurt me, and it hurt my father, him particularly because I was the apple of his eye. And it wasn't usual, back then, for a girl of sixteen to fly the family home. But of course we all realized that the circumstances were exceptional; they accepted the need for me to take off, but still ... I'm sure it devastated Dad. And now I feel at least a twinge of guilt that I was so happy to be out in the wide world."

"It seems a very mild sort of manipulation," said Sylvia. "And really necessary. Probably something similar is true with Ollie and Judy. She *needs* to feel that she's in charge, so he engineers things so that she can believe that. Hey presto – the marriage is saved."

"Yes. I suppose most successful marriages are based on successful dishonesties of that kind."

"Maybe. I wouldn't know. I've never really let a man into my life."

That was something Bettina quite understood.

11
Aftermath

The doctor came quite soon after breakfast. He said it was so Betty could get cleaned up – "a bath works wonders" he said, and the way Betty's body felt convinced her that he must be right.

Dr Merton lived in Mundehai, the third of the townships in the area, all of which he served, as well as some properties on the edge of Walgett. He was an old friend of Betty's, having seen her through measles, scarlet fever, and the usual selection of childhood illnesses. He was in his fifties, unambitious, content to work out his time in Northern New South Wales, and with no thoughts of retiring to the beach areas of Southern Queensland even after that. Beaches were good for nothing except sitting on, he said. And he could do that where he was. Above all in this situation, he was sympathetic, a calming influence.

"Try to pretend this is happening to someone else," he said, as soon as Dot had left him alone with Betty. "Or that my hand is attached to some kind of robot – you know, activated by an electronic brain."

"There's some play about that," said Betty, anxious to think about anything but *that*. "All the characters are robots."

"You'd know all about things like that. So imagine I'm something on wheels, with steel hands that send messages to some kind of radio or recording apparatus. Shut your eyes if it makes it easier."

So she did close her eyes, and tried to float away to some distant planet, only giving a small yelp when his electronic hands probed the throbbing bruises on her neck and throat, than began to raise her frock. "Burn it!" screamed something at the back of her brain, "so I can never, ever see it again." Finally, after inspecting, gently feeling and tut-tutting, he pulled the sheet over her and sat down beside the bed, making notes in a cheap notepad such as Betty could have bought in Phil Clayton's general store. It seemed to lack the dignity of a serious crime, of a possible court case in Walgett. Then Betty thought this was probably right: this was a crime without dignity.

"Now," said Dr Merton, "as I said, a bath can work wonders, and your mother has kettles on the stove now."

"What about the policemen?"

"Don't you worry about them. I take the medical evidence, and no one else."

"Thank goodness."

"They're not qualified to do that, you see. But they are qualified to investigate a crime, and I'm satisfied that's what this is. I know Inspector Blackstone from Walgett. There's no better policeman in this area. So just think – try to remember every little thing – "

"Ugh!"

"I know, I know," he said, genuinely soothing. "But you'd regret it later if you remembered something that could have been vital in a court case, wouldn't you?"

Betty thought. She couldn't admit to the doctor that the idea of a court case was intolerable.

"I suppose so," she said.

"Of course it would. He's got to be caught. So get it all over now. Then the police can get on with their investigations, and you can get on with your life."

"I never want to see Bundaroo again," said Betty loudly. "Never want people there to see me."

"Now Betty – think!" said Dr Merton, taking her hand. "Be sensible. You've done nothing wrong. Everybody knows that.

148

You're talking as if it was you who's guilty. It's not. It's the man who's done this to you. Right?"

"Right," said Betty eventually. But something inside her said: "I bet they're all saying in Grafton's and Phil's that I brought it on myself with my dancing."

As the doctor said, Betty's mother had kettles and saucepans on the Crown, and before long she was lying in a warm bath, feeling cleaner and better, and trying to think through the terrible event of last night, trying to remember anything that the policemen from Walgett would need to know. The thought of the approaching interview nauseated her, but she didn't need Dr Merton to tell her how important it was.

Betty lay luxuriating in her bath for as long as she could. It helped, as the doctor had said. How did he know? she wondered. At last her mother shouted "You'll get cold if you don't come out of that bath!" – which seemed unlikely in temperatures over the hundred. Her mother had put out a clean nightdress, and when Betty tried to insist that she would talk to the policemen properly dressed, not in bed like a sick child, her mother, unusually forceful, insisted that she had to go back to bed and talk to the policemen from there. She used words, or supposed words, of the doctor to back up her command.

"He says you mustn't *think* of getting up for the next couple of days. And what would the policemen think if you were up and dressed as usual? They'd think what happened was nothing very much."

So when the two men arrived in a police car, two chairs had been placed for them in Betty's tiny bedroom, with its musty picture of the water-babies on the wall, and the wire grille up against the open window, through which could be heard the sounds of the farm – the cattle lowing from a distance, the occasional bleat from the few sheep, and noises from the chicken run at the back of the house.

"Hello, Betty. How are you feeling now?" asked the policeman from Walgett, sitting down immediately beside the bed, and letting the local man have the seat by the door.

"Better. The bath helped," said Betty, looking curiously but she hoped not rudely at the police contingent. Inspector Blackstone was pushing fifty, with a neat little moustache and kindly but penetrating blue eyes. Less impressive and interesting was the constable Betty knew: he was laboriously getting out his notebook and pencil, then settling down to take notes, holding his pencil as if it was a screwdriver. P.C. Malley was tall, broad and heavy, a familiar figure in Bundaroo but not a greatly respected one. He was rumoured to extract confessions from suspected "crims" by threatening to sit on them.

"I'm sure it did," said Blackstone. "Now Betty, I know this is going to be distressing, but there's not much we can do about that: I'm going to have to take you through the events of yesterday evening." Betty nodded. "Let's start then, shall we? It was to be a big night for you, wasn't it? You went into Bundaroo with your parents, I suppose. How did you go?"

"We walked. We always do if we're going to something. There are always people doing the same, so we meet up."

"I see. And who did you meet up with last night?"

Betty considered.

"Oh, the Broughtons, the O'Haras. And Alice Carey – but she lives practically in Bundaroo."

"She's your best friend, isn't she?"

Information from P.C. Malley, thought Betty. She decided to be truthful.

"She used to be. Not any longer. She's got a bit jealous since Hughie Naismyth came to the district. She felt out of it, because Hughie and I have been together so much."

"I see. So you all arrived in Bundaroo, and I suppose you went to the school hall. Where did your parents go to?"

"They went to Bob's to have a bite to eat."

"Did they stay there all evening?"

"I don't know. Some of the parents walked around a bit – looked in at the school hall, or just gossiped in the street. Mum could have gone to have a chat with the vicar. She's a member of the mothers' group, and they're organising the Christmas party this year."

"Most of the fathers went to Grafton's, I suppose. We know about the little arrangement the landlord has when there's anything on in Bundaroo."

"I bet you do," said Betty, who had often seen P.C. Malley emerging from the back room late in the evening.

"What about your dad?"

"No. He said he wasn't going there."

She sensed at once a reaction from the two men.

"Why did he say that?"

"Just that he'd be in Bob's if I needed him ... He and Mum were both there when I ... when I did need them."

"Right. Now what about yourself?" Here it comes, thought Betty. "You went along to the school hall, and you met up with all your mates, I suppose."

This was beginning to feel like coming-clean time.

"I don't have many mates at the moment."

"Oh? Why is that?"

"All the school turned against Hughie Naismyth, and I wasn't going to go along with the herd."

Inspector Blackstone pondered this information.

"Well now, you'd better tell me who this Hughie Naismyth is, and why all your mates turned against him."

"His parents are migrants – his father used to have a farm in Northumberland. I think that's in the North of England, isn't it? Hughie is very artistic, and that didn't help."

"From what I hear you're pretty artistic yourself."

"I read a lot. That's not quite so bad. I mean, quite a lot of people read. Anyway, I don't make too much of it. Hughie really knows about painting."

P.C. Malley now put in his spoke from the door, where he had been taking laborious notes, which Betty would dearly like to be able to read.

"From what *I've* seen he just sits talking to Mr Blackfeller any chance he gets."

"That's right," said Betty, edgily.

"Why would he do that if he's interested in painting? That's just bullshit stuff old Blackfeller peddles. I wouldn't have it on my walls."

"Hughie's interested in aboriginal art, especially the genuine stuff, not the stuff done for the tourists."

Inspector Blackstone felt he should step in.

"Well then, Hughie is English, he's interested in art, and doesn't make any secret of it – is there anything else?"

"I suppose there's his father," said Betty slowly.

"His father's out at Wilgandra," put in P.C. Malley.

"He's manager there," said Betty, "since September. He's not very popular." She saw Blackstone look at Malley, who nodded. "I don't know much about it, but I think he's too used to English ways and doesn't want to learn Australian ones. It puts people's backs up."

"And that's rubbed off on to his son, has it?"

"Yes. And his mother's considered a bit snooty. She insists on doing things the English way, and she buys things at Phil's that he only stocks because Mrs Cheveley uses them ... Silly little things, but in a small place they influence people."

"People often set a lot of store by silly little things," agreed Blackstone.

"Anyway, what I'm saying is that at the moment I don't have a lot of friends in my year at school."

"Which meant that you and Hughie were thrown together a lot last night."

"Yes, though we would have been together a lot of the time anyway. We like each other's company."

"So you danced together?"

He obviously knew about that, from the tone of his voice. Malley again.

"Yes, we did. Quite well actually. So everyone said we were showing off. Then we came back to the refreshments table and there were one or two silly comments, so we just stood a bit apart talking to each other." Rather brightly, thought Blackstone, too loud and with no natural pauses, to pretend that they didn't mind being ostracised, when they really minded very much. "And then the trio began their medley of songs from the shows, and the first ones were slow numbers ... sort of yearning ..."

"And they struck a chord?"

"Yes. *Yes.* Wanting something else. Wanting to be somewhere else. Like being chained and aching to escape ... And first me then Hughie went on to the floor and began doing little dances on our own."

"Dances you made up, do you mean, not regular waltzes or foxtrots or dances like that?"

"Yes. Just expressing what we felt through our bodies, and through movement. Oh, I'm sure it wasn't Isadora Duncan or anything like that, but it satisfied us, felt right for us."

"So you've heard of Isadora Duncan?"

"Heard of her. Nothing more. Anyway it was just a way of expressing ourselves, like I said. It wasn't – " she tried out a word she had never used before – "erotic or anything like that. Probably pathetic more than anything else."

From under her eyelids she saw a glance go from Blackstone to Malley. This time it was not an enquiry, more a command – to keep quiet, perhaps. Had Malley been among the group at the door? And had he told the Inspector that it *was* erotic? Or perhaps that she and Hughie were just showing off, drawing attention to themselves – as if this somehow justified what happened later? Betty would dearly like to have known.

"I'm sure it wasn't either erotic or pathetic," said Blackstone kindly. "So what happened next?"

"Hughie saw his parents arrive, and he went over to the door where all the parents and the others were standing, so he could make light of the dancing, as if it was just a joke, a big game."

"Why would he do that?"

"He thought they might hear about it from the other parents. His father's rather hot on manliness – manly sports, manly occupations. Doing solo dances that you've made up yourself isn't manly at all in his book, I wouldn't think."

"So what did you do?"

"I pushed my way out."

"Out into the open air?"

"That's right. To get away. To get a breath of fresh air. It was very hot in the hall, but it wasn't just that: it was all the hostility – most of it really childish, and we're supposed to be on the verge of adulthood. It depressed me."

"So you tried to put a distance between you and them, did you?" asked Blackstone.

"That's right. I looked towards the main street, but there were people around there, and I didn't want to talk to anyone. So I went in the opposite direction."

"Down towards the river?"

"Yes."

"You weren't frightened?"

"No," said Betty, trying to remember back to her days of

innocence. "This is Bundaroo. Nothing ever happens here except occasionally men get drunk and have a fight."

"So you didn't have a sense of anyone following you?"

"No, of course not! If I had I'd have turned straight round. But I wasn't listening, because I didn't feel scared. It was very peaceful. I didn't have any notion of anyone else being there until – "

Her voice faded.

"We'll come to that in a moment," Blackstone said hurriedly. "Can you tell us exactly where you went?"

"Yes, I went to the Primary building, then behind it to the fence that cuts the playground off from the river. It's rather overgrown there."

"We know. We've been looking at the place. That's where it happened, isn't it?"

"Yes. I was watching there and thinking for some time – five minutes, maybe longer. I thought I heard an animal in the long grass, but ... Either he was there already – but why? what would he have been there *for*? – or he followed me, skulked there for a bit, and then – then *pounced*."

"Did it feel like that? Coming from nothing?"

"*Yes*. That's why it was so *terrifying*. He put his arm around my neck and seemed to be choking me. I tried to tell myself it was a joke, a prank, but I knew it wasn't. It hurt so much. I thought he was going to kill me."

"Dr Merton mentioned the bruises," Blackstone said quietly. "They'll hurt for a while yet. So you say he came from behind, and you couldn't see him then."

"I couldn't see him at all, ever. There's no light down there. All I could do was feel his arm choking me, and smell his smell."

"His smell? What do you mean? Body smells?"

"No, beer. Not just from his mouth – I don't think his mouth was ever near enough. But all over ... all over."

She saw this time a look of real significance travel from Blackstone to Malley. Her words had definite meaning for them, and that meaning was something they had already talked over.

"Was there anything else about the attack you could tell us?" asked Blackstone. Betty thought hard.

"He was taller than me. Strong ... Please don't ask me about the actual ... you know ... because I was so terrified and nauseated that it's like a big black hole. I don't *remember* anything, except the pain and the horror."

"Yes, yes. We do understand," said the inspector.

Suddenly Malley put in his twopenn'orth.

"Didn't your dad give work to a sundowner a few days ago?"

"Al?" said Betty, glad to know the name. "Al Cousens? Yes, but what? – Oh no. *No!* He moved on on Thursday – took the road to Walgett."

"Nothing to stop him doing a U-ie and coming back."

"You just want it to be someone who's not from Bundaroo."

"Well, is there anything wrong with that? This is your home, a nice little place, full of people who know you – "

"Full of your mates, you mean," said Betty, feeling greatly daring but fired by a sense of justice. "You don't want to find out who did it, you want to rule out most of the suspects from the start, and then find someone from outside the district you can pin it on."

"Now, now, Betty. You're upset," said Blackstone. "Nothing like that is going to happen, I can assure you. Nobody is going to be ruled out and nobody is going to have anything pinned on them."

"Well, you *can* rule out Al. He was probably a hundred miles away, if he got a lift. Anyway they wouldn't serve a sundowner beer in Grafton's, any more than they would an aboriginal."

"If they've got the money they can drink it outside," said P.C. Malley. It was rarely that he got an idea, but when he did no power on earth could knock it out of him. Blackstone shot him a look, and the two men took their leave, the inspector assuring Betty that she had been very brave.

They had had two very tiring days. The first had been given up to the most obvious tourist destinations, and Bettina had decided you could never have enough of the Royal Mile. It was all of fifteen years since she was last in Edinburgh, so she enjoyed the great promenade at leisure, with frequent stops. Ollie was one of those tourists who, knowing he is having a once-in-a-lifetime experience, is determined to see everything there is to be seen, and see it through the lens of a camera. This left Bettina and Sylvia with plenty of time to sit and chat together.

"I'm all in favour of Mary Queen of Scots," said Bettina, gazing down over the lower parts of the city, "and I'd be even more in favour if she'd had John Knox quietly poisoned with a potion recommended by her mother-in-law Catherine de Medici. But I must say David Rizzio was an unwise piece of self-indulgence. Anyway, what was a charming sophisticated Italian doing in this rainy, windy country going mad with fundamentalist religion?"

"Nowadays the Italians seem to sell ice-cream," commented Sylvia.

"Then it was travelling guitar. To be fair, Scotland seems to have had more need of love-songs than of ice-cream, but I still think Rizzio was a mistake. Not to mention Bothwell. OK, she may have felt the need of a ruffian to keep the awful Scottish nobles in order, but to sleep with him! Marry him!"

"I suppose after the French court she appreciated something a bit more earthy."

"Earthy is one thing. A total thug is another. You do see it today: a woman gets shot of one hopeless husband – and Darnley really was the pits, and you see his type everywhere in England today – and then crashes straight into another marital disaster. At least after Cecil Cockburn I learnt the obvious lesson: no more marriages."

"Is he still alive?"

"I have no idea. I wouldn't know him if I sat opposite him in a train." A quick look at the woman sitting beside her told Bettina that her brusque dismissal of the man she had married had been a mistake. "I'm sorry. I should have thought. He was your father after all."

"Don't worry. I know it was a very short marriage. What was he like?"

"He was twenty-five. He thought the world owed him a living, a good lifestyle, a cushy job once the war was over, admiration, deference, the best of everything. And this was in half-starving, war-ravaged Italy in 1945. Whether he'd got that way because his parents spoiled him or at his minor public school I never found out."

"You were both in the services?"

"Yes, the army. He was a transport officer, and he was brilliant at it. It was the rest of life he couldn't manage, but he hadn't realized this at the time. I was twenty-three. I'd been in Italy fifteen months, I should have been worldly wise, but I wasn't. I'd hitched a lift to Europe in a way – come as assistant to a well-known Australian war correspondent. After three months in Italy I knew the language well enough to be useful to the British Army, which was advancing up from the South, so they let me join up."

"But why did you want to? Journalism was much more your thing then, wasn't it?"

"I didn't want to report on other people's experiences, I wanted to have them myself. Even at twenty-three I knew what sort of experiences would be useful, and direct ones of war were among them."

"You knew that, but you didn't know what type would make a good husband."

"Definitely not that. But unlike Scottish Mary I only made the mistake once. That's enough about Cecil. You've put the idea in my mind that I might meet him again, and I couldn't bear that."

The next day they split up. Sylvia and Oliver went their various ways around Edinburgh, and Bettina went into Glasgow. She had decided years ago, when she was in the city on a publicity trip, that the Burrell collection was second rate, so she went to the Kelvingrove Art Gallery, had a long and delightful lunch on her own with *The Times* crossword still to do, then went back to the gallery and looked for a second time at the pictures which really interested her. When she got back to Edinburgh neither Ollie or Sylvia was in their rooms. Theatre or a concert, she decided. Sylvia had worked most of her life as a teacher, but her great love was arts administration – co-ordinating the work of hundreds of amateur bodies in Australia. Bettina didn't want another big meal, so she awarded herself an early night. She was, after all, over eighty.

She got down to breakfast late, and decided to have the works – the full English, or British, breakfast, starting with porridge and continuing with a fry-up. It was a long time since she had eaten, and she made up for it. She was on to the toast and marmalade when Sylvia came into the breakfast room, looked around for her, then came over and bent over her table, her voice urgent.

"Bettina, you're wanted at the desk."

Bettina wiped her mouth.

"At the desk? What on earth can that be for?"

"I don't know. I was just coming in from a morning walk when they hailed me because they know we're together. It's someone on the phone from London, and I think I heard the word 'police'."

"Oh Lord, Mark can't have been up to his tricks again, can he?"

"Surely they'd want Ollie if he had, wouldn't they?"

Bettina was beginning to be worried. Leaning a little on Sylvia's arm she left the breakfast room and went out to Reception.

"I can put the call through to the box over there if you like," said the Receptionist. "It's more private."

Bettina nodded and she and Sylvia went over.

"Yes? Bettina Whitelaw speaking," she said.

"That is Mrs Whitelaw of 13 Holland Park Crescent, is that right?" asked a young male voice.

"Yes, that's right."

"I'm afraid there's been a break-in at your flat, Mrs Whitelaw."

"Oh Lord. What's missing?"

"That we don't know. Nothing obvious. We'll need your help on that. But I'm afraid the lady in the flat – "

"Katie? What's happened to Katie? – "

"I'm sorry, but she's in hospital. She has bad head injuries. She's not expected to survive, I'm afraid."

Bettina whispered, "I'll be there. I'll come as soon as I can," and put down the phone.

12
Taken by Force

Bettina sat in the plane, shaking her head at all the offers of food and drink, deep in thought and memories. She was glad to be on her own with them. Sylvia had volunteered to come with her, but that was not what Bettina wanted.

"No, you stay for your last day, as we'd intended. I wouldn't want Ollie left on his own. I haven't got my old brain around what has happened yet. If I need support and comfort it will be after I've grasped the details, and decided whether I'm – "

"You don't think you're responsible, do you?" said Sylvia, a schoolmistressy note in her voice. "That it was your fault? You said yourself that she volunteered – "

"I know, I know. Let's wait and see, shall we? Just come with me to the airport and find out if there are any spare places. The police are contacting the airline to ask them to give me priority. I do so want to be home *quickly*."

So here she was, almost without registering what was happening, on the ridiculously short flight from Edinburgh to Heathrow. The thought of Katie fighting for her life in hospital – if she hadn't already lost that fight – tormented her. Why hadn't she simply refused her offer? Katie would have been offended, but it wouldn't have altered their friendship – their barbed friendship, in which Katie rejoiced in the office of the candid friend. She'd always made it clear that she preferred Peter, and perhaps she'd been right. He was one of her own, spoke her language, and perhaps was the nicer person.

But Peter, so relaxed and kind on the surface, had

always put his own needs and well-being first. And selfishness always increased as a person got older. Probably her own acceptance of Katie's offer had been selfish – to save herself further trouble. Easy options got more attractive the older you got, the more effort every action involved. And the more it didn't seem to matter whether they turned out well or not.

Bettina put herself in the dock. She had known that there was some kind of threat to the flat, and thereby possibly to herself. Someone had been in before she left for Edinburgh. Why hadn't she – rather than accepting Katie's offer – employed a security firm, or a flat-sitter? Why hadn't she asked someone like Mark to stay there for the three nights that she would be away? He had a mobile, and would not have been out of the reach of any of his potential employers.

But then she grimaced. She disliked the thought of Mark having the freedom of her flat. She disliked the thought of Mark full stop. She knew Sylvia considered she was unfair to him, and admitted to herself that she might be. But the truth was that he was associated in her mind with Sam Battersby, with P.C. Malley, and men of that type. Even if he got the Nobel Peace Prize, or for that matter the prize for astrophysics, those were the associations that would remain around him in her mind, the men she would class him with.

"I blame myself," said Bettina, after she had settled into the car in the police compound at Heathrow and had begun the drive through hideous suburb after hideous suburb towards central London. Being met at the airport by a young policewoman had given her a feeling somewhere between being a VIP and being a prime suspect.

"Why is that?" the capable young woman asked, keeping her eyes on the road.

"How stupid can you get – asking an old woman to flat-sit for you when you're away?"

"Mrs Jackson is a friend of yours, isn't she?"

"So she's still alive?"

"Yes, but very poorly."

"She's a fighter. Please God she pulls through ... Yes, she is a friend of mine. And that makes it stupider, and nastier too: how *could* I get Katie involved in something like this, when I knew that someone – God knows who it can be – had been showing an interest in the flat?"

"Yes – we'd had a hint of that from Mrs Tuckett."

"Oh, was it Clare put you on to my being in Edinburgh?"

"Yes. Mr Seddon put us on to her, and Mrs Tuckett told us where you were staying."

Bettina looked at her, her forehead creased.

"Mr Seddon? Peter? How did you get in touch with Peter? I thought he was in Bournemouth."

"No, not at all. It was he who went round to your flat, and thought there was something wrong when he couldn't get an answer. He went back a second time a few hours after, and when the same thing happened, he called us."

"I see."

But she didn't really see, and they remained largely silent until they pulled up in front of Bettina's apartment in Holland Park Crescent. It was a substantial nineteenth century house with five apartments carved out of it, and at the top of the four-step flight up to the front door there stood a policeman. He was witness to the fact that the powers that be at Scotland Yard had recognised that Bettina was a pretty well-known novelist, and the media could well get interested in the news that an intruder of some kind had battered an old woman who had been sleeping in the distinguished writer's bed.

"Is Murchison here?" the policewoman asked the uniformed guard. He nodded.

"Arrived back ten minutes ago. Waiting for you."

The policewoman led Bettina up her own stairs and into her own flat. Bettina had just time to register that there were savage cuts around the lock when she was introduced to a man pushing fifty, with a little greying moustache, rimless spectacles, wearing a smart, dark-blue suit.

"Mrs Whitelaw? I'm sorry to have to bring you back from – "

"How's Katie?"

"Holding her own, but only just, I'm afraid. Her age is against her. You mustn't hold out too many hopes – "

"That's just what I must do. Where was she attacked? In bed?"

"No. She was found in the doorway there." They were inside the flat now, and he pointed to the door between the sitting room and the study. "She was – hit around the head." Bettina had a strong sense of his holding something back, but for the moment she let it pass.

"I noticed that the main door from the landing had been forced."

"Yes," said Murchison, and Bettina had that feeling of caution once again. "We're having an expert in to examine that. If you were just to look around the flat, at the most obvious things, is there anything you notice that is different? Moved, for example, or maybe missing?"

Bettina's eyes were such that she had to walk around the sitting room, looking at chairs, tables, cupboards and walls. Then she did the same in the study and the two bedrooms.

"There is some disturbance on the desk in the study," she announced when she had concluded. "And one picture missing."

"Yes – we'd noticed a gap, and the brighter wallpaper," Murchison said quietly. They went over to the place near the door out to the landing. "What was there?"

"An Australian aboriginal painting by John Mawurndjurl. I'll write the name down for you. A bark painting – very intricate and geometrical – but not an abstract: more and more shapes emerge the more you look at it."

"But not especially valuable, surely?"

Bettina raised her eyebrows at the assumption.

"Not the *most* valuable I have, certainly. But I bought it some time in the mid-eighties – because I liked it, but also on Hughie's advice. Hughie is my friend who's an art critic. He says it must be worth now many times what I paid for it. You should talk to Hughie – that's Eugene Naismyth. You can contact him through the *Sunday Telegraph*, or I could give you his home address."

Murchison nodded, taking everything in and filing it.

"Right, I will. First things first, though. Do you know of anyone who would want to kill you, or injure you, or steal from you?"

"No to the first two. But steal – "

"Mrs Whitelaw mentioned to me someone 'showing an interest in her flat'" said the policewoman. Bettina looked at her approvingly.

"That's what it was. Shortly before I went to Edinburgh I was sure someone had been in here. Nothing was missing, but things had been moved in the study."

"Sure?"

"Absolutely sure." Murchison nodded. He trusted her, she thought. She was pleased at gaining the trust of a calm if limited mind that could weigh evidence.

"Now what about keys to the flat?" Murchison went on.

"But surely he – " Bettina stopped short. She mustn't imagine she could teach him his job. "Well, Katie had one for a start."

"Anyway? Not just given her while she was flat-sitting for you this week?"

"Anyway. She still did work for me now and then. And Clare has one – Clare Tuckett, my agent."

"Yes, she's told us that. I'm a bit hazy about agents. Why would your agent need a key to the flat?"

"She's a friend as well as my agent. I probably gave her one when I was away but wanted her to do something here, or collect something."

Murchison practically tut-tutted.

"Anyone else?"

"Mark, my nephew. He stayed here for a bit when he arrived from Australia, and I had one cut for him then."

"And in all these cases you never asked for the key back?"

There was despair in his voice that decades of trying to educate the over-trusting public had had such meagre effect.

"No, I – " began Bettina weakly.

"And all these people had a key to the front door as well as to the flat?"

"Well, one of them would be no use without the other."

"And all these keys could have spawned other sets of keys, if anyone close to the holder thought it was worth while to get one made?"

"Yes, I suppose so. You think I've been silly ... Oh, Peter may still have one. Peter Seddon. He was my partner many years ago. Partner as in lover."

"He didn't use it when he came round. He called us."

"Well, maybe he'd lost it, or given it back to me some time. I'm afraid I don't remember."

She saw, plain as the back of her hand, a thought going across Murchison's face: maybe Peter thought it unwise to show the police he had his own key. It had become obvious that the police thought the marks on the front door were a blind – a red herring. But perhaps they could explain why anyone close to her would want to steal one of her aboriginal paintings – worth something, certainly, but far from the most valuable painting in her collection.

There were footsteps on the stairs and a knock on the door. A police rider was there, helmet under his arm, a parcel of books in one hand. It made an odd picture, but Murchison merely nodded his thanks and closed the door.

Bettina's eyes went to the pile of books. Immediately she recognised *The Heart of the Land*. Murchison saw her recognition and looked a little shamefaced.

"When we found out who lived here – yesterday afternoon it was, when I talked to Mr Seddon – I asked the library to put together anything they could get hold of about you. That's one of yours, is it?"

"That's right. One of my Australian ones. About to be filmed. I had to stop writing about my own country because I was getting too remote from it ... And this is a book of interviews by a man who specialises in interviewing women. It was the only time I've ever enjoyed being interviewed, as a matter of fact ... And here's a history of Australian literature. I think they gave me all of a page, which is probably more than I deserve ..." Bettina paused, surprised. "What on earth is this?"

She was looking at a copy of *Hi!* magazine, a cheap weekly that specialised in celebrities and paid good money for home interviews with them, lavishly illustrated. Film and television stars, footballers and other athletes in photogenic sports, aristocrats, rich businessmen and game show hosts – these were the usual grist to their mill. It was a magazine that did not aim high.

"What can a common little mag like this have to do with me?" asked Bettina, looking disgustedly at a cover picture of Joan Collins, happy at last with a new man. Superintendent Murchison took the magazine up.

"Joan Collins, of course," he said, flicking through the pages. "Andy Cole, the Duchess of Westminster, that Australian barmaid from the Queen Vic, Princess Michael of Kent – "

"The Queen Vic? Is that *EastEnders*?"

"Yes. She's out of the series now. What's her name?"

"Is it Kerry Probyn?"

"Yes." He'd found the place and opened up the magazine. "About to start filming *The Heart of the Land*."

On the first page there was an Armstrong-Jonesy portrait of Kerry herself. On the second page there was a picture of Kerry and Bettina around the coffee table, as close as Bettina ever allowed herself to get in the course of the interview. "About to star in a major film," said the rubrick at the top of the page. Murchison flicked over. There was another picture, of Kerry standing at the very door they were now standing by, and to her left was the bark picture by John Mawurndjurl where now there was a mere gap.

"Pushy little bitch," said Bettina disgustedly.

When she had talked to Murchison for some time it occurred to Bettina that she could not – and certainly did-n't want to – spend the night in her own flat. The thought of sleeping, or tossing sleepless, in the bed from which Katie had been awakened and gone to the brutal attack which maybe would still prove her death made her gag. Unwilling to interfere with the SOCO investigations she went downstairs to her best friend in the flats – Nick Szabo, a refugee from the 1956 Hungarian uprising, who had proved to have a Midas touch on the Stock Exchange. He had been in the flats almost as long as Bettina, and remembered the scandal when she had taken up with a bus driver.

"Hello Bettina – still bringing trouble on us," he said genially when he found her at his door.

"No, Nick. Someone is bringing trouble on me," she said firmly. "Or on poor Katie. Can I use your phone? I need somewhere to rest my head."

"I suppose you do. Are you going to the Prince Leopold?"

"If they have got a room for me."

"They'll find one."

The Prince Leopold, one of the few family hotels left in that or any other part of London, had figured in one of Bettina's later novels – one that had contained sharp por-traits of all sorts of literary figures including Kingsley Amis, Muriel Spark and Ted Hughes. Bettina had been a favoured client ever since, had stayed there whenever she had had the decorators in, and had parked there any visitor she did not care to have in her own flat. They had heard the news of the break-in, were very concerned, and had already pencilled her in for one of their best rooms.

"Come as soon as you like," Harry on the desk said. "Get away from all the nastiness."

"I may just do that," said Bettina. "I'm only in the way here."

An hour later, having packed a small suitcase under the watchful eye of the policewoman who had driven her from Heathrow, she was installed in a small suite in the Leopold with an unasked-for pot of tea, a plateful of her favourite crab sandwiches and a cakestand with the sort of goodies they did particularly well.

"Got to pamper you a bit," said Harry, the son of the house, who brought the tray up himself. "Now, are you in hiding or in retreat here, or are you receiving visitors and phone calls?"

"Being in retreat sounds marvellous," said Bettina, "but I can't hide from what has happened. The police know I'm here, so I suppose I'm available to them or anyone else who calls."

So it was that she was hardly into her second triangle of sandwich when there was a knock on the door and Peter came in, carrying a cup, saucer and plate.

"Can I join you? They said you were receiving – like bleeding royalty, it seems. That's what being robbed does for you. Still, I suppose you need a bit of luxury and waiting on. Come as a nasty shock, this must've."

"Very nasty. But worse for you, I suppose."

"Seen worse things in Cyprus," said Peter, harking back to his brief period in the army, and apparently inclined to shrug off the horror of finding Katie. "Anyway, it wasn't my flat. It's always nastier when it's your place – like being invaded."

He sat down and tucked into the sandwiches.

"But I don't understand why you were around," said Bettina. "You were supposed to be in Bournemouth with a lady friend."

"She never turned up. We were to meet on the coach, and she didn't show her face, nor in the next day or two. Can't think why she didn't. Things were going so well."

"Hmmm. I suppose she was in her late forties or early fifties," said Bettina, who knew the way of a woman's world.

"Round about. I never asked for her birth-certificate."

"You're in your seventies, Pete. You're not much of a catch so far as the look of the thing goes. The bed bit may be all fine and dandy, but a woman that age will always prefer to be seen with a man nearer her own age, and probably younger."

"Materialistic, that's what women are," said Peter, apparently without malice. "They go for appearances. Anyway, it left a gaping hole in my holiday. Nothing but Bingo and touring Agatha Christies at the local theatre. Gave me the heeby-jeebies. By Tuesday I decided to cut and run."

"Twenty years ago you'd have found another lay," said Bettina.

"You do wonders for a fellow's confidence," said Peter. "Anyway you don't know Bournemouth out of season."

"No, I'm fortunate that way. So you came back and went round to see Katie?"

"That's right. I thought she might like me to take over. I shouldn't think it's all that pleasant being a single lady in someone else's flat."

"An *elderly* single lady. Peter, I've been very thoughtless. If only you'd *said* when it was arranged in the Duke of Sussex."

"I wasn't thinking, same as you," said Peter, with genuine regret. "Seemed a sensible set-up. Once I'd been stood up and was back home it didn't seem so sensible."

"We're a selfish pair," said Bettina, rather resentfully watching him wolfing crab sandwiches. "So what did you do next?"

"Well, when I didn't get any reply I went back home. Thought she was out shopping or something. But then I thought you'd probably left her anything she might need, and remembered that the whole point of her being there was because you thought someone had been in your flat. That made me nervous, so I went back. When I got no reply the second time I called the police."

"Why didn't you use the key you had?"

"Key? Have I got a key to your flat?"

"Yes, I gave it to you years ago. I think you were going to walk Mr Growser when I was away for the day once."

"Don't remember. I'd have given it back, surely. It's not as though we've had anything going since I moved out, is it? I haven't got any use for it."

"Is that what you mostly keep keys for?"

"Well, yes. If we have a big bust-up I might throw it at her and storm out – big gesture, you know the sort of thing. Otherwise I generally keep them. You never know, after all."

"I'm pretty sure you kept mine, even if you did think we were finished for ever – *rightly*. Anyway, you didn't use it. The police came round and you went in with them, did you?"

"Yes. It was horrible. She was lying there in the doorway to the study."

"Did you see the wounds?"

"Yes. Of course we ran over, and she was lying face down. There were nasty wounds on the back and side of her head – almost like cuts. I don't know how she'd survived that long if she was surprised during the night. You know the police don't think she'll pull through?"

"I know ... But I've got to hope. Otherwise it'll be as if I signed her death warrant."

"Don't be daft, woman. She wanted the job, remember? It's not as though you pushed her into it or anything."

"I shouldn't have agreed."

"OK, luxuriate in guilt. You intellectuals are really into guilt, aren't you?"

Oh no, thought Bettina. That's not my problem.

Later that evening she rang Hughie. She only got to speak to him after going through the filter of Marie, who doled out shock, horror and sympathy as if they were regulation portions of a school meal.

"Poor, poor Katie. You must be devastated. She was such a character. I feel like I've lost a friend, even though it's years since she was your daily, and the most I did more recently was see her around in Kensington and swap the odd word. But she was always so 'straight from the shoulder', and told you exactly what she thought."

"It's not 'was' but 'is', Hughie. She's still alive."

"Is she? That's wonderful! When I heard you'd been broken into I rang the police and it sounded as if there was no hope."

"Katie is a fighter, so I'm going to hope. I don't suppose you know that the John Mawurndjurl has gone."

"Gone? Been stolen, you mean?"

"Yes. Presumably by whoever attacked Katie."

"Oh God. It is the most wonderful thing – so intricate and so various and look-at-able. But far from the most valuable thing you have."

That was Hughie. The aesthetic appeal came first, but the monetary value came a very good second.

"I know," said Bettina. "It's odd."

"But it was in that article on Kerry Probyn in *Hi!* magazine this week – did you know? I saw it in my newsagent's."

"Hughie, I do not believe you inspect cheap little magazines like *Hi!* in your newsagent's. Pornography I'd believe, but not *Hi!*."

"Well, Marie actually saw it, and saw the picture of you. But there it was by the door – Kerry Probyn beside the John Mawurndjurl."

"I know. If I'd known that interview would be placed in a magazine like *Hi!* I wouldn't have bothered doing it. They must have known that, and kept quiet about it. Do you think it convinced someone the picture was worth stealing?"

"Quite possibly. Art thieves often need guidance."

"Well I hope if anyone comes to you for guidance on this particular picture you turn them straight in to the police. I want it back. I love it. But why did they only take that? I've got a lot of small paintings they could have grabbed along with it."

"Presumably the thief was surprised by Katie."

"But Katie was attacked on the other side of the room, in the doorway to the study."

"Maybe he was over there when she surprised him, then when he'd attacked her he grabbed something close to the door on his way out."

"I suppose that is possible. But I don't like coincidences like the picture being in the magazine the same week."

"Coincidences happen, even if they're difficult to make convincing in books."

"I know the difference between life and books, Hughie."

No one better, she thought grimly as she put down the phone.

13
Flight

The next day, after a long luxurious breakfast that included scrambled eggs almost up to American hotel standards, Bettina went up to her room, found it was already done (they knew her habits at the Prince Leopold), and settled down in front of her desk. Could she write? Could she put a clean sheet of paper in front of her and write with a pen in her hand, as she had done throughout her writing life until the terrible pains had gripped her hand? She had in fact felt much less pain recently when she ate her meals. No essential difference, surely, between wielding a knife and fork and wielding a pen? She could go and get the little tape recorder from her flat if necessary, and if the police would agree to it, but something inside her told her to leave the police alone to do their job. And she did so want to write the next chapter of *A Cry from Bundaroo*, dealing with the aftermath of the rape, because she felt now, at the end of her adult life as the rape in the school grounds had been the beginning of it, that she had at that time run away from the situation, and she must not do the same thing now.

That nagging feeling had been there almost since she left the little town of her birth and growing up. Often she told herself that she couldn't have done anything else, that she could not have gone on living in Bundaroo, and that she had made the decision to leave it long before the rape. But she knew in her heart that there were many girls, her contemporaries, who had had no way of leaving the place, no escape route, that they would be – had been, still were – there all their lives, making the best of it, or the worst.

Perhaps it was a consciousness of this difference between them that led to the general bitterness at Hughie, then at her, that had been the prelude to the rape. Jealousy, but of an understandable sort.

She drew towards her the Prince Leopold folder on the desk, took out the little bundle of stationery, and began to write.

The only thing that Betty was grateful for in the period that followed the worst happening in her life was the doctor's command that she should be kept in bed for some days. Her first instinct had been to get up and face the world straight off, say to it: "This is not my fault. This had nothing to do with me, with what I am. I'm the victim here, and I'm going to have my revenge." But lying in bed, with a sheet over her for decency in the baking heat of an outback summer day, she felt that this reaction had been childish – felt, in fact, a wave of relief that she didn't have to do anything, didn't have to meet anyone except the three people she most loved in the world.

Her father at first didn't know whether he ought to say anything about the rape.

"The police are questioning someone," he blurted out at last.

"Who?"

"Sam Battersby." That was all right then.

"What have they found out?"

"I don't know. Nobody knows. But people say he was there in the school hall, watching the dancing."

"When?"

"Nobody really agrees. He was in the little group at the door, but the group kept changing. Maybe someone who was in his back room at Grafton's will remember what time he left and came back."

"So maybe he saw me and Hughie – "

"*Maybe*. Always remember it was not your fault, darling."

Two days later, the day which she had decided was to be her last day in bed, and after visits, endured but still appreciated, from Miss Dampier and Michael Potter-Clowes, her father came in with more news. Betty knew he was putting a brave face on things.

"Battersby has been released for the moment," he said. "The police need more time to investigate – that's their line anyway. Battersby's poor little wife has been running Grafton's, but hardly a soul has gone in there. Now he's back I doubt if anyone will go there, apart from casuals in the town. And you can't make a living from casuals, not in Bundaroo."

"I'm glad no one's going there ... Why did they fix on Battersby, Dad?"

"Because of something you said ... And you kids wouldn't have heard talk of it, but people have been noticing the way he's always been out in the street at the beginning and end of the school day. We're not daft, Betty."

"No. Pity no one did anything about it."

"What could we do when he'd done nothing?" protested Jack Whitelaw. He thought for a moment. "Though there was talk about that daughter of his."

Betty thought it was best to leave things there.

"Have they talked to anyone else?" she asked.

"Oh, they picked Al up near Walgett. Murchison went back there and questioned him. He's a lot brighter than P.C. Malley."

"I should hope so. Imagine anyone making P.C. Malley an inspector."

"Stranger things have happened," said Betty's father, who knew how things worked in New South Wales, even if he didn't capitalise on his knowledge. "Al is pretty much out of it. He was having a meal at a farmstead this side of Walgett on Saturday around five. Difficult to see him getting a fast car back to Bundaroo. Difficult to see why he'd want to."

"Of *course* it is," said Betty hotly.

"Anyway there's talk that he was in bed with the widow-lady running the farm later in the evening."

"Oh ... Anyone else?"

"Oh yes. All the parents who came and watched the dancing. They were in the vicinity. Very difficult to find out who was there when, since they weren't noticing who else was there. Then there were the boys in your year – the ones who were so rotten to you."

"Steve Drayton and that lot?"

"Yes. What they did was real crook, but I don't think it was one of them, Betty."

"Nor do I," said Betty. Then thought. "But I don't see why they shouldn't get a bit of a shock."

"No. It's all very difficult, you know, darling. Everyone knows you were ... the victim – "

"Raped."

Her father put his head in his hands.

"I hate saying it, Betty. Anyway, the problem is proving who did it. Unless there were marks on him, or on his clothing ..."

"I don't think there would be marks on him. He held me so close I couldn't do anything. So you think he'll get away with it?"

"I didn't say that. There's more ways of skinning a cat ..."

"Dad! You're not thinking of a lynch mob!"

"'Course not, Betty," said Jack, shocked. "This isn't the Deep South. But you can't go on for long if folks won't do business with you."

Betty felt the need to change the subject.

"I'm getting up tonight, Dad. We can all have a bit of supper together – maybe have a game with Ollie."

And so things started to get back to normal. Ollie had begun to be depressed by the atmosphere in the house, so they played hide-and-seek and hopscotch with him, and ate braised mutton. Betty could see how happy it made both her parents to see normality – slightly strained normality – returning to the house. Two days later she decided to go into Bundaroo.

There was nothing she wanted to buy there, and certainly no one she wanted to see. She had to badger her mother to tell her something she could find a use for from Phil's. Her mother understood what was at stake, but was unsure whether it was the right time for Betty to go into Bundaroo on her own. Eventually, as usually happened, she gave way.

The walk to town began bravely enough. She waved to her father in a far paddock, and then to one or two people in cars or on horseback on the road into town. "Betty back to her old self" they probably said, to themselves or their companions. But as she approached Bundaroo there was a tightening in her throat (the throat that the surprisingly strong arm had nearly throttled), and that tightening seemed to spread to her entire body, so that she hardly knew how to hold her shoulders naturally, could barely put one leg in front of the other to get herself to *that place*.

But she got there. Feeling like nothing so much as a doll or a puppet she reached the main street, walked past Grafton's Hotel, though not so much as a glance did she cast in its direction, past Mr Won who was arranging cauliflowers in a box in front of his shop and raised a tentative hand, past Bob's café, not yet open, and at last, as if the walk had been miles instead of merely yards, out of the merciless sun and into the shade of Phil's General Store.

"Well, hello Betty. Good to see you. What can I get for you?"

Give Phil his due, he did exactly the right thing. Just the tone he would always have adopted if she hadn't been in for a few days.

"Hello Phil. Mum wants a tin of tomato soup and a tin of pineapple chunks please."

She watched, aware that she was relaxing, as Phil reached up behind him to get down the tins and put them down on the counter. As he did so Betty was aware of someone else entering the store. She handed over her shilling and waited for the change, then heard a sort of shuffling behind her. As she turned to go she saw Steve Drayton.

"Betty, I – "

"Hello, Steve." She was conscious of putting a warmth into her voice that she did not feel.

"I wanted to say I'm sorry – we're sorry – "

"I'm sure everyone is. Nearly everyone."

"They are, they are! But I meant what happened before. We all got screwed up about things, and it got nasty. Maybe it was the Leaving doing funny things to us. Anyway, it became just silly."

"Yes, well, I think we all became a bit silly. But then we were all doing the Leaving. It doesn't seem quite so important now."

"I suppose not. We *were* so sorry, Betty – "

"Thank you, Steve ... Steve, would you do something for me?"

"O' course."

"Will you just walk me down the main street – just till we're past Grafton's?"

"O' course. No probs."

"That's right," said Phil, "keep the little girl safe," thus losing most of the Brownie points with Betty that he'd earned earlier.

182

They left together through Phil's door on to the street and walked back in the direction Betty had come. Steve didn't seem to have much conversation for such a situation, and Betty would not have had much attention to pay to small talk. Eventually Steve said:

"I don't think he'll try anything on."

"We'll see," said Betty.

"He'd better not!" But as they neared Grafton's there he was, pushing his way through the main door, intent on bearding them. He seemed to have lost weight, though he was still bulky and menacing, dwarfing Betty's defender who was clenching and unclenching his fists. Sam's eyes had a wildness to them, very different from the creepy and insinuating gleam they had had before when he talked to Betty.

"Betty! Stop! You've got to tell them – "

"Get lost, dickhead. Now," said Steve, and they both continued walking, Betty quickening her pace as she walked within a couple of feet of Sam, and Steve immediately following suit.

"Betty, you've got to tell the police I had nothing to do with what happened to you. They've got this daft idea – "

"Cut it out, will you?" shouted Steve.

" – this daft idea that it was me. And you know we've always been friends, always had our little jokes together. Betty, you've got to tell them – "

Betty turned around, and Steve put a restraining hand on her arm, but couldn't stop her.

"How can I tell them you didn't do it? I don't know you didn't. I don't know who it was. But I do know you make me want to throw up."

And she turned and almost ran till they were on the dirt track, past the last shop and house, Alice's, and on the way to Fort George. Betty stopped, drew breath, and turned to Steve.

"Thanks, Steve. I'm very grateful."

"No fuss, Betty. You told him, anyway. Bloody bullshitter."

Suddenly Betty seemed to crumple, lose all her fire. She hid her face in her hands.

"I can't stay here. I can't stay any longer."

"Don't say that, Betty. It will get better, really. They'll arrest that mongrel – "

"They won't. They've no evidence. He'll always be here, leering at me ... Tell the others, Steve: it's nothing to do with what happened at the dance. Tell Hughie too. I just can't stay here any longer."

And when she got home she walked straight out to her mother, feeding the chickens.

"Mum. I can't stay here any longer."

Bettina's second morning at the Prince Leopold was marked by a flying visit from her agent.

"I heard this was where you were," she gabbled, "though I could have guessed. Rellies still in Edinburgh? Do Australians call them rellies? No – well, that was a fair guess too. Now, I thought you'd want to work, so I rescued your tape recorder from the police."

Bettina was breathtaken by Clare's barnstorming style.

"That's very kind of you, Clare," she said quietly. "But yesterday I managed to write several pages longhand."

"Really? *Really*? Well give them to me and I'll photo-copy them just to be on the safe side. I'm glad I brought the tape recorder though. I mean, if you've got arthritis you've got arthritis, haven't you? I should stick to the tapes. They're probably safer here than in the flat. You can put them in the hotel safe every night, can't you?"

"Oh yes. Along with my diamonds and Fabergé easter eggs."

"Humour was never your style, was it, Bettina? Satire,

yes, but not much in the way of fun in your books, is there? I hear Katie's still hanging on."

"Yes. Katie's a fighter."

"Is it worth it at her age, I wonder?"

"It's her nature. I don't suppose she has a choice."

"Of course you have a choice. The most lively dog decides at some point that it's not worth going on any more ... The police seem very interested in Mark."

"*Mark*? How do you know that?"

"You know my wonderful hearing. Better than a bugging device any day. While I was unplugging the tape recorder and getting the whole caboodle into a bag, I heard the big chief – Murchison, is it? – talking on the phone in your sitting room. It was something about Mark having a police record back in – Victoria, is it?"

"You know perfectly well Australia has a state called Victoria, Clare. You're just trying to make it sound like Botswana or the Galapagos Islands. Yes, Ollie and Mark live in the suburbs of Melbourne, though I think Mark tries to spend most of his summers in Sydney or Surfers' Paradise."

"Places as unknown to me as Samarkand or Xanadu, darling. Well, I have heard of Sydney, what with the Games and the bushfires. Pure magic, I'm sure, both places. Anyway, that's who they're interested in."

"Only as one of several possibilities, I'm sure. I don't think if they've talked to Mark for long they'll take him very seriously as a suspect."

"Why not?"

"Too dim. And Mark is just weak. A bundle of trivial vanities. A child who doesn't see why he shouldn't have any and everything he wants when he wants it. It's not on the cards he could do anything like this."

But when Clare had gone, Bettina sat thinking about Mark. She had classed him in her mind with P.C. Malley and Sam Battersby and other body-orientated types she had met on three continents since her Bundaroo days – simple-minded, small-brained men devoted to their own obsessions and satisfactions. But P.C. Malley had made it to Inspector, as her father had more or less predicted he might, though his time in Grafton had been cut short by a case of evidence-fixing so blatant that even the NSW authorities couldn't ignore it. And of course Sam Battersby ...

But Sam had signalled danger, even to an ignorant young girl. Mark had never done this. But should she have been alert to other signs, different messages? Was Mark more complex, more mixed-up – above all more dangerous – than she had imagined?

Everyone was very kind. Of course her parents were more than that: they were loving. And in fact when she thought about it after she had made her escape from Bundaroo, the kindness of most of the people close to her had been concerned, responsible, well-judged.

Her father, when he got in from the paddocks, had gone into Bundaroo and talked to the Reverend Potter-Clowes. Unwilling to telephone from Grafton's Hotel, the vicar had got on his bike early next morning and cycled out to Wilgandra. As a consequence, soon after breakfast Bill Cheveley had appeared at the farm, and all four of them – Betty definitely included and listened to – held a Council of War. After that Jack Whitelaw had gone back with Bill and telephoned to his sister in Armidale, at the department store, Cummings's, where she worked. By the time Jack arrived back to Fort George it had been arranged that Betty would go and stay with Auntie Shirley for a while. Jack had established that there was a bus from Walgett to Brisbane that passed through Armidale, and ran every Saturday. Bill was with Jack when he came home and spoke very kindly to Betty.

"I'd like to have loaned your dad the car so he could have driven you to Armidale," he said. "I just don't like being without it for too long – because of Peg."

"Of course Peg comes first," said Betty, who was really fond of Bill's wife, even if she did suspect that her illnesses were mostly imaginary. "And it'll be rather exciting taking the bus."

As soon as she had said it she realized that excitement was about the last thing she wanted at that time. What did make Betty feel guilty was the general agreement that she was going to stay with her Auntie Shirley "for a while". That wasn't her intention at all. If she had her way she would never come back to Bundaroo. Not "never" never, of course: she would come back, she thought, if her parents were ill, when Ollie got married – family events. She would come back for a few days, even a week or two, but never more than that. Armidale was the haven that beckoned at present, but it was only a stepping-stone on the road to Sydney, and to who knew where else?

Before Saturday came she had a visit from Michael Potter-Clowes. Perhaps the vicar sensed the truth – that this was a real goodbye. They sat in the sweltering lounge and he stumbled to say how much knowing her had meant to him.

"Having you to talk to, watching your mind develop, has been one of the pleasantest things in my life," he said. "And it will be wonderful to watch you from afar. I *know* exciting things are going to happen to you."

She felt like saying that one just had, but she knew it would be the wrong note to sound.

"Oh, I don't know," she said deprecatingly. But her smile said that she thought he might be right. "Will you – can I write to you?" Tentative as the suggestion was, she knew it was she who was conferring the favour.

"*Would* you? Oh, I'd so like that. I've never had a real correspondence in my life."

Thus began an exchange of letters every three months or so that lasted till the end of Michael Potter-Clowes's life, when Betty had published all her Australian novels and gone on to London subjects. It was a correspondence that gave as much pleasure to her as it did to him.

On Saturday Kevin Drayton arrived with the car before sun-up, and Betty said goodbye to her mother and Ollie on the dirt road outside the farm, crying at losing them, crying at the end of one movement in her life – which had begun, unsymphonically, with a long slow movement, but which she was sure was now about to speed up. Then she and her father got into the car, drove through the silent landscape to drop Kevin back at Wilgandra, then continued on to Walgett. By nightfall she was in Armidale, being met by her aunt in Beardy Street. It was lucky she was the only girl of the right age unaccompanied on the bus or they would have had difficulty recognising each other.

She soon got on to her aunt's rather spinsterly wavelength, and found the taboos in her world-view rather comforting. She registered to take the Leaving year over again at Armidale High School. This had been agreed with her parents before she left. They all knew she was in no mental or physical condition to start teachers' college or university. The comparative coolness of the place – now and then, even in mid-summer, feeling to the girl from the outback positively chilly – began the work of healing. Away from the roasting sun everything seemed more balanced, more understandable, more susceptible to rational solution.

There was one thing, however, that she found it

inconvenient not to be able to talk to her aunt about. As she met Shirley's friends and neighbours in the next few days, though, she began to suspect that they all knew what had happened to her. She was bemused, because she couldn't imagine her aunt sharing her knowledge around the town. She later found out that the woman on the switchboard at Cummings's, who spent most of her day taking down orders from the surrounding graziers, listened in to every private conversation that promised to be interesting and spread the information gained. So Betty chose the most sympathetic of Auntie Shirley's neighbours in Dangar Street, and went to talk with her one pleasantly sunny afternoon when her aunt was back at work.

"I think you know what happened to me, don't you?" she said, over tea and biscuits. She ignored the look of apprehension that spread over Mrs Brighthouse's face. "How will I know – and how soon will I know – if I'm pregnant?"

The neighbour was quiet for a few seconds. Even in Armidale minds were not easily adapted to new situations, and giving sexual counselling to a victim of rape was way outside Mrs Brighthouse's experience. But she rose to the challenge, and the main sign of her nervousness was the fact that she sank her voice to a whisper, as if her weatherboard walls had ears. When she had finished, and answered Betty's questions, she got off the subject as quickly as she could.

"I hear you're in for a competition in the *Bulletin* for a young journalist," she said. "How exciting! And your auntie says you have a good chance of winning."

"Oh, that's probably just Bundaroo talk," said Betty, unconvincingly. False modesty never came easy to her, even before she was mildly famous.

They talked happily, avoiding difficult subjects, until Mrs Brighthouse's son came home, dressed in flannels and carrying a cricket bat. He was to be in the Leaving Year that Betty

189

was joining at the High School, and they talked for a bit, beginning the very mild romance that occupied her first few months in Armidale. This provided the basis for the heroine's romance in *The Heart of the Land*, where it became much less mild. But then fiction, including Bettina's fiction, never tried to capture the lukewarmness and unformed nature of life as it is really lived.

When Mrs Brighthouse said goodbye at the front door she whispered:

"In a few years you'll find a husband and have a family, and all this horrible business will be forgotten."

No I won't, thought Betty. And it won't be forgotten by me.

Over Christmas and the weeks after it Betty began to settle down in Armidale. Everything there seemed attractive after the baking dusty summers in Bundaroo. She couldn't wait for the two days in winter when the locals told her they would have snow. Every week, and sometimes more often, she got a letter from her mother or father. They told her which of her female classmates was said to be going with which of her male classmates. They told her that Miss Dampier had got a teaching post in Bathurst, and that her replacement had not been appointed yet. They told her (briefly, with no embroidery, as if their letters were read by a Gauleiter or a Commissar) that Sam Battersby had given up the Grafton Hotel and left the area for South Australia, and that his poor little wife had gone to live near her daughter, who was engaged to be married. They told her that Bill Cheveley had blown up when he had heard Paul Naismyth tearing a strip off a raw recruit to the property's workforce. They had come to a parting of the ways, and the Naismyths had decided to return to Britain. Paul Naismyth had changed his mind about the likelihood of war, and decided that his country needed him. With his usual tact he had enlarged on this decision for all to hear in Phil's.

"We'll be fighting by year's end. And make no mistake, Australia won't be with us this time. This country's got no backbone. It's rotten, it's lazy and it's yellow to the core."

The letter from the *Bulletin* came in mid-January, just after Betty had received her moderate-to-good Leaving results and before the start of the new school year. There was nothing on the envelope to say who it was from, but the postmark was Sydney, and it was typed and addressed to Miss Bettina Whitelaw at Fort George, Bundaroo, NSW. Betty's parents had decided that it could not be from a friend or relative, and had sent it on unopened, thinking she had a right to read it first.

It congratulated her on winning the first prize. It said her article was evocative, mature and beautifully written. It said what a wonderful tribute it was to Australian life and education that a tiny place like Bundaroo could produce the winner of a competition that had attracted more than a thousand entries. It said that the editorial board of the *Bulletin* thought it appropriate for a member of the journal's staff to come out to Bundaroo and present Bettina with her prize of one hundred Australian pounds at the High School there.

Before her aunt returned from work Betty had written a reply, expressing her joy and gratitude, but asking, since she had always longed to see Sydney and did not know when she would get another opportunity, if the prize could be presented to her there.

14
Prophesying War

That afternoon, phoning in advance to make sure a visit was acceptable, Murchison came to the Prince Leopold to see Bettina. He brought news that Katie Jackson had shown more than one slight sign that she responded to voices.

"The other thing I wanted to tell you," he said, settling down in the little armchair, "is that we're finished with your flat. You can move back in whenever you feel like it."

From the upright desk chair, where she sat with a stiff, upright posture that Murchison ought to have envied, Bettina thought for a moment then screwed up her face.

"I don't know ... Not yet, I think. I just can't imagine settling down there, or getting a good night's sleep ... On the other hand the longer I leave it the more difficult it will be ... I've never been weak about making necessary decisions, but somehow everything has become very difficult."

"Anyway, it's up to you. What about your brother, and – and the lady he's with?"

"She's not his partner or anything like that. She's my daughter. Unacknowledged."

"Actually I did know that. That's why I hesitated."

"Mark, of course." Murchison gave a bob of his head. "Men are such awful gossips."

"Couldn't she stay with you?"

"Do you really think I can ask the daughter I abandoned to put herself out for me in that way? That flat won't be pleasant for *any*one to sleep in until the whole

193

horrible business is put out of all our minds. That will be months away, and Sylvia will be back in Australia by then."

"You say you can't ask your daughter to do this. Does that mean that you don't get on?"

"No. We get on better than politely, better than I ever could have imagined. We're friendly and interested in each other. But I can't pretend we're mother and daughter in any real sense. Maybe I can't ask her because I feel guilty."

Murchison nodded.

"It sounded like that ... I gather you're writing your memoirs."

"So people tell me. It's news to me."

"Tell me what you are writing then."

Bettina paused, wishing to be as precise as possible.

"I am writing a novel based on my life. I've kept all the names, or most of them, but it is essentially a novel. I go into thoughts, I give lots of dialogue when of course I can't remember what was said sixty-five years ago. I probably get things wrong, put shops in the wrong streets in Armidale – not in Bundaroo – I couldn't get little Bundaroo wrong. The book is my own life novelised."

"I see." It was Murchison's turn to think. "When my grandparents died I had to see to their effects. They had lots of books, some of them left over from their childhoods. I remember a series of titles like "Lives of the British Queens", "Lives of the Great Explorers", "Lives of British Murderers". They were either sentimental or sensational, and they were told as stories, but I think essentially they tried to stick to the facts. Is that what the book you're writing does?"

Bettina laughed rather sharply.

"You make it sound quite dreadful, but I suppose you're right. But you mustn't think I'm sentimentalising or sensationalising the story of my life. I'm just writing it in the way I know best, recreating it as a novel, hoping to make it more interesting, and to dig deeper than most autobiographies, by presenting it in the way that the modern reader knows best and feels happiest with. And I hope it will appeal more than an autobiography would to the younger reader, who knows nothing or very little about the period, and perhaps who gets her ideas about Australia from the early evening soaps."

"Thank you," said Murchison. "That makes it clear. What period in your life is this novel going to cover?"

"Oh! I'm not sure I've decided that yet. But in the back of my mind there's always been a feeling that it shouldn't be one of those loose baggy monsters that just meander on and on until they splutter and die like an old car. That would be awful. So it will be about my young life, like *Sons and Lovers*. In a way that means my relationships not just with people – parents, schoolfriends and so on – but also with my own country, my real home. It began to wear thin when I became assistant to a war correspondent in Italy in 1942. That's going to be very difficult to write, because in the nature of things records get lost in wartime, or don't get written at all. I may postpone doing that until last. I suppose the real end of my childhood and adolescence was in Trieste, in 1945 and 6, when I'd joined up with the British army, got married, and somehow committed myself to Europe."

"I see." Murchison pondered for a moment or two. "And was Sylvia Easton a product of that marriage?"

"Yes."

"And you never went back to Australia?"

"Twice, briefly, when my parents died. I think I'll have to include those deaths somehow, as flash forwards. That was when my last real links with Australia were cut."

"And your brother – "

"My brother was so much younger than me that I never really saw him growing up."

"I see. But you said earlier that people think you are writing your memoirs."

"That's what people keep telling me."

"Which would mean a much wider picture of your life – up to the present day, or near it."

Bettina pondered.

"I suppose people could have that idea. But people writing their memoirs often choose to cut the story short, because of the difficulty of dealing with people still alive. Or they just deal with one section, like the war, for example, or growing up."

"So people could be interested in what you're writing who weren't known to you in your early years. People who think they won't like what you might write?"

"In theory, possibly. But mine hasn't been an exciting, controversial, headline-grabbing life. I'm no Germaine Greer. Or even a Graham Greene. I don't quite see why you're so interested in my novel."

"You said yourself someone has been into the flat – before the current break-in or entry – and has been at your desk."

"Ye-es. Yes, of course. But my desk is the centre of my professional life. Not just what I'm writing, but what I'm earning, what I'm spending, what I'm paying the tax man, what I'm *worth* – it's all there. People who live in flats, with adequate but limited space, have to be a bit methodical, and for most people like that their desk is in a way the *business* centre of their lives."

"Agreed."

"So it's a logical place for a thief to go."

"Maybe."

"I'm not quite sure, you see, that you should be concentrating on my book. There are other things: you could be looking at what I'm worth, for example."

"All right – let's do that. Let me guess roughly. The highly lucrative lease on the flat. A very well-chosen collection of twentieth century Australian art. The proceeds of a life of novel-writing, probably wisely-invested. Any royalties or film-or-TV rights in the future. A nice little fortune. Anything inherited from your parents or other relatives?"

"Dear me no," said Bettina, shaking her head humorously. "We were always poor, and the drought of the early 'forties was my father's death-blow as a farmer. Anything there was was left to Ollie. I asked my dad to do that when I went back to be with my mother when she died. Even then I preferred to rely on myself."

"Anyway, a nice little fortune. A million or more."

"More like two, I suspect. I sometimes react if people call me rich, but my dad would have gaped at how much I've got."

"Who gets it?"

"At the moment the National Portrait Gallery."

It was Murchison's turn to gape.

"I can't see the National Portrait Gallery organising a murder, or even a break-in."

"Not in this country. Some of the sums given to cultural institutions in America are so vast that I sometimes wonder whether some public-spirited individual might organise an early voyage to the shades for the Midas figure concerned. Anyway, you can rule out the Portrait Gallery for other reasons than unlikelihood. They don't know. And it's probably only a temporary, emergency will. It leaves token amounts to friends and relatives, and the rest to the Gallery because it's one of the London places where I feel happiest."

"But you may change your will?"

"If I can think of anything better. Nothing occurs to me at the moment, but something may emerge from all this ..."

"Just one more question: suppose that you were to die intestate – who would inherit then?"

This rather threw Bettina.

"I suppose ... she's my legitimate daughter."

"Mrs Easton?"

"Miss. She's never married. And was never legally adopted, because I would have had to be consulted, wouldn't I?"

"I imagine so, but I know nothing about Australian law. Did you never make enquiries as to whether the foster parents wanted to give a legal basis to their custodianship?"

"No. That was up to them, wasn't it? I wouldn't have put any barriers in their way, however." She saw that she was making a deplorable impression on the policeman, and felt she had to elaborate a little. "I didn't feel ashamed about that then – I mean about just getting rid of her and forgetting her. So it seems a bit hypocritical to start feeling shame now."

"I'm not here to judge you," said Murchison, but Bettina was pretty sure he already had. "The point is that if there was no will, Miss Easton would probably be your legal heir."

Bettina got impatient.

"Yes, but there is a will."

"And before this one, this temporary one, was there an earlier one?"

"Yes! Some of the people named had died, but yes, there was. And Sylvia wasn't named in it. There's no way you can start suspecting Sylvia. It's nonsense!"

It occurred to her to wonder by what process of emotional change or development she had become so protective of her daughter. But then she had been protective of Mark, if much less passionately.

"On the day before the attack on Miss Jackson, you and your brother and your daughter had gone your separate ways in Scotland, hadn't you?" asked Murchison.

The five days she spent in Sydney in February 1939 were the most exciting in Betty's life so far, though in her later memories they were destined to fade in comparison with the experiences of war. Her parents came down by bus and train from Bundaroo, and she enjoyed the last period happily together of their long companionship. They went to the theatre, wandered through the seedy glamour of King's Cross, saw the most beautiful natural area Betty could imagine – the harbour. It all passed like a dream. She wanted to pay for their hotel out of her winnings, but her father wouldn't allow it, and when they went to settle the bill they found that it had been paid for by the *Bulletin*.

The presentation of the prize was in the journal's offices in George Street. Reporters from Sydney newspapers had been invited, and those in tune with the *Bulletin*'s political views had accepted. They were polite rather than genuinely interested, but when Betty talked to such elevated beings she felt like a star.

"Shall we call you Betty or Bettina?" one of them asked.

"Bettina," said Betty firmly, beginning the process of transition.

Cameras clicked as the prize was handed over. In addition to the cheque there was a little silver cup. Betty prized the cheque infinitely more than the cup, and her father said "Quite right!" When she was told that the competition was to become an annual event she felt pleased, because writing her entry had given her so much satisfaction that she enjoyed the thought of others following in her footsteps. She also felt something of a pioneer.

Lunch in a Sydney restaurant with her parents, the editor and some of his senior staff was an ordeal to be got through. She had seen her father, before the presentation, deep in conversation with the editor, and she knew that her recent horrific experience must have been the subject for the hushed encounter. That depressed her. She tried to sparkle, but knowing that they knew dampened her spirits.

"Are you reconciled to losing your daughter to the wider scene?" the editor asked Jack Whitelaw over coffee.

"It's what we've always wanted for her," he said simply. "She's good. She's better than just talented. What could she find to do in Bundaroo?"

Later that day, when her mother had taken a Bex APC tablet for a nervous headache, Betty and her father sat alone in the lounge of the hotel, and he took one further step in the process of loosening the ties on her.

"You go for it, little lady," he said, taking her hands. "There's nothing for you in Bundaroo. Even if you'd been a boy, I'd tell you to get out. We're at the mercy of everything – the elements, insects, the rains or lack of them, disease, the bastard earth of the place. We're just camped out on soil not fit to crap on – pardon my language. You get out, darl; make your way to something different. We'll be watching you, your mother and I, and we'll be so proud!"

Why, remembering those words in later life, did Bettina have an aching sense of loss?

The war changed everything. In the spring and summer of 1939, while she was again ostensibly studying for the Leaving, Betty had two articles published in the *Bulletin* – one was on Armidale, one was a thought-piece on the over-dependence of Australian radio on British material. Then came September: Britain declared war and – almost without thinking, it seemed – Australia declared it as well. Radio brought the war into Australian homes, the cinema intermingled it with Jeanette MacDonald and Clarke Gable. Men volunteered. The Brighthouse boy, with whom Betty had been mildly flirting, spent much of the war on the Burma railway, and wrote to Betty in the 1950s, when her aunt died. War altered the fortunes of politicians. Robert Menzies, who had been keen to ship iron ore to Japan in the months leading up to the war, found himself newly christened Pig Iron Bob when the iron ore came back in the form of bullets, putting his political fortunes on hold for a decade. Soon there was talk of a Japanese invasion, or submarines in Sydney harbour. Men volunteered in still greater numbers. Men in the *Bulletin* offices volunteered or talked of doing so.

The offer of a job in the journal's Sydney office came to Betty in mid-October. The letter made no bones about the fact that she would be a glorified office-girl, but stressed that they had faith in her and that she would be given every chance to make her contribution (judged on merit alone, of course) to the periodical. Bettina went straight down to Cummings's and phoned them from there. She felt she was owed this, since her private affairs had been spread round town from the switchboard. The *Bulletin*'s managing editor already had in mind a good home near the office where Bettina would be made part of the family. Betty's parents, after all, had to be given peace of mind, especially after what had happened in Bundaroo.

Leaving Certificate was forgotten. Betty never committed the (to her) great irrelevancy of going to university. Within a week she had a job, a new home, a new destiny. For over two years she worked on matters trivial and matters vital, in her spare time writing special articles and – more importantly – her first short stories. Then in early 1942 she joined the staff of an Australian war correspondent, first in Cairo, then in Italy. Thus she edged her way into the theatre of war, and into Europe.

Sylvia arrived at the hotel in mid-afternoon. She and Oliver had got an early train from Edinburgh, and she had learned where Bettina was staying from Clare Tuckett.

"Mark had her number," she said, sitting on the bed without being asked. "He knew Clare was selling your film rights and he thought she must be a theatrical agent as well. When he rang her to push himself she was very kind to him, and I think he's still under that impression."

"Kind? Doesn't sound like Clare," muttered Bettina.

"Feeling grumpy, are you?" Sylvia asked, rather daring. From anyone else the question might have brought a put-down, but in fact it brought an uprush of feeling from her.

"*Yes*! Yes, I am. And it's all my own fault. I don't know what to do Sylvia. The police have finished with the flat."

"And you don't know whether to move back in?"

"Yes. Half of me says I can't bear to. The other half says if I don't do it now it will only get harder and harder, especially if Katie dies, so I should pull myself together and get it done. It's the only place in the world I really feel at home in. I only need to throw a few things into the suitcase I brought with me, and call a taxi."

"Then let's do it, shall we?" Sylvia said briskly, getting up from the bed. "When we get there I'll either stay the night, or two nights at most, or I'll make myself scarce if you feel happy and safe."

"One night, Sylvia. I'm sure I'd like you to stay for one night. After that I'll have to bite the bullet and get back to normal. I'm going to sleep in the little bed in the guest-room ... Oh! Where will you sleep?"

"On the sofa, on the floor – maybe even in your bed. Now come along. Is this the suitcase? Just the one then. Let's get it done and be on our way. Shoes first, then all the bathroom things, clothes on top."

Any impulse she might have felt to protest or call for more time was suppressed by Bettina. She let herself be chivied along, went down to pay the (remarkably cheap) bill, had Harry call her a taxi, and half an hour later she let Sylvia help her out of the taxi on to Holland Park Crescent. She looked up at her destination.

"I've always liked these flats," she said glumly. Then she stomped up the steps, opened the main door, and made her way heavily up to the first floor. She felt a strong temptation to behave badly: to be the elderly cur-mudgeon, to quarrel with every little decision made for her. The only thing that held her back was that she was with her daughter. Sylvia had known enough bad behav-iour from her – even if she was too young at the time to register it.

Sylvia made tea, found biscuits and some fruit cake that was still moist and fresh, acting on the idea that old people seemed to need pampering more than most, and usually had a sweeter tooth than most. And it seemed to work. By five o'clock Bettina was sitting back, asking about her and Ollie's last days in Edinburgh, and generally trying to put behind her the fact that they were in the room where Katie had been so horribly attacked. But comfortable though she was, that attack now and then obtruded itself on her mind. Once she had hoped that serving in the army all the length of Italy as the Germans reluctantly and violently retreated had calmed her fear of sudden attacks by acquainting her with worse things, but she had long realized that that had been a vain hope.

"So what has been going on since you came back as far as the investigation is concerned?" Sylvia asked eventually.

"I don't really know much. Murchison was round this morning asking me questions about my will. He seems to have his eye on Mark, which I pooh-poohed, though I don't imagine he'll be taking much notice of *my* views."

"I just dropped into the flat briefly with Ollie, but I gathered Mark had been grilled."

"How has he taken it?"

"With his usual breeziness. Apparent breeziness. He did say he thought they were turning their attention to Peter Seddon, but he had no idea why. He said he thought Peter and Katie were old friends."

"They are."

"I suppose Murchison has decided it's a man's crime."

"Hah! Clare is worth two of Mark or Peter."

"You don't think? – "

"No, of course not. I only mean that if I was in some hairy situation in wartime – as I sometimes was in Italy – I'd much rather have Clare with me than either of those two men. Mind you, it won't worry me at all if the police give Mark a bad time for a few days if it makes him think. But I don't think it will."

Sylvia's sharp eyes gleamed.

"It's Peter, not Mark we were really talking about."

"Ha!" thought Bettina. "She thinks I still hold a torch for Peter. As if!"

"Hmmm," she said. "Peter's a bit more capable of thinking than Mark. But perhaps I am biased. I suppose I came as near to loving Peter as I've ever come with a man. But that was long ago. And he's another one who tries to shrug off any unpleasantness or any threat to his peace and quiet – he'll turn away from anything nasty as if that cancels it out ... You've been awfully good to me, Sylvia. I'm conscious I've not deserved it, and that this was not how we said things would be when you came over."

"No, it's not. I thought the letter I wrote was sensible at the time."

"It was."

"But it's rather been overtaken by events, hasn't it? And it wasn't entirely honest. The truth is that since I've known I had a birth mother who was rather famous I've collected anything I came across about you, piled up little bits of information in scrapbooks and looked at them from time to time. I've not done it obsessively, I don't think, but just tried to build up a picture for myself. Ollie was one of my sources, of course. Occasionally I met someone who'd known you: at Bundaroo, or Armidale, or Sydney. We have an amateur music festival every year in Bairnsdale, and I met someone years ago with the Chamber Orchestra of Northern New South Wales – someone who'd known you at Bundaroo. Played the flute. Drayton the name was. Would it be Steve?"

"Steve Drayton would never play in an orchestra! Not in a million years!"

"I'm sure that was the name. Said he was in your year at school. Said he'd known you quite well at one time, but only talked to you once after the rape, when he'd walked you down the main street past Sam Battersby."

"Good Lord! It must have been Steve."

"People change, you know, Bettina, and Australia is often a surprising place."

"I know people change. Of *course* I know it. Perhaps they change more than we ever have the space to let them do in a novel."

"That's right. Except the big nineteenth-century ones, perhaps."

"Oh dear. If I was offered that much space to fill with one set of characters I don't know how I would cope."

Sylvia hesitated for a moment, then clearly decided to dive straight in.

"There's something I've been wondering whether to tell you, Bettina. I don't know that it's relevant to anything, but it's something I don't think should have been kept from you."

Bettina's heart stopped, but she tried to put on a determined face.

"Then tell me."

"It's a piece of information ... background information ... that they thought would upset you."

"Tell me now."

"You know I've always loved the people that I think of as my natural parents – the couple who in effect adopted me. And particularly my mother. She was someone your dad and Bill Cheveley knew slightly, as I suppose people in small places like Bundaroo do know everyone."

"Bundaroo?"

"Yes. They already knew her, and knew she and her husband couldn't have children ... She was the daughter of Sam Battersby."

15
Marriage, Birth and Living Death

"Sam Battersby's daughter."

The words came out almost flat, yet Bettina felt a wave of relief washing over her: I was right.

"Yes. You must have known her."

She had thought about her often enough over the years, so that every little thing, and there had only been little ones, was firmly lodged in her brain.

"Yes, a bit, as everyone knows everyone else in places like Bundaroo. But she was four or five years older than me, so there was very little real contact."

"How do you remember her?" persisted Sylvia.

"Very quiet. And that's the word everybody used about her. She was always known as a good student – not brilliant, but very conscientious. But she was *unnaturally* quiet, with a quiet that was hiding something. Cowed is the word that springs to mind."

"Did people wonder why she seemed cowed? Did you?"

Bettina screwed up her face.

"I've thought about her quite often since ... since the rape, and it's difficult to sort out what I thought then. Did I realize she was cowed *then*, when we were both at school. I suspect not. I feel that people generally, while she was still living in Bundaroo, just thought she was quiet – the shy type. But I think there was a change in people's attitude when she went away to teachers' college and never came back for the holidays or even for a visit. She was still in her late teens, so that seemed odd, unnatural, to need an explanation. There was talk.

Someone said that Sam Battersby's wife – Marge I think the name was – "

"That's right. My gran."

"Of course. That she visited her daughter in Lismore, but did it in secret. And possibly paid for it afterwards."

"I think she probably did. One thing I never talked to her about was her husband."

"To tell you the truth, if I thought about Hettie then, I think I maybe would have guessed that she was beaten, treated cruelly, but sexual abuse was so little talked about that as a child it hardly entered my consciousness."

"But that's what it was. Persistent, over a number of years, and both women terrorised into silence about it. Probably it was this that made Hettie incapable of having children. She was lucky in the end: she had a good marriage, and I came along – my good luck as well – to make it complete."

"Sam Battersby wasn't so lucky, was he? But he hardly deserved luck."

"No. He had to get out of Bundaroo."

"It was clear he would have to before I left myself."

"He put a lot of miles between him and the rumours about what he had done. Went to South Australia. It worked for a time. There's less shifting about from state to state in Australia than you'd expect, and still less then. But eventually someone turned up in Peterborough who'd worked at Wilgandra, and then the rumours started floating around there too. Then it was move on time again. They say he died in a Salvation Army hostel in Darwin."

"I see," said Bettina, pensive. "I didn't know that. Sam Battersby was someone I never enquired about. I hope his wife fared better."

"His wife fared much better," said Sylvia, smiling happily at some good memories. "I remember my gran as a good-humoured, loving person who spoiled me rotten. Sam left her behind to hand over Grafton's at Bundaroo to the next tenant, but she scarpered to Hettie in Lismore, then moved with her when she got a teaching job in Bathurst. She lived with or near her for the rest of her life, and was almost part of her marriage. She was always there to look after me, and I went between them as if they were my two mothers. No – Marge was happy as a sandboy after she escaped from Sam."

"I'm glad. And glad your mother was happy."

"She was. She tried to live for the present. But once I knew about her childhood I felt there was always something in the background of her mind – something she didn't talk about but couldn't get away from. Maybe when a child's been abused, particularly sexually abused, that's always how it is. Memories of the experience *seem* to go away, but they lurk, waiting."

"Maybe," said Bettina. She thought for a long time. "I've thought I really escaped. I've never felt the need to use that particular experience in a book."

"I've noticed that. Wondered a bit."

"A rape may be different from the drip of constant abuse ... I know I didn't get away from the attendant things: cutting myself off from my roots, and to a degree from my parents. That can be liberation, but it can be impoverishing too."

"Yes. I would have felt it impoverishing. My happy home in the background was always the basis, the bedrock, of my life as a single person ... But it doesn't worry you, my connection with the Battersby's?"

Bettina's eyes widened.

"No! Why should it? I don't believe in visiting the sins of the fathers on the sons, so I certainly wouldn't blame the wives and daughters for the sins of the husband and father. Your mother was Battersby's *victim*. Of course one has more doubts about her mother. Why did she remain silent? Could she really not have found somewhere where she could be safe with her daughter? But then you think of the pressures: the violence, the fact that she probably was never *sure*, the fact that what was happening was practically unmentionable in the English-speaking world at the time."

"And remember too the unemployment. How was she to get a job and keep them both?"

"I'd forgotten that. I'm glad you remember her as happy. But how did it come about that Hettie and her husband were the ones that fostered you?"

"Hettie was the one they knew about, your father and Bill Cheveley. The married woman who desperately wanted a child."

"But by that time she and her mother had been left Bundaroo for years."

"Bill Cheveley had kept in touch almost from the start. He had something of the old paternalistic feeling about the people around him. He liked people he knew, thought he should be good to them – as your Dad found when the drought forced him out of farming. One of Bill's workers, in Lismore on Wilgandra property business, thought he saw Marge Battersby. A week or two later, when his wife was going through a good spell, Bill went over and had a couple of days in the town. Eventually he saw Gran, as he was pretty much bound to."

"What did he do?"

"Nothing spectacular. Just sat her down in a café,

walked with her in the park – I don't know the details – told her he was always there for the two of them if they were ever in real want. He didn't act the Father Christmas and hand over lavish amounts of cash – that wasn't his way, and would have been more worry than anything else to someone like Gran. He just made it clear he was willing to act as a back-stop. Hettie had her first teaching job at this time, earning a pittance, of course, but they were just about managing, with Marge doing some scrubbing and bar work. The main thing that he asked them to do – he talked to Hettie too, after school – was to write every now and then, keep in touch."

"And he knew about Hettie's childhood?"

"Oh yes. Marge told him – very ashamed, going at it in a very roundabout way. Yes, he knew. He didn't talk to Hettie about it, though. There are things best left unspoken."

"Of course there are," agreed Bettina. She knew that better than most. "But they kept in touch?"

"Yes. Marge usually did the writing, and Bill wrote brief notes back. He wasn't a great one for writing. Hettie got the job in Bathurst, a better job. They moved there, she met my Dad, and they married. Eventually they moved to Victoria, to Ballarat, where she was a Deputy Head, and that was where most of my childhood was spent. Dad worked in the tax office there, and Gran looked after me when necessary, and it was a very nice, stable, enriching childhood, thank you very much."

"Don't thank me. The most I did was in the early stages, when I entrusted you to Dad and Auntie Shirley, though when I heard that Bill had helped with the placing of you I was glad, because Bill usually judged people sensibly. Apart from that, the whole business of your conception and birth was an appalling mess, totally mismanaged by me. Which only shows that we shouldn't despair when we seem to have mucked things up entirely, doesn't it?"

They went to bed early, and Bettina slept fitfully in the guest bedroom and Sylvia slept well on the couch in the living room.

Bettina and Cecil Cockburn walked from the Merceria San Zuliàn toward San Marco in the hazy May sunshine, their khaki uniforms prickly and uncomfortable in the nascent heat, but putting no bar on their optimism and their exuberant high spirits. The Venetians, better fed than the Southerners but still thin from privation, were nevertheless tough and active-looking and they helped the young couple's mood, often saluting them with broad smiles or miming applause – one gondolier even did a little jig of happiness in their honour. Others, it is true, scurried past, faces averted, tense and grim in defeat. *Il Duce* had been dead less than a fortnight.

"You can say this for stringing up Mussolini and his Clara by their heels," said Cecil with his usual nonchalance: "at least everybody knows it's all over."

Bettina had been shocked by the pictures in the Italian papers, but less than she would have been if she had seen them in Australia. The last two years had inured her somewhat to savagery.

"Probably better the way it was than putting him up before some tribunal," she agreed. "They say that by the end he was as silly as a two-bob watch."

"I take it that means he was losing his marbles," said Cecil in his most pukka voice.

"Something like that. He was reading all his horoscopes and

believing the ones that promised him the rosiest future. And going on about a death-ray that the Germans or Italians were developing – in his mind at least."

"The Italians haven't invented anything since Leonardo," said Cecil. "And most of his things stayed on the drawing board. It must be a German brainchild. Probably some crazy notion of Wernher von Braun."

"Never heard of him."

"Hitler's prize boffin. Generally thought to have something nasty up his sleeve."

"Well, it won't save them!" said Bettina, almost whooping out her prophecy. "Everyone's closing in on them. It's too late for spiffing wheezes!"

They laughed, and people laughed back at them, and they turned towards the great open space of San Marco, where the sun had lifted the mist and the whole world seemed bathed in gold. Ahead of them was the Saint's own canal, pigeons, and Venetians scurrying hither and yon.

Across the space where the street opened into the Square a British uniform strolled. The soldier's eyes, alert as they still had to be, travelled in their direction. His feet slowed down, uncertain, and then he stopped. Bettina had stopped too. Seven years did not drop away so easily.

"Hughie?" she said.

"Yes," he answered, a little crack in his voice.

"Hughie!" She ran forward, threw her arms around him and kissed his cheek and danced round and round in joy. Then she was conscious, from around her in the Square, of the sound of applause. Blushing, she disengaged herself, and saw that a little knot of Italians had gathered – men and women in drab, worn, mended shirts and dresses, but smiling joyfully and banging their palms together.

"*Inglesi?*" asked one of the men.

"*Si*," said Bettina. She had had trouble sometimes when people mistook Australian for Austrian.

"*Inglesi amorosi*," said the man, turning round to announce it as if it was a hitherto unknown phenomenon. Everybody laughed again. Bettina shook her head, and went over to Cecil and dragged him over towards Hughie.

"Cecil, meet Hughie, Hughie, meet Cecil," she said, and they all laughed at nothing in particular. The men shook hands and Cecil looked at Bettina.

"You seem to know each other from way back," he said. "How was that? You've never been to England."

"English people come to Australia, or didn't you know?" she said. "In fact practically everyone in Australia is descended from someone British or Irish, since Asiatics were barred years and years ago."

"You're forgetting the Aborigines," said Hughie. "Like most Australians."

"Sorry. Yes, we were the invaders." She turned to Cecil. "Hughie used to be interested in Aboriginal art when he was in Australia."

"Never heard of it. Should I have?"

"I still would be interested in it," said Hughie, "if I could get to see any."

"Where can we *go*?" shouted Bettina. "Where can we get a cup of coffee? Or wine if we must?"

"The back streets are a better bet than Florian's," said Cecil. "Let's dive into the narrowest and darkest we can find, and before long we're bound to come to some little local bar that will have something."

The first ten minutes of walking didn't support his claim, but they talked and laughed and commented on the sights and waved to old ladies in windows and eventually they came to a place dark and stuffy, but with a little table already set out

216

outside. They ordered three cups of coffee and eventually –
after the proprietor, beetle-browed and suspicious, had decided they were reliable – agreed that they would like some pasta
and some wine.

"But how come you are here, Betty?" asked Hughie. "With
the British?"

"Bettina," she corrected him. "It just happened. I was assistant to an Australian war correspondent, and doing a bit of
reporting for Australian papers on the side. My Italian had got
to be pretty good. I decided I wanted to be part of the war, not
just see it and report it. The British Army recruited me because
I could speak to people, find quarters for the officers when
necessary, negotiate with local politicians, who are slippery as
hell. It's been great."

"Yes, it *has*," agreed Hughie. "Better than any war ought to
be."

"What are you doing?" asked Cecil. "I'm in transport."

"I'm in art," said Hughie. "They found a use for me after I
proved pretty duff with a gun or a bayonet. For the past year
I've been monitoring the American and British advance from
the South and advising on buildings and art collections that
call for special protection in the towns they're about to come
to. The Americans have had a lot of good propaganda out of
this. The Germans have been calling them philistines and bar-
barians and worse where the black soldiers are concerned.
This proves they're not, and contrasts with the Germans
destroying all the historical archives in Naples. So there, you
see: it's very important work."

"Of course it is," said Bettina. "Though I bet all you really
do is get out your Baedeker and write a list of all the obvious
things that need protection."

"*And* the map readings," said Hughie, with a comically
exaggerated sort of complacency. "Vital that. It ensures that

the buildings get one hundred per cent protection – provided the troops get *their* map-readings right."

Their pasta came – drizzled with olive oil and with a tiny spoonful of parmesan already sprinkled on. Venetian food, always considered a bit Spartan, had become meagre. But they plunged their forks into the long, thin lengths of pasta and twirled with all the expertise of more than a year in Italy.

"Who's to say they're eating any better back home?" said Cecil.

"Better this than corned beef hash," said Bettina.

"Home they have rationing. Italy has intrigue, bargaining, barter, sex, blackmail, family connections, Mafia – a much richer brew." Hughie took up the glass into which the proprietor had poured a villainous-looking thick red liquid. "*Salute!* May the war last for ever!" said Hughie.

They drank.

"Well, it won't," said Bettina, "not the European part, anyway. They'll get rid of me as surplus to requirements within a month or two of Hitler being hanged from a Berlin lamppost. Cecil will have to wait longer for demob."

"Won't stop us getting married," said Cecil with a broad smile. "If necessary we'll get a backstreet priest to do it. My mother is a Catholic."

"Marriage!" said Hughie. "My! I didn't realize it was that serious."

"Well, we can't go on living in sin indefinitely," said Cecil. "The British army would like that even less than marriage."

They all laughed.

"The British army!" said Hughie reflexively. "You wouldn't believe them, would you? When you look at the C.O.s you wouldn't think they could organize a school bun-fight, and here they are defeating the great German military machine."

"With a little help from our friends across the pond," said

Cecil. "God – I need a leak. I suppose they've got a little cupboard somewhere here."

He left the little triangle of sunlight in which the table was set, overlooking a landing stage, and went into the bar where, with the help of graphic mime, he made the proprietor understand what he wanted. Bettina gazed out at the few passing boats on the canal. If this wasn't pure magic, she thought, it was near enough for her.

"We're not actually living together," she said suddenly, without quite knowing why, "but only because we can't find anywhere to do it. Cecil has to sleep with his unit, and my billet is a large and springy sofa in a cold old palazzo. You'd probably love it, Hughie, but I find it palls after the first day or two."

"He's not worthy of you," said Hughie, ignoring her remarks but looking at her clear-eyed. "He's nice, and funny, and very approachable, but after a time he'll know that you've got a much better brain, and he won't be able to live with that. I know I've no right to give you advice, but can't you just stick together and see whether it works? Because it won't."

Bettina remembered these words in the months ahead. Remembered them in the tiny, backstreet church with the dirty, unshaven priest who married them without a smile or a word of good wishes or advice. Remembered them in the up and down of the first months of their marriage, when she resumed writing for the *Bulletin* and the *Sydney Morning Herald* and started work on her first novel, which Cecil tried so hard not to resent that he seemed to resent absolutely everything else she did. Remembered them when she found she was pregnant – Cecil's carelessness, that, and the stupid boy didn't want a child any more than she did. Remembered them on the way back to see her dying mother, remembered them when she heard her mother's account of how she met her husband-to-be, which oddly seemed so much more romantic than her own marriage. Remembered them when she gave up her child to her father and Auntie Shirley, then travelled for the first time to London to resume her single state and begin her career as an English writer.

"God, that place was indescribable!" said Cecil, coming back. "I'll smell it on my uniform for weeks."

"There speaks someone who has never known a dunny, and certainly not one in a baking climate, hundreds of miles from the sea," said Bettina.

They went shares on the meal, and Cecil put down the notes and coins, with the regulation small tip the army recommended. Then they linked arms and walked towards the nearest bridge that would take them in the direction of the Grand Canal. As they walked over the bridge Bettina turned back. The dark, gnome-like proprietor, stowing their money away in a pouch at his waist, turned in their direction and spat.

Not all Venetians welcomed the coming of the Allies.

The hospital where Katie lay in a world or non-world of her own was about ten minutes' walking time from Holland Park Crescent, and when Bettina got permission to visit her, ten minutes after Sylvia left the flat to go back to Mark's, she put on her summer mac and set off with her umbrella for stick. She had never come to trust English spring days.

The hospital was, for London, a small one, specialising in brain disorders. There was a private security man on the entrance, and when Bettina found the room where Katie lay she found a policewoman dying of boredom near her bed.

"I don't think you'll get much reaction," she commented when Bettina introduced herself. "I try of course now and then, and sometimes she squeezes my hand back, or there's a flutter of the eyelids, but that's about it."

Bettina suspected the young woman to have a natural garrulity that was currently suffering from disuse, so instead of going over and taking Katie's hand she detained her in conversation.

"What is Superintendent Murchison guarding against?" she asked. "Does he think she might be attacked again?"

"Well, it's possible, isn't it? Officially I'm just here for if she wakes and manages a few words, but the other possibility is there. Even if it was just a common-or-garden burglary there's a chance he will be afraid she saw enough to identify him and that he'll come back to finish the job."

She was intolerably breezy, but Bettina suppressed her irritation.

"But Murchison obviously doesn't think it was a casual burglary."

"Oh, I didn't say that. But there are other possibilities, aren't there? She may have told any number of friends – or enemies – that she was going to look after your flat for a few days."

Bettina pursed her lips in disbelief.

"Katie has a very sharp tongue, and strong likes and dislikes, but I don't see her as having 'enemies' of the sort who would want to do her in."

"She was your cleaner, wasn't she?" Bettina nodded. "Do you really know all that much about her private life?" Sharp, thought Bettina.

"Maybe not enough to say what I just did," she admitted.

"And then there's the possibility that whoever was in the flat didn't know that you were in Scotland."

"That she was attacked in mistake for me?"

"That, or he didn't intend to attack unless he needed to, but was willing to do it even if it was you."

"If Murchison thinks that then he should have put a guard on me."

"Are you quite sure he hasn't?" She was still horribly breezy, but she now changed her tack. "I say, I'm dying for a cup of coffee and something to eat. Could you man the fort for ten minutes or so? It'd save my life."

"Of course. Get along."

She didn't query how much use the girl thought she would be if the imagined attacker turned up to finish the job on Katie or to get the right person this time. She simply watched her depart, locked the door of the small room, and went over to Katie's bed. Through the maze of tubes and masks she saw the injured head with a sinking of the stomach. If only she'd thought. If only, when the suggestion had been made of Katie as flat-sitter, she had taken a few moments to consider it first. It was Peter's suggestion, and a bloody silly one, but her responsibility. She sat down on the little chair beside the bed and took the other old woman's hand.

"Katie, it's Bettina."

She squeezed the hand, feeling a sharp arthritic pain as she did so. She thought there was a feeble return of pressure.

"Katie, I wish to God I'd never let you be in that flat on your own. Can you forgive my silliness?" She wondered if the eyelids had flickered, but she felt no answering squeeze. "If I'd only thought I would have hired a firm. Maybe asked Peter if he had a friend who could do it, or got Ron from the Duke of Sussex. If only I hadn't brought you to this." She thought there might be a very faint return of pressure. Comforting her perhaps? But that didn't sound like Katie. "If only I'd thought," she repeated. "You can never tell with people. Never tell what they might do."

She sat there till the policewoman returned, but the hand in her hand remained limp and the eyelids motionless. If she had ever emerged from it, Katie was now back in the non-world.

16
Commercial

Two days later Inspector Murchison rang Bettina. He said he knew she was alone in the flat now, and wondered how she was faring. Newfangled police PR, Bettina thought to herself. Or old-fashioned covering his back.

"I'm 'faring' perfectly well," she said, a touch of tartness in her voice. "As I always have."

"I'm sure you have," said Murchison. "But when a murderous attack has occurred, and on someone you are quite close to, a place is not quite the same, is it?"

"No," Bettina had to admit, "it's not. But I'm coping."

"I thought I should come round some time and bring you up to date with investigations," Murchison said.

"You'll be very welcome," said Bettina. "Is it worthwhile? Are you close to making an arrest?"

"If we were close to making an arrest I probably wouldn't come. I'd wait till it was made and talk to you after that."

"I see."

"What I mean is, since you were well away from Holland Park when the attack took place, your evidence is unlikely to be crucial when we come to make an arrest. But what I would value is your knowledge of the background – the facts and tensions surrounding the attack."

There was a pause while Bettina thought.

"Yee-e-es. Assuming, that is, that it isn't an attack by a casual intruder."

"Yes. And we're not assuming anything at this point."

"No, I see ... Well, please do come and see me."

"What are you doing tomorrow?"

"Well, Sylvia and Ollie are going to watch Mark filming a commercial at Margate. Mark regards it as a breakthrough. Of course normally I wouldn't bother, but they did ask me to go with them, and at the moment I feel I should take any opportunities that occur to be with Sylvia."

"Well, shall we say the day after? Tuesday morning? That would suit me quite nicely. I hope you'll keep your eyes and ears open tomorrow."

"I normally do. It's what I earn my living by. What in particular am I to be on the alert for?"

"Anything that seems to you to be revealing about character, about the particular situation at this time of the people you're with, about their hopes, aspirations, disappointments, hang-ups."

"'The people I am with' in this case are pretty close members of my family."

"I pay you the very big compliment of thinking this would not lead you to hold back anything that might be significant. There is a defenceless old woman who was savagely beaten in this case, as you've seen for yourself recently. You'll be even keener than I am to catch her attacker."

Again Bettina had to think. How age slowed the thinking processes!

"Katie was never defenceless. I'm sure in this case she was just unlucky. But of course you're quite right. I will look and listen."

"It's true, isn't it, that you've never been a family person?"

"Yes, it's quite true," said Bettina with a sigh.

Bettina was picked up next morning by Ollie and

Sylvia in a rented Honda. Mark had already been at Margate for two nights rehearsing – doubtless with deleterious effects on the health of all those who employed him as a personal trainer. Ollie was a tense and cautious driver at first, but before he was even out of central London he relaxed and drove as if he had been perfectly acquainted with British roads and regulations for years. He was a child of the car age. Bettina herself had never had the slightest urge to acquire a car or to learn to drive – though she had done a bit of emergency driving in Italy during the war, when no one was in the least bothered about driving licences: the lack of anything much else on the roads was a plus, but the possibility of being shot at was a minus.

"So what are we going to be watching?" asked Bettina as they all untensed themselves.

"Oh, the usual garbage," said Ollie genially. "I thought British television was supposed to be so much better than the Aussie rubbish, but it's pretty much the same."

"Yes, it is now," said Bettina.

"It's for something called Munchets," contributed Sylvia. "I think it's a variation of the 'bully kicking sand in my face on the beach' formula."

"Mark being the bully, I suppose," said Bettina.

"Well, he's so big it would be difficult to imagine anyone intimidating him," said Sylvia.

"And if he was the 'before', it would be terrible to think of the 'after'."

Ollie was sensitive to the tone of the conversation.

"You'd never think, would you, that Mark was the one who was bullied at school?" he said.

"I can't believe there was anyone big enough to try it," said Bettina. "Or was it psychological bullying?"

"No, no. Mark wasn't big then. Well, he was quite tall, but he was one of the bean-pole kind – skinny and weedy. They picked on him. Of course he was never too bright – always in the bottom two or three in the class, so that didn't help. But he pulled himself up. Went to gyms, took up weight training."

"Took steroids," said Bettina before she could stop herself.

"Never asked. Best not to," said Ollie cheerfully. "Anyway after a time it wasn't in anyone's interest to take him on. Did wonders for his confidence."

"I can imagine," said Bettina.

"The other one in the ad is a high-powered footballer," Ollie went on. "Plays for Chelsea or somewhere like that. Mark tells me he's the only Englishman playing for them, which seems a bit odd. Anyway Mark won't take any crap from him. Mark's always man-to-man, whoever he's with."

Bettina could imagine that too.

When they got to Margate they got a parking space not too far from the beach. It was not yet high season, if English seaside towns still had a high season. Their habitual bleakness was mitigated today by a hazy sun, and they had a pleasant stroll to the end of the promenade where they could see a little knot of vans and all the apparatus and busyness of filming. When they got nearer they saw it was not just a little knot of vans but one of people too: locals, with the odd visitor, glad to vary the monotony with a glimpse of something that they might in the future see on the thing that was the centre of their lives – the TV set.

They watched for half an hour as down the beach, well-barriered from the spectators, the figure of Mark was filmed over and over again running in gaudy Hawaiian-style shirt and beach-shorts towards the recumbent figure of the famous footballer, apparently consuming things from a silver-papered packet. Just when her interest was on the point of evaporating entirely Bettina was relieved to hear the man in charge call for a break. The little knot of people started moving away, but when it became clear that the two performers were coming up towards the promenade the more devoted stayed on.

Mark and his friend hadn't got far up the walkway before there was a shout from the director, if that was what he was called. Mark didn't bother to stop walking, but he turned round and the man bellowed something incomprehensible.

Mark shrugged his shoulders.

"It's my oldies. My dad and my auntie. No worries."

As they turned again the director renewed his shouting. Probably various parts of the footballer were insured for ridiculous sums on stringent conditions. Mark, barely modifying his voice, said "Oh, go to buggery" and came up to his little party beaming a big smile that told them he was very chuffed with himself.

"Hi Dad. Hi Sylvia. Hi Auntie Bet. This is Mel. He plays that English game with the round ball."

Mel looked about eighteen, and had probably gone straight from school to earning fifty thousand a week. By now he was quite likely used to wall-to-wall adulation rather than Mark's jokiness, but he smiled weakly while he was trying to get his emotional bearings.

"Good to meet you," said Ollie to him. "Australians know perfectly well what soccer is. Won't be long before we beat the world at it."

229

Bettina remembered Hughie teaching his classmates the rules, when it was virtually a foreign game. She had to tell herself that countries changed, their people changed. She should not confuse Mark with Sergeant Malley. He was a different generation and mind-set. Even about the people she had known as a child her confidence had been shaken by Sylvia's revelation that Steve Drayton had played flute in an amateur orchestra.

"How did you think it went, Auntie Bet?" asked Mark, turning to her, presumably as the expert on film due to the forthcoming *Heart of the Land*. It was an impossible question to answer.

"Difficult to say really," Bettina said. "I'd heard about doing the same thing over and over, but when you see it actually happening it's still hard to see why it should be necessary."

"Oh, they'll find the take that best fits in with the whole sequence, won't they, Mel?" said Mark sagely.

"Suppose so," said Mel.

"The next bit's the difficult one," resumed Mark. "That's the bit where I snatch the packet of Munchets."

Bettina cast a covert glance at him, hoping to see some sign of joking, even a degree of self-irony, but there was nothing of that. She was relieved when the two boys were called back to perform this dramatically challenging section of the commercial, though her interest waned during the twenty or thirty repetitions of the manoeuvre. Is this the peak of civilisation we have been aiming for all the years of my lifetime, she wondered?

Eventually a halt was called. It was after twelve o'clock. Mark was allowed to come up and fraternise with his oldies, but Mel of the precious limbs was spirited away with the director and crew. As they walked off in search of the nearest presentable pub for lunch Mark showed himself still incurably self-satisfied.

"I thought that went really well, didn't you, Auntie Bet?"

"Awfully well," she replied, straight-faced.

"The director's a beaut bloke, underneath. We went over it a fair bit yesterday evening. Mel had a lot of problems, not being used to this kind of work. But I got him through it all right today."

"I suppose there are all sorts of possible reactions to having your Munchets snatched on the beach," said Bettina.

"Too right. But the director's got clear ideas about everything like that, and it was just a question of getting Mel to understand what was required."

They were interrupted by a woman in her twenties, someone Bettina had noticed when they first joined the little knot of onlookers on the promenade. She was looking diffident, but proffering a book in her hand.

"This is awful cheek I know, but I recognised you and ... I managed to find this book in a bookshop here. I wondered if you would sign it for me. Could you write 'For Caroline'?"

"Of course," said Bettina, taking the book and pen. As she turned to the title page she caught a glimpse of the faces around her. While Ollie and Sylvia were looking pleased and rather proud of their subsidiary part in this piece of unexpected homage, Mark was looking in what seemed like bewilderment at the book, as if he remembered what they were but hadn't seen one in years, and wondered what a woman of about his age could be doing with one, and why she should read a literary work by a very old woman.

"Oh, *The Chattering Crowd*," said Bettina with practised friendliness. "My first book set in London."

"I'm sure I shall enjoy it," said the woman, slipping tactfully away.

"I suppose that's a book about the arty mob, isn't it?" said Mark.

"Something like that," said Bettina, though that was in fact precisely what the book was about.

"You'd know about them. But how did she recognise you, Auntie Bet?"

There was no mistaking his expression now. There was on his face the most naked, naive, childish jealousy.

"Oh, I used to appear on arts discussion programmes on television," said Bettina. "Before the BBC dumbed itself down."

But something in Mark's reaction – not the jealousy but the naivety – made her remember her father's reaction, shortly before his death, when she gave him one of her books. She dictated it into her tape that night, knowing she would have to fit her father's death into the novel somewhere.

Bettina flew back to Australia in three laborious stages in 1961 to see her father, who was dying of kidney failure. He had been living for the last three years in Ollie and Judy's home in Bendigo, northern Victoria. She brought with her one of the first copies of her book *The Chattering Crowd*, which she had great hopes for. It was an exciting time to be part of the British literary scene. Angry young men vied with sparky young women for critical attention, and once again, as in the Brontës' time and Arnold Bennett's, writers from the provinces, soon to be renamed the regions, had pushed their way to the forefront of public attention.

Bettina could not compete with writers from Stoke-on-Trent or Nottingham. She had quarried her first twenty years of life in four novels set in Australia and it was time to move on, as she had moved on in actual fact fifteen years before, to London. The Australian novels had done respectably, but they had certainly not managed to go with the tide of popular interest aroused by Shute's bestseller *A Town Like Alice*. Bettina had not been surprised. She had not aimed at or expected bestsellerdom. But it was time to move on, time to make use of that sharp, satirical intelligence that she had only intermittently brought into play in the first novels: it was the age of the Discontented Migrant, and there were too many people sounding off about the awfulness of Australia for her to want to join them. It would have been the emotional equivalent of rejecting mother's milk.

Jack Whitelaw lay in the bed, gaunt, seeming to lack totally the grit and vigour that had been his when Bettina really knew him, twenty-odd years before. They kissed and cuddled, and Bettina lay beside him in the bed.

"How are you *really*?" she asked at last.

"I'm a bit worried," said Jack slowly. "I'm trying to juggle the date of my death so it doesn't interfere with one of Judy's Tupperware parties."

"Oh *Dad!*" Then she looked at him and they both giggled.

"She doesn't actually have Tupperware parties," admitted Jack, "but she does love having the young married set around so they can discuss the price of frozen peas and tinned baby food."

"I don't see why Judy should worry about the price of baby food," protested Bettina. Ollie and Judy's first child, Marileen, had not been born until two years later, and Mark's birth was all of twelve years away.

"She has her family planned. Judy's good at long-term

strategic planning. Now aren't I an ungrateful mongrel, going on like that? They've both been very good to me, and I expect I've been a dead weight on them since this happened."

"Why didn't you stay at Wilgandra, Dad?"

"Bill's getting old and sick himself, and he's grooming one of his nephews to take over. I'd've only been in the way ... That was my happiest time, you know, Betty."

"Was it, Dad? At Wilgandra? I thought giving up Fort George – "

"No! I knew that place couldn't be long-term. It was never going to come good. Oh, I hated that blasted drought, and the look of the cattle and sheep, and I hated being defeated by it all. But I knew I couldn't win. You needed plenty of capital to come through a time like that terrible drought. But only half of me – less than that – hated giving up my independence. I enjoyed managing a big place, having cash reserves to spare so I could really make plans – big plans sometimes. And Bill always supported me. That was his nature. He hated not being able to support that bludger Phil Naismyth."

"He was a disaster."

"Bill never hired anyone sight unseen after that. Not even a kitchen hand. He was good-natured, you know that, but he hated being imposed on. Did you know Phil and his snooty wife split up, and he was arrested for conning elderly ladies out of their life savings soon after the war?"

"I knew the first, not the second."

"Worked the English seaside hotels. Was banged away for two years. You could use him in one of your books."

"I don't use real people," said Bettina, an automatic response. Then she pulled herself up. "Well, I do, but I always have to say I don't." They laughed again. She dived into the travelling bag beside the bed and brought out a copy of *The Chattering Crowd*. "It's not quite published. Out next week."

Jack Whitelaw took it. His eyes widened. He seemed to be struggling to find something to say. It was almost, like Mark, as if he never saw books, as if they were not part of his life, which was not true. Bettina knew from her letters that he had read her early books. She took pity on his sudden attack of inarticulation and kissed him on the forehead. He grasped her round the neck and gabbled something about how proud he was.

The cover of *The Chattering Crowd*, not chosen by Bettina but atmospherically drawn by Ardizzioni, showed a collection of fashionably-dressed people in little groups clearly engaged in gossip and spite under a sparkling chandelier. Later, in the bath, trying to wash away traces of the last leg of her plane-trip, Bettina decided that her father had been moved by the well-heeled people on the cover, the splendid setting, and they had been an image for him of how far his daughter had travelled from her origins in Bundaroo.

She herself was not inclined to think that the in-group of London literati which she had satirised in the book was so very different, or so much more elevated, than the society which she had grown up in.

"So what do you think actually happened here that night?" Bettina asked Murchison as he sat opposite her drinking coffee. "Not who was in here, but what did he or she actually *do*?" Murchison took his time before replying.

"He or she took the aboriginal painting. But Mrs Johnson was found battered at the door between this sitting room and the study. We feel he had in fact been in the study – it's nothing more scientific than a matter of disturbed dust on the desk."

"But speaking of scientific evidence, what about DNA?"

"Nothing much of interest yet. It takes a hell of a time. And criminals are getting wise."

"So you haven't ruled out a professional?"

"I've told you, nothing is ruled out. If you look at the evidence the idea of a professional has a lot going for it. An article appears in *Hi!* magazine. There is a photograph of Kerry Probyn beside the John Mawurndjurl. Not only that: have you read the article itself?"

"I couldn't bear to. Silly little bitch."

"The article says that the Mawurndjurl is part of 'a choice and varied collection of Australian art.' A thief would only have to check a telephone directory to find your number in Holland Park Crescent – obligingly named in the article: don't they have *any* sense? – and come at night into a not-particularly-well-protected building and case the joint to see what's worth stealing."

"Would he be likely to know that?"

"He could be, if art is his speciality. If not he has only to go to a book on Australian art and note down the big names: Nolan, Drysdale, Boyd and so on. He could have been looking for the big names on your pictures when he was disturbed."

"Yes, he could ... On the other hand? – "

"On the other hand, it's difficult to account for his presence in the study, if there was one. There's only two or three pictures in the study, and the presence seems to have been at the desk. Of course the person disturbing the dust could have been Mrs Johnson herself."

"If Katie decided to do some housework, reverting to old routines, she'd have *dusted*, not just disturbed some dust. She had no interest in my writing, and no reason for snooping around on my desk."

"Right. So if we take it that the intruder was at the desk

this gives us an alternative scenario. The painting then becomes something he grabs as he leaves the flat to give credence to the idea of a burglary. It was just by the door, remember. Probably he'd always intended covering his tracks by taking some paintings, but having to attack Mrs Johnson panicked him and he made it less convincing than he intended by just taking the one. In this scenario it was the desk that was the object of the break-in – or the entry we might call it, if he had his own key."

"I see. And what in particular about the desk. My memory-novel?"

"Yes. Someone could be afraid of how you might present them, what you might allege about them, in the book."

"I don't see why."

"I'm sure you do. You have a reputation for putting pretty cruel pictures of real people in your books."

Bettina became frosty.

"Oh? Had you anyone in particular in mind?"

"I've been reading up about you. There was a book about the London literary scene. A lot of people recognised themselves, and a lot of critics claimed to recognise real writers. It made the book's fortunes."

"*The Chattering Crowd* ... " Bettina was forced to go through a thaw. "There was Kingsley, of course. I thought him a loathsome man ... and Philip. And poor Iris. Awful to think of the Alzheimer's, then that horrible book, and the film. No one pays even lip-service to dignity and privacy these days ... And Olivia Manning had a bit part – she hadn't made her name then, but she *had* made herself felt ... And Ted and Sylvia, the happy young pair – all glamour and poetry. Yes, I'd have to plead guilty that there were sketches of people in that book. But they're all dead."

"So I believe," said Murchison. "But if you can do that to mere literary acquaintances, someone today who's a close friend or someone who's *been* a close friend of yours at some time, might be afraid about what you are intending to do to them in this new book."

"Who in particular?"

"Many people – some whom I know, some whom I don't know yet. Peter Seddon, your agent Clare Tuckett, Eugene Naismyth whom I haven't had time to talk to. Then there's your brother Oliver and your daughter Sylvia – "

"In Edinburgh."

"Late plane down, early morning flight back. Perfectly possible. I'm just throwing the full range of suspects at you."

"Yes. You haven't mentioned Mark."

"No." He looked at her closely. "I thought you might tell me about yesterday." Bettina nodded.

"Ah, yesterday. I'm not sure there's all that much to tell. I learnt that filming a commercial is a thing of mind-bending monotony."

"All filming is, I suspect," said Murchison. "I once had a case at the old Elstree studios."

"But there the end product might have some weight, or some style, or some intellectual content. But a commercial about sweets, filmed by grown men playing around like boys? Sometimes I really yearn back to the time when we only had one television channel, no colour supplements, when advertisers didn't rule the roost, and when the billboards were not packed with smutty innuendoes and glossy status-symbols."

"Well before my time," said Murchison.

"Of course. This is just an old woman's ramblings. I

had the impression that Mark was getting the hang of doing commercials. But he also has the traditional Australian attitude to people in authority – thumbing their nose at them, not taking any bullshit from them, as he would probably call it. That may well harm his prospects over here, but I must say I found it rather refreshing." She thought for a moment. "Though when it was aimed at *me*, as a matriarchal figure in his family's life, I didn't like it at all."

They both laughed together.

"He and the other chap, a footballer, came up and talked to us in the break, both very conscious of the young women among the spectators; then they filmed the dramatically demanding sequence of Mark stealing the bag of Munchets from Mel Whatever-his-name-is, and after that they all knocked off for lunch and Mark came along with us to find a suitable pub to have lunch."

"Yes ... You're missing something out, aren't you?"

"Well, not really. It's just a matter of impression."

"Your impressions are what I want."

"All right: here they are, however childish. A young woman came up to me on the promenade with one of my books. She'd recognised me earlier and slipped into town to buy it. Mark looked at the book quite bemused, as if – I don't know – he didn't realise people still read books, couldn't understand why a young woman would read one of mine, and then finally ..."

"Go on."

"I don't think I imagined it: a look of jealousy, almost childish, that I was getting attention. *Public* attention, the sort of thing he would like."

Murchison left a long silence.

"I recognise that sort of childishness. You often get it in

criminals. In others too: actors, opera-singers, *stars* of all sorts. In aristocrats too, particularly ones who have nothing much apart from their birth to recommend them. It's a craving for attention, a need for it, an inability to understand why anyone else should be receiving it when only *they* deserve it. Politicians have it in spades."

"I can't think why Mark thinks he's worthy of it, has done anything to deserve it."

"I don't think that enters into it. I had the impression when I interviewed him that it was the old notion of being God's gift – to women, of course, but to everyone else as well."

That chimed in with Bettina's own observations.

"Yes, and yet with it there is something else. Uncertainty. He, and others like him, *acts* like he's God's gift but somehow behind the facade you sense that he doesn't believe it."

"But that's part of the childishness, isn't it? Always needing reassurance. Being the centre of the world's interest in his own eyes, but always finding evidence that the world has other, more important things to think about."

"Yes. That seems to make sense. But I must say I can't see Mark having the nous, the perseverance, the nerve, to carry out a burglary and an attack such as the one in this flat. And what could be the motive in his case?"

"Your memoirs? As we said before, they could have gone up to the present day, they could take in living people you know."

"They could. But why should Mark imagine he would figure prominently?"

"He didn't need to figure prominently. Vanity hates pinpricks. Just a casual aside, a dismissive sneer, a cruel joke, would be enough. He could easily have feared that sort of treatment. He knows you don't like him I'm sure."

"He certainly knows he doesn't impress me. I'm so old I don't think he's thought about liking one way or the other. When he stayed here, when he first arrived, he tried to treat me as an irrelevancy, but I wasn't going to put up with that."

"This all ties up with *vanity*, doesn't it? The child or adolescent thinking he's the centre of the universe."

"Maybe. But I still don't think Mark is capable of this ... I tell you one thing: if he *did* do it, you'll find evidence against him. He's not bright enough to have thought of everything."

"Then we don't have to worry: there's no danger of his not getting caught, is there?"

17
Declaring Allegiances

"Bettina?"

"Hello, Hughie. Who else could it be?"

"Sylvia's voice is quite like yours. But of course a bit more Australian."

"Of course. But Sylvia moved back to Mark's flat several days ago."

"You're not nervous on your own? You really are all right?

"I really am all right," said Bettina, concealing her exasperation. "What are you ringing about, Hughie?"

"I have a very faint trace, a possible trace, of the John Mawurndjurl picture. Don't get your hopes up – "

"You've already raised my hopes. I love that picture. Hughie, why don't you come – both of you, of course – to a little farewell drinks gathering I'm giving for Ollie and Sylvia? It's at the Prince Leopold – early evening, about five. They're off to the National later on."

"At the Prince Leopold? I don't know why you bothered to move out."

"It's at the Prince Leopold because the alternative, here, wouldn't be exactly conducive to jollity."

Hughie cleared his throat, chastened. Bettina knew very well how to chasten him.

"Of course not. I'll be there."

Jollity reigned only fitfully at the gathering. Ollie and Sylvia still had two more days in London, and Bettina was taking them to Windsor – one of her favourite places – the next day. This was the only time the Prince Leopold had one of their smaller private rooms available. Clare didn't add much to the jollity, and Hughie's manner suggested that attending such a gathering involved bending – even stooping – to a level he did not normally function on. Bettina was just glad that Marie had been on one of her monstrous shopping binges and sent her regrets. Peter, as so often, was the jolliest, and swapped stories with Ollie about British roads and with Mark about the sporting scene and television advertisements.

"These days they're the best things on television," Pete said.

"Too right. Little miniature dramas," said Mark. "That's what our director calls them."

Seeing Pete looking at his watch Bettina said:

"And how are your miniature dramas, Peter? Someone lined up for later?"

"Nothing gets past you, does it, Bettina? Old X-ray eyes, that's you. Yes, actually I have got someone lined up to take to Bingo. Quite young for a Bingo fanatic, and definitely interested. We'll be going back to her place afterwards, if her hints have been anything to go by. It's a minor triumph, because there are lots of others sniffing around."

"She must be a very odd younger woman if she finds hordes of pensioners sniffing around her a turn-on."

Mark had been hugging himself with impatience.

"Auntie Bet, about that film of your book – "

"Oh, Mark, I was wanting to make you and Clare better known to each other. She has *lots* of contacts in the advertising world, and could be *very* useful. Clare, darling – "

That done, she and Hughie got into a huddle with Sylvia listening in, all of them now and then reaching out to take one of the delicious nothings from the Prince Leopold tray.

"So what about this 'faint trace' of the Mawurndjurl?"

"It's a contact in Melbourne. He's been offered a picture from a British source. It's aboriginal, or aboriginal-inspired. It's been described to him as a matter of intricate lines and shapes, in browns and greys."

"That could describe a lot of aboriginal work," said Sylvia.

"It doesn't seem to amount to much," said Bettina.

"It's a lead. If it doesn't amount to anything it still alerts people, and that's what we want. Dealers noticing and making contacts."

"I love that picture so much!" said Bettina.

"I could look around a bit when I'm back in Australia," said Sylvia. "It seems logical that that's where the thief would try to sell it. And I remember it quite well. It sort of brought me up every time I went out the door."

"*Would* you keep an eye open?" said Bettina, feeling oddly pleased. "I'd be so grateful. And we would be keeping in touch."

For a moment Bettina thought: "I'll leave my art collection to my daughter." But then she thought: "But what will happen to it after she dies?" She might even leave it to Mark. Better to leave it to an English gallery, maybe one of the regional ones. Australian art *should* have a strong presence in Britain. It was international, like Australian fiction.

"These little fishy things are gorgeous," said Sylvia, into the moment's silence.

"They do me very well here," said Bettina complacently.

"So they should," said Hughie. "You put them on the literary map."

"The literary map!" scoffed Bettina. "You're obsessed with league tables and ratings and values at auction. It's very vulgar."

"You're wrong, Bettina," said Hughie, for whom this was an old charge. "I'm obsessed with *quality*. I like all the other stuff associated with quality – standing, current values, that sort of thing – but they come very definitely second."

"Anyway, I don't suppose the Leopold gets anyone staying here or dining here because *The Chattering Crowd* put them on some imaginary literary map."

"As you please," said Hughie. "I don't suppose any-one ever drank at the bar of the Folies Bergère just because Manet painted it."

"Actually, I bet thousands of tourists have."

"So how is the good Inspector Murchison going?" asked Hughie casually.

"You've talked to him?"

"Oh yes. He came to quiz me on Tuesday night. I told him quite a lot about Australian art values, but I didn't have a lot else to add. Since the thief was obviously disturbed by Katie while he was on the job, the one picture he took doesn't tell us very much about whether he was an expert or not. He grabbed the Mawurndjurl either because it was just beside the door or because he had seen it in *Hi*! magazine. Or both."

"I still can't get my brain around the idea of art thieves in Britain specialising in Australian art," said Sylvia. "I suppose in an odd way it proclaims that it has arrived."

Hughie raised his eyebrows. He had hastened its arrival, in his estimation, and that several decades ago.

"Don't knock your native land," he said. "Artists,

opera-singers, novelists, even poets. You name it, Australia is in there buzzing."

"Still a bit short on playwrights, architects and one or two other things," said Bettina. "But I'm sure Sylvia was not knocking it. And I'm not either."

"You could have fooled me. I should think you know less than nothing about Australian architects. And not much more about playwrights."

"More than you think, Hughie. Australia won't need you as a cheerleader while I'm around. You loathed the place, remember?"

"I loathed small-town and outback Australia," corrected Hughie. "That's only a tiny segment, population-wise. Essentially Australia is a big-town place."

"Maybe. I'd certainly prefer to live in Sydney than in Bundaroo if it was still my country ... Anyway, I'm not sure how seriously Murchison took this art thief notion."

"He certainly seemed to be taking it as a distinct possibility," said Hughie. "And he struck me as a pretty bright man."

"Oh, I think he is. But talking to me he seemed more interested in my little memory novel. I'm thinking of calling it *A Far Cry from Bundaroo*, by the way. I don't suppose Muriel Spark will sue."

"You know there's no copyright on titles, Bettina. Why would Murchison be interested in that?"

"Victims of my vitriolic pen trying to sabotage it, that sort of thing. I take that with a pinch of salt. I can't see that my pen is that savage."

"How can you say that? We just mentioned *The Chattering Crowd*. Kingsley Amis must have felt *flayed* by that book."

"Odious man – served him right. And I'm glad I cruci-

247

fied the young Kingsley rather than the old man. He was a monster and a bore who everyone could have a go at in his later years, but he was horrible back in the 'fifties, well before he whizzed over to the lunatic right."

"Well, Kingsley is dead – "

"Exactly. And if Martin is going round exacting revenge on people who didn't like his father, he'll have his work cut out."

"So who does Murchison think might be wanting revenge or pre-empting revenge?"

"Any and everyone I'm in contact with at the present time, apparently," said Bettina briefly. She turned aside abruptly and drew Ollie and Sylvia together. "How is K – " began Sylvia, but Bettina just shook her head and silenced her before going on. "I know we'll see each other tomorrow, but since this is in the nature of a farewell I did want to say, from the bottom of what heart I have, that I have been so happy having you here. It's been, somehow, reviving – what people mean when they say 'a tonic'. Can we keep in better touch in future, Ollie?"

"That suits me fine," said her brother, grinning widely with pleasure. "And Dad would have been pleased."

"Dad and Mum," said Bettina. "Dad was only half the man I knew when he lost Mum. That's not my observation, of course. It's what he said to me just before he died ..." She turned to Sylvia. "And I meant what I said about keeping in touch."

"I'm really glad about that." The warmth in her tone was patently sincere.

"You're wonderful because you don't expect from me what I can't give."

"You mean love, don't you? I understand that, and

maybe why. I'll settle for interest. Interest lasts longer usually."

Kissing her and turning away Bettina felt that that last remark was an acute one. She would part from Sylvia with genuine regret, and look forward to whatever contact they could maintain with interest, and she felt the same would be true for Sylvia. She was sure they were both similar souls – or at any rate natures: if they had met without the emotional baggage they did have, they would still have felt a kinship in attitudes, in their psychological make-up. But love? Bettina felt that love did not enter into it. Had love ever entered into it with her, in the years since the closeness to her parents? Hughie had been a wonderful intellectual stimulus, the Brighthouse boy had been just a flirtation, Cecil Cockburn had been a bit of fun which marriage had turned sour, and Peter had been "something else" – something different in her life, something comfortable to be with. All the rest had been just bed.

Peter was the first guest to go – off to meet his Bingo queen. Then Ollie and Sylvia disappeared in the direction of the Underground, which their stay in London had made them quite expert in negotiating. That left Clare and Mark. She hadn't noticed how they'd been getting on, but she did notice that, though they pretended to be going their separate ways this involved some acting on Mark's part that he was not quite up to. Bettina raised her eyebrows at Hughie and they both went over to the window that overlooked the main entrance. A minute or two later they saw the two of them leave together and go towards Mark's car. As she waited for Mark to unlock the passenger door Clare looked up and gave a cheeky wave in the direction of the window.

"Good God! Whatever is Clare thinking of?" said Bettina.

"I'll give you one guess," said Hughie. "Actually I think Clare is exactly the type of managing middle-aged woman that Mark stands in need of," he added in his prissiest tones.

"I'm not worried about what Mark needs," protested Bettina. "What on earth can *he* offer *her*? ... One guess for that too, I suppose. Forget I spoke. What do I know about such things? One day some critic will discover a great gap at the core of all my novels and realize it's an absence of heart ... What time are you meeting Marie, Hughie?"

"Not till eight."

"Would you walk me to the Park then? It's a lovely evening, and we haven't had so many of them. The café will still be going, and we can have coffee sitting out."

They walked through the tediously well-painted streets until they got to the Park, where the winding paths soothed her: the abundant and varied flowers, the shade from the trees, around her the nursemaids with prams, the foreign students, the people staying at the Youth hostel, and the world and his wife walking in the late sunshine. They had hardly spoken so far, Hughie only to show solicitude for her greater walking difficulties. Once they were rid of all the traffic noise and fumes Bettina said:

"I'm worried, Hughie."

"Of course you are. You don't get over something like a break-in in a matter of days."

"It's not that – not *just* that. It's the police. I didn't want to talk about it in there, but they have everyone in their sights. Even Ollie and Sylvia, though they were with me in Edinburgh at the vital time."

Hughie considered.

"There are planes."

"That's what the Inspector said. Down on the last one at night, back on the early one from Heathrow. It all sounds rather silly and fantastic to me, like one of those detective stories based on railway timetables."

"I don't see why the idea is fantastic."

"Well, planes are pretty small, particularly ones on internal flights. They would surely be recognised and remembered by the hostesses and stewards."

"That might not bother them if all they were planning on doing was robbing the flat. When did you see them that morning?"

"Sylvia about half past nine or so. Ollie later."

"And the day before?"

"We went our separate ways."

"I should think at that rate they could even have taken the train."

"That seems hardly less fantastic. In any case I barely know Ollie, and only met Sylvia – apart from holding her as a baby – three weeks or so ago. They can hardly be living in fear of my memoirs."

"In Sylvia's case there could be a long-cherished resentment."

"I know. I hope not, but I do realize there could be. But if there is one, why would she go down to London to work it out, when we were together in Edinburgh? ... Murchison seemed more interested in Mark, oddly enough."

Again, Hughie thought hard.

"Apart from watching him today I only met Mark briefly when he first came. I did realize it wasn't love at first sight as far as you two were concerned."

"Oh, I could well put Mark down with a poisoned arrow or two if I was carrying the memoir up to the present day. But I'm not, and even if I was I don't think I'd bother with him. He's hardly worth the trouble."

"I bet he wouldn't think that," said Hughie with a grin. "Why is Murchison directing his cold gaze on him?"

"I didn't say he was direc – Oh well, yes, maybe he is. He's talked to him, of course, and I think he's been struck by the vanity, the self-love."

"Who wouldn't be? You were. And even watching him just now it rather *thrust* itself at me. A modern narcissus."

"Yes. I forgot to tell Murchison that according to Ollie Mark hasn't always been like this."

"I'm glad to hear it. I'd hate to think of a baby as full of himself as Mark is."

"I rather think babies are, though neither of us would know much about that. It seems to me that the basic fact about growing up for most people is becoming aware of others. What Ollie said was that when he was at school he was the tall, beanpole type of kid, picked on by others."

"Difficult to imagine."

"Yes. Apparently it was partly because he wasn't too bright, partly the gangling physique. The ridicule sent him to the gyms and the weight-training courses."

"Probably to steroids as well. That's the way men get Mark's sort of body-bulk. And they can send you off course, steroids."

"Well, don't say that to Murchison. I had the same thought, but I let it out to Ollie, not to Murchison. He's fixated enough on Mark."

"Why should you protect him? He's less than nothing to you. Anyway, the mere talk of gyms and weight-training will have suggested steroids to a policeman."

"I'm not trying to protect Mark," said Bettina, becoming a little heated, "except that I don't want innocent people accused or suspected where there is no evidence. There have been far too many fit-ups in British crime history in recent years."

Hughie nodded, but kept with the subject.

"So though you don't like Mark, though he gives you the heeby-jeebies, you feel pretty sure he didn't do it?"

Wanting to collect her thoughts, to approach the subject in the way that suited her best, Bettina put it off.

"Ah, here we are. Coffee is just what I need. I'm parched."

They sat down in the open-air part of the cafeteria near to the house, and ordered coffee and cream cakes from an exuberantly Italian waiter. They talked about little nothings till they were tucked into them, and then Bettina took up the subject again.

"You asked me if I felt pretty sure that Mark didn't do it. I do, though I can see the way Murchison is thinking: Mark is vain and yet unsure of himself; he has a child's mind in a very powerful body; he seems to be pretty unsure of his sexuality; and he has the sort of vanity that needs constant feeding – for example from women, who may be casual paid pick-ups if nothing else is available. Poor Clare – I wonder how she's doing ... You get this strange breezy confidence and at the same time the constant *asking* for admiration, for acceptance, for some kind of status. It seems to bespeak the uncertain persona, with a history of non-acceptance."

"So? What holds you back from agreeing with him?"

"I can't for a moment see Mark conceiving the idea of destroying my book because it might contain some bilious picture of him, or going to the lengths of savaging Katie – he would know it wasn't me who was disturbing him, since I was with his father in Edinburgh. Mark just doesn't have enough determination and joined-up thinking to do that."

"So who does? I must say Mark sounds more likely than most of the alternatives."

"I'm not accusing anyone. I'm just saying 'Why pick on Mark?' Clare has the grit, the thinking-through, the ruthlessness."

That surprised Hughie.

"Clare? I've always suspected Clare of preying on you, wanting her pound of financial flesh, though I suppose that's her job as you always say. But have *you* thought it through? Why? – "

"There's no why. I'm not making a case against her. She has custody of the tapes of the new book, so if she were to have done it that couldn't be a motive ... Then there's Peter."

"Peter? I'd never even thought of him."

"Yet he's got a lot in common with Mark. You know how I've said that everything washes over Mark. I remember I told you how I had him walking round the flat practically naked, and when I told him in no uncertain terms that it wasn't on, he just said 'OK, Auntie Bet' and added an item of clothing or two. Then he was accused of kerb-crawling and all he did was say it was a silly law, and that it's a good way of picking up someone for sex. Nothing sticks. And why? Because there are no known standards or norms of conduct there."

"Are you saying Peter is the same?"

"Yes, I think I am. In a milder form. I love Peter, you know that: I enjoy his company almost more than anyone's, and my time with him was I suppose emotionally the best time in my life. But he has always been so much the boy, the wilful, lustful *boy*, who must have whatever he craves at any one moment, so that he goes after it even if it means losing something infinitely more valuable to him. And he's always enjoyed the boy's pleasure of taking anything he wants *off* someone else. When he left me to go after a floozie he crowed at the thought of giving one in the eye to her existing 'protector'. Very like Mark, don't you think?"

"I don't really know either of them well enough to say. I don't think you want Peter to have done it, though."

"No, of course I don't. And I can't think of a reason why he should have. If he were to appear in my memory book he'd know it would be with affection ... And if it wasn't he'd just thumb his nose at me and laugh."

"And you think Murchison will have all those people in mind?"

"I imagine so, since he obviously knows his job. For all I know he's added you to his list since his talk with you."

Hughie seemed unfazed.

"I expect he has. And I suppose you're going to add that I have something of the self-love that Mark seems to embody for you."

"Yes," said Bettina nodding. "I think I would add that." She was sitting opposite him now, and she held him with her stare. It was Hughie who spoke.

"We know each other so well, Bettina. There's hardly a thought of yours I don't spot in your face as soon as it comes into your mind."

"Maybe, Hughie ... Did I tell you I went and had a look at your current popsy the other day?"

"You didn't even tell me that you knew about my current popsy."

"Oh, I knew. Clare is a great one for collecting gossip among the scribbling classes. I hope the popsy is satisfactory?"

"Very, thank you, Bettina," said Hughie in his primmest voice.

"At least you don't have to crawl kerbs for them."

Hughie seemed inclined to fire up, but damped himself down.

"But the instinct is the same, you're implying?"

"The *need* may often be the same: for reassurance, bolstering of the ego, ministering to your self-satisfaction. And compensating for being shunned by your peers in your early days."

Hughie, apparently on impulse, pushed aside his plate with a half-eaten cake on it.

"That was lovely, Bettina, but I think I've reached my limit as far as cakes are concerned."

"So have I, I think ... It does go back to school, doesn't it?"

Hughie shook himself.

"Sorry! I was dreaming. What goes back to school? A taste for cakes?"

"The need for reassurance, the need to assert a conventional sexual identity. Both you and Mark were the objects of ridicule and suspicion."

"But I was ridiculed because I was a Pommie. Quite different from Mark."

"That was part of it. You tried to become one of the boys by teaching some of them to play soccer. To which, I am quite sure, you were supremely indifferent, and of which I imagine you were almost as ignorant as they were."

Hughie laughed, and Bettina laughed back.

"But there were other elements," Bettina went on. "You were the intellectual in a thoroughly anti-intellectual climate. You were called 'Mardarse', 'back-door merchant' and suchlike because that was an assertively heterosexual climate – though some of those loudly hetero men wouldn't bear too much examination into their feelings, I suspect. But your sexual identity was under challenge, as I suspect Mark's was at school."

"Maybe," said Hughie, shrugging. "And is this, in your analysis, why I've usually gone in for bimbos on the side? And why you and I were close as close, but never attracted to each other in that way?"

"Partly, maybe. I think I've always gone for fun in my men. You were never fun in that way, Hughie. Wrapped up in yourself, just like Mark and Peter and poor Cecil Cockburn, but in a much more knotted-up way. Perhaps if I'd been interested in taking up a challenge rather than just having a superficial sort of good time we could have made a good couple, or an interesting one."

"If I didn't continue to go after bimbos, like Peter."

"Yes. Eventually I drew the line at that in Peter, so I suppose I would have in you too ... Do you remember, Hughie, when we met up again in Venice?"

"Of course. It's a moment I've always treasured."

"Cecil and I were in that little street, and you were crossing St Mark's in the sunlight. You stopped and saw us. We stopped."

"I just couldn't believe it could be you."

"That wasn't the reason. It was only six or seven years

since you'd seen me last. You were uncertain of your reception, though I'd sent a message to you long before by Steve Drayton. It was to say it was nothing to do with what happened at the dance, my having to get away from Bundaroo. Then, in the Square, I went up to you and we hugged and kissed. It was so good."

"Yes. Yes, it was. Golly, is that the time?"

"Hughie, I had a phone call from Murchison before I came away. Katie has died."

He stopped momentarily in his getting his things together.

"Oh – poor thing! But I suppose in the circumstances – I mean, after what happened to her, perhaps this is for the best."

"Maybe. It makes things more serious, Hughie."

He started gathering up his things from the table again.

"Yes, of course it does. I must dash. I promised Marie I'd meet her at the Leighton Gallery at a quarter past. They've got a preview of a new exhibition on."

"Well, you mustn't disappoint Marie."

"Bettina – " He had stopped between the table and the path running beside the cafe. She had not been able to look at him closely during the last minutes of their talk. Now she saw that there was on his face a pleading look – a beseeching call to her to remain compassionate and understanding.

"Bettina, I never meant – " he said.

She should have replied "Oh, but you did, Hughie. Why else did you malign all my friends, hoping that I'd make you my literary executor?" But she could not break the habit of a near-lifetime.

"I'll do what I can, Hughie," she said.

He swallowed hard and hared down the path.

Bettina signed to the waiter for another pot of coffee. She had needed most of the first pot to get through their talk, and now she needed still more. She was glad she had kept a clear head. It had prevented her giving Hughie assurances she had not wanted to give, and had presented to her that typical author's ambiguity: "I'll do what I can." But it had not helped her to come to a cold, hard decision.

There was every reason for making one: poor battered Katie calling for retribution (as the doughty old woman would have done, if she had ever regained her voice); justice, the proper fitness of things. And, above all, her firm conviction that she herself had been the intended victim. "I never meant –" Hughie had begun. Oh, but he *had* meant! The theft or destruction of the tapes of her new book only made sense if she was incapacitated from making a new tape later. The tool which made the botched attempt to suggest a break-in was really meant for that darker purpose and it had been used for it, but on the wrong woman. If Katie had not heard a noise and got up she would have been attacked in bed – Bettina's bed. And the only one of her close friends whom she hadn't told of the Edinburgh trip was Hughie.

And all for vanity. All to protect his silly public persona as a latter-day aesthete, a man with a funny accent who lived for Art, from a charge concerning something that happened over sixty years ago.

It all cried out for a different decision, for a strong, determined one that said: enough is enough. She knew why, in all those years since Venice, the thing had never been brought out into the open. She knew it because she understood how the decision had been made that

Hughie was her burden. It had been made when his strong, farm-boy's arm was around her neck and she had smelt – not beer, as she had told Inspector Blackstone – but the insidious scent of Parma Violet soap. Then she had known she was being raped because it was what Hughie needed, and because he knew she was one person who would never betray him. Or perhaps she had made the decision further back than that: when she had seen that solitary figure for the first time, trudging its way to school, in short trousers that were not Australian short trousers, somehow giving off to her alert sense a feeling of helplessness, of being adrift, but at the same time being excitingly different, instinct with possibilities that Bundaroo had never till then had. She had never until now seriously questioned that decision. Now she realised it had given them a sense of invulnerability, of being unlike other men, of being one of those that lived by their own rules, made their own moral codes.

And Katie was the one who had suffered. And it was she, Bettina, his protectress, who had been his intended target. Hughie, shuffling off hurriedly, pleading for mercy from her, had been pathetic. But the inner Hughie, the one she had helped to make, was monstrous.

She finished off her coffee and slowly, reluctantly, made her way back to the flat to phone Inspector Murchison. The burden had been borne long enough, God knows. Borne long enough.